DAWN AND QUARTERED

PRETERNATURAL CHRONICLES BOOK 2

HUNTER BLAIN

ARGENTO PUBLISHING

COPYRIGHT

Hunter Blain

Dawn and Quartered

Preternatural Chronicles Book 2

ISBN: **978-1072400103**

info@argentopublishing.com

A MESSAGE FROM HUNTER BLAIN

My name is Hunter, and I'm a wordaholic. I'm also about to break the fourth wall...of your mindhole. Because there is a true story behind this... well...story.

It begins with two best friends who grew up together, breaking rules and raising hell as they shaped each other's personalities into the shameless assholes they are today. Well, at least for one of them, but I'll get to that in a moment. These two boys—let's call them Hunter and John—were all but inseparable. John excelled at creating music powerful enough to make angels weep and being the funniest asshole in Texas while Hunter dabbled—poorly, I might add—in his humble writings. Because they were self-declared brothers from other mothers, John respected Hunter's humble writings as much as I—I mean *Hunter* (stupid third person perspective)—respected John's musical magic. John's tunes could have changed the world, one day...

One evening, after reading one of Hunter's horrifically detailed short stories about a serial killer, John asked Hunter to write a story about him.

"Hell yeah, dude! What do you want to be?" Hunter asked, brimming with honor and biting back a very manly *squee*.

"A vampire," John responded with a mischievous gleam in his eye. "But not one of those sparkly ones. A true bad ass!"

"Done!" Hunter crowed with a smile and an accompanying high five.

"No, dude. *Promise*. Promise you'll write and finish a book about me. You are the most prolific writer of our generation!" John said. (*Something like that. I might be paraphrasing a little, but you get the gist of it*). "I would consider it an honor to live on for eternity with your words as my life's blood."

Hunter agreed, never to realize the weight of that promise until one Sunday morning when his mother called, crying incoherently.

John...had died.

Hunter was left in a cold world without his best friend and doppelgänger, and still thinks about that phone call to this day. How the morning light crept through the bedroom window while Hunter stared at the ceiling, noticing how the popcorn texture created cruel, jagged shadows. How everything started to blur as his chest was crushed beneath the weight of what he was hearing, each word stacking heavily upon the other until only fitful, ragged gasps of air could escape his throat. Only fiery tears existed, especially after the horrific realization that Hunter now had to make some of the hardest phone calls of his life to the circle of friends who orbited around John's solar pull.

Their bright star was no more, extinguished in an instant, leaving their universe a colder and darker place.

John not only left Hunter, but a friend named Valenta as well. There was also Nathanial and Depweg. The friends were each stricken numb with the loss of such a beloved flare of life. But...

When the three found out that Hunter was keeping his promise to write the greatest story ever told—starring their dear friend, John—they *demanded* to be a part of the adventure. Each of them immediately knew what type of supernatural character they wanted to play in this urban fantasy eulogy. It would be a funeral pyre of words, and their fictional personas would be John's pallbearers.

So please, as you read the following pages, feel free to laugh. Laugh at the situations John is placed in and his dickish dialogue to those around him, because John is 100% in this story without alteration (*albeit he is a vampire*). Laugh and let his memory live on inside the theater of your mind. Like he does in ours.

Thank you, sincerely, from the bottom of my beating heart, for giving my best friend the chance to live again. You are part of this magical ritual, and that would make him the happiest man in the...well, wherever the hell he is.

Cheers,

~Hunter

EPIGRAPH

"I doubt, therefore I might be."

— *Anonymous*

"I'm no sell out. Unless you give me money, then yeah, whatever you want."

— *Hunter Blain whenever Netflix calls to offer a series contract*

"Hunter Blain and Shayne Silvers are the best fantasy authors ever to be born."

— *Abraham Lincoln (probably)*

SEAL OF THE COUNCIL

1

A plume of green hellfire cascaded overhead, erupting from the mouth of my new friend as I slid on my knees over the wet concrete. My head shot backward, lifting my chin to protect the top of my head from the fire. The flames were beyond intense, and I could feel the skin of my nose and cheeks hovering on the edge of the conflagration. The smell of singeing hair from my perfectly Irish red beard pierced my nostrils as the flames bellowed a deafening roar in the alley.

As I slammed into the legs of the flame-spouting demon, I wrapped my arms around his slimy hips while shifting my weight to my left and placing my right foot on the ground. My body connected as I exploded up from my posted right foot, throwing the demon off balance with an—I assumed—look of confusion on its grotesque face. I couldn't exactly tell what his face looked like while my head was in prom night position at his waist.

As we tumbled to the ground, I moved up his body so my chest would smother his upper torso as we slammed down. I could feel as much as hear the exploding bubble wrap as the demon's ribs broke under my weight. This skinny bugger was more of a caster than a melee fighter, and I took full advantage of his lack of physical prowess.

I brought my head up for a better view of my prey. He...was...hideous.

A layer of slime coated his naked body, making him slippery. His gray skin was loose, like the jowls of a bloodhound, increasing the difficulty of keeping him down. Speaking of keeping things down, "Don't throw up. Don't throw up," I said in a mantra as I wrestled over the loose chicken skin. A...

Twisting in my position, I threw a leg over his abdomen in a full mount maneuver. As I did that, the monster slipped a hand between our torsos and began summoning a green ball of hellfire. With preternatural speed, I willed a blooddagger through my palm and swiped at the demon's wrist. The green light extinguished as the hand smacked wetly onto the ground next to us. The demon shrieked in pain and surprise as thick, black gore oozed from his nub of a wrist.

I looked into his wide, babyshit green eyes, and was reminded of those ugly jeeps I sometimes saw on the road. Mr. Flabskin took advantage of my momentary lapse in thought and snapped at my face with teeth made from needles. I reacted by putting my left forearm against his throat and pushing down with my body weight. I supposed he didn't like that because he started squirming with renewed vigor while choking gurgles escaped his mouth.

"Locke's gone, you skinny fat fuck! Who summoned you?" I demanded through clenched teeth.

A scratchy, high-pitched voice, similar to Sméagol's, answered with, "Locke was but a puppet, mosquito. The master has many servants to follow his will."

"Who is your master?" I asked with impatience. In my best Alan Rickman voice, I said, "I'm going to count to three. There will not be a four."

"One." I smiled, showing my teeth.

"Two." My fangs elongated to surgically sharp points.

"Three." I moved my forearm and placed the palm of my hand against his forehead, keeping him steady. I shifted my head closer to his neck.

"Okay," I said just before sinking my fangs into his neck and yanking his artery apart. Black sludge erupted in a torrent, hitting the concrete. Some got in my mouth as I pulled away, and I began spitting vigorously. I had already discovered the hard way that demon blood gave me heartburn and daymares. Fun stuff!

I pushed myself up to my knees and then stood, staring down as Babyshit McSkinnyfat writhed in pain. As his sludge blood began to slow, his skin started turning translucent. After a few moments, he had melted into pure ectoplasm and was evaporating before my eyes. I pulled out a pack of gum from my leather duster, which Da had miraculously repaired, and freed an entire row of the minty goodness from their aluminum prison, only to make them fall prey to my mouth. I chewed with gusto to get the taste of shit, piss, and diesel oil that the demon had given me as a parting gift out of my mouth.

"Ugh. No wonder they're all so surly," I said with an overly full mouth to the now empty alley.

With the task complete, it was time to return to Father Thomes Philseep with a progress report.

As I casually walked down the alley to the road, I pondered the influx of summonings since I had killed my archnemesis, Locke. Locke, the bastard who had killed my parents under the name Godwin centuries ago. I still enjoyed thinking about his decapitated head, about how I had laughed into his blinking and twitching face as he'd died. Revenge was hollow, and I found myself glorifying the brutality in which he had died to fill the vacant hole in my chest. I had lost my parents and had been given a mentor in return—Ulric. During the most helpless moment of my entire mortal life, he had promised to give me the ability to avenge my father and my mother. In exchange, I had given my word that I would walk this mortal plane with him, teaching him the ways of the modern world. Apparently, Ulric had been asleep for some time and had needed a guide and companion. Eternity could be boring without the right company. And misery loved company.

My hand absentmindedly stroked my singed beard, burnt hair beginning to grow back like a turtle poking its head out of its shell after the perceived danger had dissipated. At least my gray beanie was okay. I loved that thing almost as much as the patched-up trench coat I had stolen off the body of a Nazi officer back in Germany.

"Hello, Jonathan," a silken voice purred from above.

My eyes lazily slinked up, almost in an eye roll, to find Lily of the Fae Court sitting on the edge of a two-story industrial building. Her toned legs were shiny in the pale light of the full moon.

"It's just—" I started.

"Whatever I want it to be," she interrupted, displaying her authority over me.

After she saved my unlife by spilling her ancient blood over my decimated body, I was forever locked into a life debt with her, powerless to refuse her commands until the debt is repaid. The thing is, she's lived for countless millennia and hasn't died yet. I'm pretty much her immortal plaything. It's only been a few months since she saved my sexy ass, and already I'm growing tired of doing her bidding. It seems she has something for me to do at least once a week. I've even painted her damn toenails and detailed her car with my tongue. She insisted it was a lesson for trying to fight her commands by "interpreting her meaning" in my own way.

Whatever that means.

"Now, I need you to do an itsy-bitsy favor for me," she said with a devilish smile as she pushed off from where she was perched and landed gracefully next to me. She was wearing black spandex shorts and a neon-green sports bra with matching tennis shoes. Long, curly blonde hair flowed out the back of a black baseball hat and into a ponytail. She... looked...ravenous. Ravishing! I meant that one.

As she closed the distance between us, her flowery scent wafted into my nose and paralyzed me. A part of me even exhibited symptoms of rigor mortis. Lily reveled in my longing for her soft, succulent flesh.

Standing next to me she only came up to my shoulders, so she had to stand on tiptoes to kiss my mouth. I immediately gave in and returned the enthusiasm. My eager hands roamed barely covered flesh as hers went up to my face and then the back of my head. She pulled on my long hair while pulling away from my lips with a mischievous grin. My head jerked back and my chin faced skyward yet again; but this time, I was all for it as long as she held on to the strands of my mane. She slipped her tongue from between her lips and ran it up my throat in a carnal gesture of dominance. Her other hand slipped down the front of my jeans and found my buried treasure.

There was something magical about the way she touched me. Literally. I was confident she had infused her Fae magic into every sensual movement.

Right as we started getting heavy into the action and I was removing my trench coat, she pulled away and said, "This isn't the favor, lover." She let her scent fall away from me, clearing my mind but leaving my body wanting.

I had already pulled one hand out of my patchwork of a coat before she broke our connection, which left me stunned in place. I fought my Predatory Self for control over the wheel, but he was insistent that we finish what had been started. I reminded him that I was the one in control and that she wouldn't let us finish unless it was her idea. PS relented, albeit reluctantly, like a child giving up on getting a toy while at the store.

After my mental struggle with PS, I was able to grasp the wheel at ten and two and take control of my body. I commanded the blood in my member to retreat in a show of control and defiance.

"I don't think so, lover," Lily said. "Fill it," she commanded with a coy grin, authoritative pleasure showing at the corners of her eyes.

"That's not how this wor—WHOA NOW!" I gulped as my own blood revolted against my will and raced to try to rip my pants.

"More," she cooed, eyes now sparkling mischievously. She was biting her bottom lip.

I moaned in pained panic as I broke all racial stereotypes and unofficially took the world record.

"Lily...please..." I pleaded, but then realized that's what she wanted, so I added, "...call the Guinness World Records. Do you have a measuring tape? Maybe a yardstick?" The pain was excruciating yet interesting. I constructed a smile onto my face, forcing each muscle in sequence to reverse from the grimace they so desperately wanted to form. My teeth were seconds away from shattering through the facade.

"Relax," she commanded. At the release of her power over me, I dropped to my knees and hunched over, cradling my shrinking package.

With strings of drool slipping from my mouth, I willed my member to heal with a focus of mind that even a monk would be jealous of.

On a side note, I learned a new trick today; I can force blood into limbs and swell them to gargantuan proportions. I can't immediately fathom a scenario where that would be helpful, but it's still neat to know.

"Thank you," I panted as I got back up to my feet. "Now, what can I do for you, m'lady?" My right hand was now shielding my junk from her trunk.

"I need you to lay low for a while. More specifically, don't go looking for a fight, my dear. I would hate for my favorite plaything to be taken from me," she said with a dramatic frown complete with pouty lips.

"I'm your favorite?" I asked.

"That's all you have to say?" she asked dubiously.

"Depweg owes me five bucks!" I exclaimed triumphantly, my free fist shooting above my head in mock celebration.

A perfectly proportioned eyebrow went up for the briefest of moments before descending again, effectively returning Lily's astonishingly symmetrical face to its supermodel rest state.

Lifting her closed fist in a show of control, I was immediately captivated against my will. Sure wasn't getting tired of that. Not at all.

"I'm serious, John. Do not directly engage with any supernatural or preternatural. And I mean *anyone*." She then hashed out all the fine-print details. The gist of it was that she didn't want me to continue hunting demons or those that would summon them until further notice. Father T wasn't going to like this. I could at least continue to hunt mortals and interact with other supernaturals, aka supes, but I was on strict orders to not attack any of them unless they posed an immediate threat to my existence. Not a lot of wiggle room, but I decided to play along. At least for the time being. Then again, what other choice did I have? Oh, right, insanity.

Those who refused even the simplest of commands in a Fae life debt ran the certainty of going completely insane.

"Fine. I needed some time to myself, anyway. I have a backlog of games and movies to catch up on," I said.

"Good," Lily purred while letting her gaze violate me from toe to beanie. "Now, take off your clothes."

"Like, right here? In the alley?" I said with a touch of trepidation as I mocked covering my nipples with the index and middle finger of each hand.

"Yes. Right here. Right now." Her smell invigorated the senses and removed all inhibitions. I had to fight PS for enough control to not rip my clothes off. Hell, I wanted to rip them off myself, but damn it, I loved that trench. Her own attire evaporated off her firm body. It was at this time that I used all my mental capacity to utter the most romantic sentence in the history of romance novels: "Soooo hot. Want to touch the hiney." Lily giggled in response as her body pushed into mine.

We broke concrete.

Claw marks healed immediately. I used bloodwhips when commanded. It was the only time I didn't mind being told what to do. A real creep of a passerby stopped dead in his tracks and began gawking at us with a smile that was fit for his own Netflix documentary. That is, until he saw us start levitating while in mid-coitus. I looked over at him and said, "There is no Dana, only Zuul." We both tittered at the man as he stumbled away, his legs trying to sprint without giving his body time to balance—inebriation at its finest.

After a super impressive four minutes, we were finished—at least I was. I was sure she would have said something if I hadn't completed my duties. Maybe I should say something.

Say something? Since when did I care about the needs of my capture? It had always been use and use alike between us. Well, she *had* saved my unlife, but she had already gotten something in the form of a perfectly obedient slave toy out of the ordeal. What's funny was, I couldn't convince myself that I didn't enjoy it to a degree. Lily was something else.

I watched her as I dressed. She simply willed her outfit back on. I saw a look of worry cross her face for a nanosecond and then vanish again. I chose not to comment on it and instead took a moment to pause and reflect. Lily had never been one to show all her cards, and I knew that look meant she knew something but wasn't about to enlighten me. Or hell, maybe she was doing it on purpose. I couldn't tell.

"Be careful, John," Lily said with sincerity before winking out of this plane. There was no sonic boom like there normally was.

"She could control it this whole time?" I asked out loud. On one of our last impromptu meetups, she had created a sonic boom in my car by shifting planes, which had caused a vacuum that the air had rushed in to fill. It had shattered all of my windows and put me in an interesting position. I still had over four years left on that tanning membership.

Feeling both physically relieved and mentally concerned, I made my way back toward the street. A featureless black cat darted from behind a dumpster and disappeared into the shadows.

As my foot crested the threshold between alleyway and sidewalk, a blast of wind struck me as if a jet engine had just been turned on full blast directly in front of me.

I shielded my eyes and gradually retreated into the alley, fighting the force pressing against me. After a few beats—because that's what was causing the wind—the air went still and a voice boomed, "Abomination, I have come for you!"

Opening my eyes, I saw an armor-clad Goliath with a flaming sword and imposing wings that filled the width of the alley. His armor was marble-white with sparkling gold linings, and the flames of his gladius burned with heavenfire. His eyes blazed a white-blue that mirrored the flames of the holy weapon and illuminated the alley almost as much as the magnificent sword.

Reflexively, I pulled out a bloodwhip and...nothing. I froze in place, poised to strike. I couldn't attack. The angel smiled at me from under an impressive helmet that looked like it belonged in World of Warcraft.

"What do you want?" I asked while tilting my chin up to stare into a face that seemed to be several feet above my own. If my heart could beat, it would have been racing at that moment.

In a reverberating, commanding voice, he said, "I have a message for the cursed one; deception is afoot, and continued involvement will result in swift retribution and a punishment, eternal." As he spoke, he lifted his flaming gladius to point right at me. PS mentally nudged me and expressed that we both felt that we were in immediate danger. I concurred. Plus, he was celestial, so not super or preternatural, right? She hadn't mentioned anything about angels.

I swung the whip around in an obvious telegraph of my intentions. The angel reacted by bringing his flaming sword straight up to try and catch my attack. That would have resulted in quite the predicament, as I was willing to bet that heavenfire would burn my essence just as effectively as hellfire, and that it would have destroyed the energy I had willed into my weapon. At the last moment, I pulled my wrist back and forced the whip to crack by the blade instead of wrap around it. I put in a lot of strength in doing so and created a baby sonic boom that disoriented the angel for a moment, causing him to reflexively bend backward ever so slightly, which was all I needed. I willed my own gladius through the palm of my left hand and gripped it tightly in my fist while dropping into a crouch. Before the angel could recover, I thrust my blade between the armored pieces and into the now exposed stomach, where only cloth offered any defense. The armor allowed for quick maneuvering at the cost of full protection. He was surely regretting his choice of attire as my blade pierced his robe underneath his armor plating and plunged into his angelic liver. I had never imbibed angel blood before, and the thought momentarily froze me.

The angel took advantage and swung widely down at me, forcing me out of my indecision. I tried to step out of the way, but my blade kept me less than mobile. Instead of splitting me right down the middle, my right arm tumbled to the dirt-covered concrete below. The holy weapon had been swung with enough panicked force that it lodged deeply into the ground. A torrent of electrified pain ripped through my body, like being hit by a tidal wave of nearly freezing water.

I was vaguely aware that my trench coat was going to have new stitch scarring where the arm connected to the shoulder.

Note to self, buy Da an iTunes gift card for all the work he puts into my loyal coat.

Where was I? Oh yeah, almost being vertically bisected by an angel.

In my haze, I knew I didn't have much of a choice now. It was all or nothing. I willed the angel's life force from his blood-soaked liver to flow into my gladius and up my arm, becoming a part of me. As his blood infused mine, a new world was revealed like a curtain dropping at the theater. All I had ever known was the curtain, but now, the show was starting.

Hairs prickled over my entire body. My eyes rolled in elation. My jaw fell open as a moan of delight escaped my mouth. The fingers on my remaining hand tingled, along with my toes, lips, and nose. I was vaguely aware that I could feel tingling on my right hand as well. Through my angelical inebriation, I barely opened one eye enough to see a stream of blood connecting my severed arm and shoulder socket. The appendage was being lovingly hoisted off the ground and toward its rightful home.

The angel was huge and had a lot of eternally old blood to give. He fought, pushing at my chest with his free hand as the other tried desperately to wedge the sword from the stone. I lifted my elongated right arm and wrapped it around the angel's neck once before placing it on my left shoulder. My hand gripped my shoulder hard, and I pulled myself closer, choking my attacker as I did. His hand moved up from my chest and to his throat, where it was met by his other hand after giving up on the sword. The angel's strength waned as I drained him, and his eyes began to flutter as his giant body began to slump over. His arms fell limply to his sides as his final breath was slowly exhaled.

As the last of his blood flowed into me, I pulled the blade out and uncoiled my arm from around his neck, letting the massive and beautiful corpse collapse to the ground. The clang of the armor against the concrete reminded me of a garbage truck ungracefully setting an industrial-sized bin on the ground.

In my blissful inebriation, I waited for the angel to turn into translucent ectoplasm and evaporate, but it didn't. I just stood there, drunkenly dumbfounded that this was an actual body.

"Holy shit. Did I just kill a real fucking angel?" I asked, feeling the seriousness of my actions sink into my core and then blossom outward to my limbs as the realization grew. This was probably the worst thing I had ever done, and it was mixed with the best, most powerful blood I had ever consumed. Drunken pleasure warred with the preternatural equivalent of adrenaline. There was NO WAY I was getting into Heaven now, man.

I expressed my worry with elegance and class.

"Oh fuck, oh fuck, oh fuck, oh fuck!" I paced back and forth, pulling my gray beanie off and running my hands through my shoulder-length black hair. My arm had returned back to regular length, and the feel of my own touch was electrifying. The light from the moon rippled like the water's surface after you had barely touched it with your finger. I wanted to scream in both delight and terror.

Replacing my beanie, I set my jaw and used all my willpower to focus.

"Okay. What do I do first?" I asked myself as if I were super hammered at a party, the hot cheerleader wanted to have sex with me, and I was doing my best pep talk in the bathroom mirror—even though I knew I had consumed way too much to perform.

I looked around and immediately noticed we were at the end of the alley. I grabbed one foot of the giant corpse before me and dragged him behind a building and away from the line of sight of the street. Though it was empty due to it being so late—or early, however you wanted to look at it—it was still not worth risking a late-night patrol or some poor mortal making a diaper run or something.

Picking up my cell phone, I unlocked it and pushed the green phone icon. My fingers trembled in ecstasy as my Favorites list popped up and I quickly tapped Depweg's name. After what felt like an eternity of me pacing a hole into the concrete, Depweg's voicemail picked up. Cursing, and then giggling, I pushed the End Call button and looked again at my Favorites list. Without much choice, I called my silver medal go-to guy.

"What have you done this time, John?" Da's curtly cultured British voice answered.

"How did you..." I began, and then shrugged off the absurdity of the question. "I really should call my friends more in a social setting. Teehee."

"Probably. Now, what do you need?" he asked absently, as if being distracted from a task. He better not be watching *Stranger Things* without me. "Wait a moment. Did you just 'teehee' me?"

"Ikilledanangelandneedhelpmovinghismassivebody," I blurted out quickly as I kicked the armor-plated thigh of the giant sack of meat, but it didn't budge. "This is *your* fault!" I cried to the stone-cold angel.

Both Da and the angel met me with deafening silence.

Oh dear. He might not be pleased that I'd killed one of his kind. Da was a faerie who believed himself to be an angel and unironically hated fairies.

"What was his name?" Da asked somberly.

"He didn't say. Only mumbled something about sending me to Hell or something." My voice shook like a meth addict. I was losing the battle between the blood high and my higher brain functions. I let loose a moan that belonged in an adult video and rolled my eyes. I just wanted to fall backward into the lazy river of eternity and float while stars danced in the sky.

"Where are you?" he asked flatly, concern and annoyance evident in his voice. I gave him my coordinates, i.e. dropped a pin and shared it on my phone's map app. It took several tries to get the pin just right. I might have sent one in the middle of the ocean for all I knew.

Da hung up without so much as a goodbye, but at least he was on his way to me and hopefully not the ocean. Excuse me, gulf, technically.

While I waited for him to arrive with my Kia Optima, Mortis, I examined the remains while tittering uncontrollably. An impulse struck and I—not surprisingly—went with it. I wrestled to unlatch a gauntlet and then regarded it at arm's length as it slid off the muscled forearm. It was absolutely awesome in size and quality. I could probably fit at least three digits in just one of the glove's fingers. For some reason I couldn't explain, I pulled the white, smooth armor up to my face and dragged my cheek across it, closing my eyes and moaning as I did. This angel armor was just so smooth.

Angel. Shit. Snap out of it, Lilith damn it!

I opened my eyes, slid my hand into the glove, and held it up. The gauntlet swallowed my entire forearm. It looked cartoonish on me, like a child wearing his dad's boots.

"Grrr. Avengers, bow before the might of Thanos!" I dramatically exclaimed while shaking my fist. I tried to snap my fingers, but my coordination was slightly impaired for some unknown reason that I shouldn't be blamed for.

After giggling to myself again, I removed the gauntlet and set it down. My eyes peered at the angel and then locked onto his empty scabbard.

"Oh, shit!" I said as I rushed to where the angel had lodged his sword into the ground. It was gone. It. Was. Fucking. Gone. Only broken concrete that spread out in a spiderweb pattern with a cavern in the middle remained.

I had just lost an angelic weapon. Pretty sure this was going to come back and haunt me.

Another wave of euphoria washed over my body, and I collapsed to my knees, laughing. I grabbed the gauntlet and held it close to my chest like a safety blanket. I mean, comforter. Safety comforter, you know, for adults.

"I lost an angelic sword," I said between fits of manly giggles. "Oh, man, I killed a real angel." Tears streamed down my face from both the mirth the beyond ancient blood forced on me and the direness of the situation. I slid the comically sized gauntlet back over my hand and then put my face into its palm. My body shuddered with the most confusing laughter I had ever experienced in over five hundred years.

"Oh, man. Is this what being blitzed is like? Now I get all those stoner movie references!" I said into the massive palm while the laughing fit relented for the time being. I was aware that my cheeks hurt from the aggressive smiling.

The LED lights of Mortis appeared and made their way down the street. I could tell my baby from a mile away. Sure enough, the white Optima pulled down the alley and stopped in front of me. I stood up, wiping my face with the sleeve of my trench coat that was falling down my arm, and walked to the passenger's side. The window rolled down leisurely, and I rested my elbows on the door and leaned in.

"A high five is five dollars. A hug is ten. Cuddling, that'll be twenty, big boy. Or, if you're feeling frisky…" I said while holding up the giant gauntlet in an R-rated suggestion, eyebrows bouncing up and down.

"Get the body," Da said. He was only five inches tall, which you would think would make it hard for him to drive; nevertheless, he managed, *with magic!* He just floated above the seat enough for him to see the road, and pantomimed driving actions. It was adorable, and I had almost giggled to death the first time he insisted on being behind the wheel and I saw him throw the car into drive.

"Little help?" I said. "Get it? 'Cause…'cause you're little."

Da turned and looked at me, a serious expression etched into his face.

"Got it. Riding Han Solo on this one," I said to myself as I turned and walked to where I'd laid the body. My head was swimming, making it hard to walk a straight line. It felt like I was floating rather than walking.

I approached the body aaaannnnnddddd it was gone. I did a Looney Tunes double take at the spot where I *knew* I had left him.

"The fuck!" was all I could manage with a gaping mouth and bulging eyes. My hands were open and outstretched, as if in doing so, the body would miraculously appear and say, "Just kidding. Here I am!"

But, it didn't. And yet, I remained in the same position, unbelieving of my luck and not willing to trust my cartwheeling mind high on angel blood.

A feeling of unease settled over me like a storm cloud swallowing the sun. Out of predatory instinct, PS sent out our senses in all directions. My eyes sought heat signatures, even through stone walls. My ears listened for the pumping of a heart, the subtle squeaking of muscle fibers moving, or the barely audible whistle of air passing through nostrils. I reached out my nongauntlet hand in front of me and sent out my will, searching for the electrical impulses created by thoughts. Nothing on all fronts. Reeling in my senses, I tried one last trick and clicked my tongue, hard. I listened for the echo and was drawn to a bulk that seemed out of place on top of one of the roofs. A second click a moment later and the shape was gone.

"Damn it," I said to myself as I decided to let the situation go. If I couldn't feel the presence of whatever was up there using all my abilities, I didn't think I wanted to confront it just yet.

Or maybe I was flying like a kite and barely had the mental capacity to stand on my own two feet.

Reconciling with my situation, I turned and made my way to where Da was waiting. His eyes shot daggers at me. I gripped the door handle and ripped it off like it was being held by a popsicle stick. I held the handle up to my eyes and said, "Odd. Never had that problem before." Reaching inside the open window, I delicately pulled on the door handle with one finger. It clicked, and the door latch released.

I climbed into the passenger's seat and stared forward, feeling Da growing impatient and silently demanding an answer as to where the angel's body was.

"Sooooo, here's the thing..." I started as I set the broken handle in one of the cup holders.

"You lost the body? Are you bloody kidding me?" I always loved it when he used that apropos British expletive.

Holding up the gauntlet and lightly shaking it once in a show of victory, I said, "I got this!"

Da wasn't amused. In midair, he threw the car into reverse and backed us out of the alley. Once on the street, he mimed shifting the car into drive, and we started forward down the road.

"Tell me everything that happened, John. Leave out no detail."

"You sure?" I asked.

"Yes, of course," he responded, frustrated.

I told him everything that had happened, going into needless and excruciating detail about my romp with Lily. He cut me off with a look of distaste, and I continued with only the important details, though I was smiling and laughing like a schoolchild who had just told a boob joke.

At my conclusion, Da sat in silence with only the noises of the road for company. After a few minutes, he said, "It's not a coincidence that the Jezebel appeared first."

A pang of annoyance bubbled in my core, surprising me that I was slightly offended at the reference to Lily. I thought on this as I stared out the window in silence.

"John," Da derailed my train of thought. "Focus."

"Yeah. You're right. She knew something," I agreed while absently watching the lights of the highway run up and over the car only to retreat behind us.

"She's not going to be happy that you interpreted her commands in your favor. We both know you were itching for a fight, and she will too." After a few moments of silence, he finished with, "I wonder what dominoes are going to tumble as a result of tonight." Worry crept into his voice.

Shit. He's right. I was already up to my tits in demons—now I'd probably added angry holy warriors to my watchlist. I was sure this wasn't going to end with me getting a big, shiny medal.

"You need to bring Father Thomes into this," Da said.

"Fffffuuuuucccccckkkkk," I breathed out heavily. "He's going to be so pissed."

"Rightfully so, I imagine."

"But maybe he can help make things right. I mean, the dude had a flaming sword pointed at me and was talking about eternal punishment and shit!" I pleaded, grasping at dead vines as quicksand sucked me down.

"Mm-hmm," Da agreed with absolute sincerity and not an ounce of obvious doubt.

2

I got lost in thought for the rest of the ride. Worry grew like a plague inside my chest, both at my imagination playing scenarios of punishment from heavenfolk and from thinking about what Father T was going to do. The last time I had done something stupid, he had chained me up in a special room made specifically for me—which was both touching and horrifying. After keeping my ass locked away for several days and being driven to the brink of dipping my toe in the pool of insanity from thirst, I had managed to escape, only to almost be incinerated by his holy magic. That's where it got good; after that, I had to face scary ass stone gargoyles that literally ripped pieces of my supermodel body apart. Depweg had saved my ass that day, and unlike Lily, hadn't evoked a bullshit life debt.

Father Thomes and I had made up since then, and I was convinced that he only had my best interests at heart. Sure, the mortal priest couldn't fully understand the power of the thirst, but he had to have some semblance of an idea. It's what drove me and kept me sane. Blood was both my elixir of eternal life and purest joy. There was simply no pharmaceutical drug on earth that could even remotely compare to the elation and sense of completeness from imbibing pure life energy straight from the tap. I had even discovered I could drink from the supernatural community, though I was quite confident that was frowned upon.

As we pulled further away from the scene of the crime, the thought of absorbing blood from an angel who had been alive since the beginning of time shot through my mind. I noticed that my legs were slightly bouncing up and down and that my fingertips, lips, ears, nose, and toes were all still tingling. A rogue giggle escaped my throat before I could cover my mouth with my free hand.

Da looked over at me with one raised eyebrow. Keeping my hand over my mouth, I shook my head a couple times in a show of "don't worry about it." Now that the danger was over and PS had given back full control of the wheel, all I could feel was the dizzying high from timeless, powerful blood. It was starting to feel more akin to what I assumed heroin to be like. I closed my eyes and rested the back of my noggin on the headrest, trying to ride out the wave. I quickly realized that closing my eyes had not been the best idea as my world began to spin. I shot my hands and feet out with a terrified yelp, trying to catch myself from the fall I wasn't actually experiencing. Da responded appropriately by screaming and losing control of his focus and the car. He fell to the seat with a whoosh of air from his tiny lungs as Mortis ran amok, free from his commands.

Looking forward, I saw and felt that we had just jumped the curb and were about to smash into a telephone pole. I quickly grabbed the wheel and corrected our course, hitting a side-view mirror with the pole. Cursing, I steered us into the middle of the road, where the car began to slow down.

Da was just now inhaling his first breath of air. He held his chest and gulped widely, appearing to suck in more air than he ever had before.

"WHAT...WAS...THAT?" he asked between breaths. In answer, I began tittering like a schoolgirl while shaking my head and trying to say, "I don't know!" but all that came out were high-pitched vowels, like a whining dog on a YouTube video.

Looking at me intently, Da regained focus and floated above the driver's seat, pantomiming the ten and two position at the wheel. A scowl creased his brow as he set his jaw.

I had never felt anything like this after a feeding. Not from Lily when she had brought me back from the brink of death. Not from Ulric when he had first made me. Though they had been good, it was as if the energy had been filtered. This angel blood felt like discovering a fine wine that had been aged for hundreds of years. But it wasn't just the fact that knowing the rarity of the wine made it better. This blood had been the purest I had ever had, and I wanted to strip my clothes off and dance naked in the moonlight. I wanted to buy a big farm, adopt every puppy in the whole world, and roll in the grass as they clamored over me with puppy kisses. I wanted every homeless child to have a puppy they could roll around in the grass with. Then I wanted to fall back into a beanbag chair and listen to reggae music while not moving for hours. Lilith, what was wrong with me? I *hated* reggae.

Mortis abruptly coming to a stop brought me slightly out of my trip enough to see that we were in front of the creepiest fucking church in existence. My eyes instinctively shot up to where two of the gargoyles were now missing, having been turned to kitty litter by Depweg. The urge to close my eyes and fake a coma rose up. I couldn't put my gauntleted finger on whether this was really because I really, *really* did not want to see Father Thomes right now or if my high was wearing off—or maybe I just deserved a little rest and relaxation once in a while.

Da cleared his throat. It was intolerable in my stupor. I sighed, loudly, while opening the door. I stepped out and turned to look at Da, dropping the trophy on the seat.

"That gauntlet is going into the cabinet with my collector's cups," I said while pointing at the seat where the only remaining evidence of my super sin sat.

"Be honest with him, John. He can't help if he's in the dark," Da reasoned, ignoring my comment about my Eternity Gauntlet.

After a moment's contemplation, I nodded my head in agreement while shutting the passenger door and turning to look at the ancient building in the middle of Houston. The church looked like it was as old as the castles you'd find in my homeland of Ireland. Moss crept around the corners with the goal of covering every square inch of stone. Original stained glass windows decorated the walls evenly, but provided no actual light. I assumed the growth kept the windows intact like duct tape, especially considering Houston had been hit with its fair share of harsh storms.

I set one hand on the—hopefully—rust-covered wrought iron fence, and fell on my ass. I lifted my hand and saw where I had ripped the iron apart as if it was made of corn dog sticks.

"Why is everything made from cheap wooden sticks all of a sudden?" I asked as I dropped the metal and brushed the dirt off my ass. Realization dawned on me, and I looked down at my hands. Consuming blood made me increasingly powerful, but it took scores of mortals over long periods of time to gain a drastic increase in strength. Even then, how much energy I could permanently store seemed to correlate with how long I had been undead. I had never questioned why, just simply assumed it was a checks and balances system of the universe. Maybe it prevented fledgling vampires from rampaging and eating entire continents of people.

I walked over to where a jagged rock protruded from the ground and kneeled down. I set my hands on the corner, gripped it, and pulled the entire fixture from the earth. It came away as if ice cream sticks held it in place (last one, I promise). The stone looked as if a teardrop and a lightning bolt had had a metaphorical baby. I lifted it up, grabbing either side, and was impressed that it spanned a little wider than my body.

"And if my theory is correct..." I started as I brought my hands together, turning the impressive rock into sand. It was as if the entire thing were made out of some sort of cheap, food-holding apparatus. You know, like a multiuse tool available across different platforms, like at a doctor's office. The word escaped me right now.

Dust fell onto and settled in the fabric of my clothes and on my black boots.

"Dang it," I said as I went to pat my stomach, only to be struck with a baseball bat to my gut. I barked in surprise and then looked at my hands. "Oh, right," I chuckled to myself. I noticed that at least most of the dust had been knocked off my shirt. Small victories.

"Must be careful when I pee," I said cautiously as I turned my hands over in front of me.

Just as intrigued as I was satisfied, I approached the cracked stone of the stairs leading to the giant weathered doors.

Standing at the threshold, I prepared to *carefully* bang out my secret knock when thoughts of the impending conversation with a frowning

Father Thomes passed through my mind as if looking out the window of a train and seeing a billboard shoot by. Worry froze me and gripped my chest like a vise. He was going to be so disappointed and upset with me.

Turning to look at Da for reassurance, I noticed that the road was empty. Great. Maybe I should just pop down to Valenta's Saloon and grab me a Jack and Blood to build my courage. Yeah, that's what I'd do. One drink and I'd come right back.

I instantly chastised myself for being weak. Let's add enchanted alcohol to the cocktail that's flowing through my veins! What's the worst that could happen?

As I stood on the landing of the church, being disgusted with myself, I heard the clacking of sturdy locks being released. I lowered my hand and took in a deep breath, preparing myself for one of the most difficult conversations I would ever have. The door creaked open, revealing an empty doorway.

It was pitch black inside, as if the church had a restraining order on all outside light. My preternatural eyes scanned the inside, searching for my holy guide. With an audible gulp, I stepped forward and through the empty doorway. As I cleared the entrance, the door slowly creaked shut behind me as if on its own volition. My eyes adjusted, and I could see a lone figure sitting in his usual pew on one side of the aisle. Without saying a word and while looking forward, I slid into the adjacent pew, and waited. The father had a knack for knowing exactly what I had done. It's like he had a direct line upstairs or something.

A match was struck and brought to a wooden pipe. The flame was tugged toward the tobacco by unseen breath and brought to the herbs, which began to glow a bright orange before settling into a light smolder. Before the match self-cannibalized, the eager flame was brought to an oil lamp, which was then set on the ground between the pews.

"You attacked and killed an angel, my son?" Father Thomes Philseep asked while staring down the aisle to where Jesus hung on the cross above the dilapidated stage.

Speaking in all seriousness in light of the gravity of the situation, I said, "He was hostile. I felt threatened."

Father Thomes' head shot my way, and I reflexively turned to meet his gaze, not in challenge but surprise. He had a deep scowl creasing his forehead, as if the Grand Canyon had been teleported onto his face.

"You KILLED an ANGEL! Do not presume me a fool to fall for your flagrant lies. If you had been an intended target, he would not have given you the opportunity to attack." Anger infused his harsh words as they exploded out of his vein-bulging face.

"I didn't know it was a *real* angel. I thought he would have a body made out of ectoplasm, like demons! How the hell was I supposed to know?" I asked, throwing my hands into the air.

"Poor choice of words, child," Father Thomes scolded.

"Sorry. 'Heck,'" I said with air quotes.

The father relaxed visibly, but not from release of tension. Instead, he deflated like a balloon with a small hole in it as he looked at me.

"I can't protect you from Heaven now, John," the father said with full sincerity and weariness. There were heavy bags under his eyes that were visible with every toke of his pipe. Orange light bathed his features with each breath.

I slowly turned my head toward the holy figure on the stage. The personification of all things holy. My new enemy.

"Let them come," I said defiantly, but only just above a whisper.

I expected a nuke of rage to drop on me from across the aisle, but nothing did. The silence was deafening and more impacting than any fury he could have spat at me.

After a few tokes of contemplation, the father broke the silence, "I'm afraid they will, child. We have drawn the attention from both sides now. Perhaps this is too big an undertaking for just us."

"Father, all the good we've done—the people we've saved, the demons we've sent back—it all means nothing now, doesn't it?" I was referring to the scale of my soul. I'd been working with Father T to try and win favor with Heaven since we'd first met. It had been determined that when it came time for the big sleep, my soul would find rest if I used my preternatural abilities for the Light. At this point, I was pretty damn sure that the demons in Hell would wait in a line that wrapped around the cosmos twice in order to get a chance at punishing me for ruining their time on Earth. I had only sent a couple dozen back, but a slight on one was a declaration of war on all.

Oh, shit. I had also killed Locke, who was a direct lackey of Satan himself. I knew from firsthand experience that he knew how to torture both physically and mentally.

"Maybe a Barnes and Noble gift card would help smooth things over?" I half joked. It was draining to attempt humor right now, and I immediately felt my eyelids getting heavy. Fuck it. I was going to have that drink after all.

My comment went ignored as Father T continued to smoke his pipe while deep in thought. The flame from the oil lamp danced, causing shadows to crawl over his weathered face, and intermixed with the weak light from the pipe, as if they were wrestling for control. His white hair was tinged orange in the glow as the air filled with the aroma of tobacco.

"I'm going to have to reflect on the situation," he said without looking at me. My heart sank. If he had looked at me, it would have meant there was hope that he could somehow fix this. At least, that's what I felt. I could be making a mountain out of a molehill, but somehow, I doubted it.

"Return tomorrow night, my son. In the meantime, remain with allies at all times to discourage further incidents." With that, he stood with a groan while placing a hand on his lower back. He stepped into the aisle and bent at his creaking knees to grab the lamp with his other hand. Without another word, he hobbled toward a hallway on the side of the room that contained several places, including his chambers. I took note that he walked with a slight hunch for several paces before straightening as his body loosened slightly with every step. Though I was 559 years old, the impacts of age would always elude me. It was sobering to see my friend of almost two decades slipping into his twilight years. Without him, I'd be lost. My soul would surely be dragged to Hell when I danced off this mortal coil, and I was not particularly fond of the idea of dancing with the devil in the pale moonlight.

A pang of guilt struck me like a broken guitar string; was I worried that the father was going to die, in what to me would be a blink of an eye, because he was my friend? Or because he was my only hope for eternal salvation? It disgusted me that I couldn't convince myself that the answer was the former. I was selfish, I could admit that, but when it came to why I had certain people in my life, it felt more like a chess game than companionship.

If I sat and thought about it, I could break down each of my so-called "friendships" into useful and distinct categories: Depweg was a loyal soldier. Da kept me grounded and watched over me while I slept; he was my devil's advocate when it came to most of my actions. Valenta provided me with drinks and sage advice, keeping me up to date with the supernatural community. Father Thomes Philseep provided bleach to my darkened soul and gave me a sense of purpose.

I had always done the right thing on a small scale, like saving a family from a house fire or stopping the massacre of a small religious village in Africa. But if I was being honest with myself, I didn't know if I had done these good deeds because of the "big responsibility comes with big power" equation, or if I simply felt good for doing it. I had no qualms about ending the existence of someone who I deemed to be "bad" if it meant the good shall live. But even the latter part of that didn't matter to me. It was simply how I justified my actions.

If I used my power to do something good, was it considered selfless if I got a sense of pleasure from doing so? To me, it felt as selfish as people posting selfies on social media after buying a few cheap toys for a child whose name was on the Angel Tree at the local mall. It wasn't about the child; it was about being better than everyone else, complete with a look-down-their-nose feeling of superiority. Whether they were aware on a conscious level was beside the point.

The other side of that coin was that at least good things were happening to the people who needed it most, so why shouldn't the do-gooders receive an increase of serotonin and dopamine as a reward?

ON A SIDE NOTE, MY BODY DOES NOT OPERATE THE SAME AS A HUMAN'S IN terms of hormones and the like. Though that doesn't mean I don't *feel* things. It is theorized that super- and preternatural's have evolved to mimic humans in order to better blend in. I perceive stimuli and my brain responds appropriately. On top of this, I am fully aware of how much my Predatory Self wants to take complete control over my actions, which means my humanity has been fighting to remain dominant all these years.

I shudder to think what would happen if PS overtook my mind permanently. However, I digress.

FEELING A MIX OF EMOTIONS, I STOOD AND WALKED TOWARD THE WOODEN doors that led to the outside. I needed a drink.

3

Valenta's Saloon was within acceptable walking distance from the church, and closer still to the cemetery that I called home. Cliché you may say, and you'd be entitled to your wrong opinion.

As I approached the lone surviving business located in a district plagued by abandoned buildings, I decided it was best to use the back entrance.

Val's Saloon catered exclusively to the supernatural elements of the region, which meant I needed to tread lightly. Not so long ago, I had accidentally exposed myself to mortal authorities who had shown a recording of me using not-so-human abilities to the public. Mortals, afraid of the truth, had dismissed it as trickery or editing. Nonmortals were not so quick to forgive or forget.

It was well known that if someone broke the laws of the supernatural community—by, I don't know, exposing themselves to mortals via a bodycam—that their life, or unlife in this situation, was forfeit. It was open season on John Cook, the last vampire on Earth, and there would be no repercussions for taking me out.

So, with that in mind, it was best to use the back door if I wanted a drink at Val's.

Two concrete steps that were a sneeze away from being rubble led up to the back door. A lone doorbell illuminated the darkness, as the only light on the outside of the premises was out front, overlooking the parking lot. I gently pushed it and waited. Instead of a chime, a small light hidden underneath Val's bar would come on. In response, Valenta would buzz me in, allowing me into his modest kitchen, which was surprisingly spotless and well lit for that of a bar; all except for a dark corner were a set of heavy metal doors led to a basement.

A sound that reminded me of an electrical current, like a transformer on a country road away from the sound of cars, told me the door was unlocked.

I stepped inside, turning my head to glance over my shoulder, ensuring the coast was clear. I froze as two amethysts glinted in the darkness about a foot above the ground. Even with my eyes, it was too dark and far enough away that I couldn't quite make out what I was seeing.

My phone, sensing an opportunity to make me piss my pants, decided to shatter the silence by belting out the music to *Beetlejuice*. I yelped in surprise and fumbled to grab it. Pulling it out of my pocket, I saw "Deppyweg" splashed across the screen. It was he who had decided it was necessary for me to get a phone in the first place. I had gone my entire existence without one until now. I answered his call as I brought it up to my ear.

"Ya, man, what's up?" I asked while looking back out at the blackness. The amethysts were gone, if they had even been there at all. I stepped into the kitchen and let the door close behind me, unsettled.

"Where you at, brother? I downloaded the director's cut of *Aliens* and I'm ready to 'get away from her, you bitch.'" Depweg chuckled at his own joke.

I stared at nothing as the theater in my mind played the events again in vivid detail.

"Hello?" I heard the phone ask.

"Huh? Oh, yeah. Game over...and stuff," I attempted to quote while lost in my thoughts, as if in a dream. The perfect recall of my memory did see two purple orbs in the darkness, but I couldn't be sure what they belonged to. It could have simply been a broken bottle glinting in the moonlight. My gut told me otherwise. I shouldn't stay here.

"You alright, John? What's going on?" Depweg asked, concern evident in his voice.

I forced myself back to the present. "Yeah, man, I'm good. I'll be coming home soon. At Val's, grabbing a quick drink."

"Alright, buddy. If you say everything's fine, then I'll see you soon." Trust was interlaced with doubt, but he knew I could hold my own.

We hung up and I slid the phone back into my front pocket. I was still getting used to having one. I got why people joked about being slaves to their technology. It was like having a crying, shitting, hungry baby that demanded all of your attention and could fit into your pocket.

Val entered through the door that led to the common area. As he did, it swung back toward the patrons, one of which straightened as his eyes curiously followed Valenta and locked onto me.

"Shit," I said curtly.

Val followed my gaze to the swinging door and then looked back at me. "Shouldn't be come'n here, boy. Y'know that," he spoke with his thick Southern drawl. He was rocking a thick mustache that covered his lips and was fashioned into circles at the ends. "What'd' ya need?"

"A bottle, please. It's been...weird lately," I said, leaving out the part where I starred in *Leaving Las Houston* after draining an angel.

Val eyed me dubiously for a moment before walking through the swinging door. I wasn't sure if that had been a yes or a no. What I was sure of was of the now empty table in eyeshot of the doorway. I took in a deep breath, held it, and repeated, "Shit," while exhaling.

Valenta returned a moment later with a bottle and a disapproving look on his face. He extended his arm and I took my prize from his hand. I nodded once and turned to walk out the back door.

"B'careful, John," Val warned. "I know y' can take care o' yerself, but at some point, ants can o'erwhelm an elephant. Ya'hear?"

"I think...so?" I responded over my shoulder before stepping outside, letting the metal door click closed with a thud.

The night's air was cool on my skin as I took the two concrete steps in one stride. Bending over, I set the enchanted bottle of Jack and Blood on the ground before straightening again.

Taking in a deep breath, I called out into the night, "Who will be the first contestant on Wheel of Execution?" I enunciated the last part like a TV show host, with dramatic pauses in the made-up title.

In answer, footsteps echoed from the darkness. I smiled my predatory grin of delight. Both PS and I immensely enjoyed punishing those who would do me harm. I let PS put one hand on the wheel as I relinquished partial control.

Closing my eyes, I let my senses flow in all directions. I could feel my pupils shift, changing from a purple shade to a dark crimson. An unseen pressure in my gums forced my canines to elongate and sharpen to surgical points. The air became a distinguishable mixture of smells, each with their own trail leading back to their origin.

I opened my eyes to see three heat signatures approaching from my ten, twelve, and two o'clock. The thermal silhouette from the blood donor in the middle didn't match his visual body. It was an ogre wearing an expensive glamour. I'd have to reflect on this later, as ogres weren't your everyday thugs, mostly because it was incredibly difficult to mask their size. Those who could afford such expensive glamours usually didn't do basic-level dirty work. Ogres were not intelligent beings—but they were good at following the commands of their bosses, at least to the best of their limited abilities. Someone else had probably bought the glamour for him. I suppose it would make sense why they had been waiting for me at my favorite hangout if a nefarious, unseen bad guy was directing them. This gave me plenty of ammunition to chew on. I could probably trace the source back far enough to get substantial answers to at least move the plot along until the next book.

Now, I knew this was serious and that I shouldn't play with my food before eating, but sometimes I couldn't help myself. The thug to my left rushed me impatiently, forcing the other two to follow suit just behind. This caused a staggered approach, which was just fine by me. I lifted my arms above my head and bent them at the elbow, hiding my hands behind my upper back. I focused on my palms and willed blood to flow, molding it into a giant, Looney Tunes–type hammer.

As the thug approached, I kicked out my leg at preternatural speed into his solar plexus, stopping him dead in his tracks and emptying his lungs for him. As he bent over with a wordless cry of surprise, I said, "Stop! Hammer time!" before obliterating his head in an explosion of skull fragments, blood, and chunks of brain. I took notice that my super strength, well, extra super strength, was diminishing, but I still had enough in the tanks to be considered overkill for these jokers. The supe's body dropped to the cracked pavement, spasming violently as chunks of loose cement shifted. Val really needed to fix his foundation.

"Wait, is Gallagher still relevant? I feel like there's a joke here somewhere."

The cranial explosion caused the remaining normal-sized thug to slow in shock. The ogre just behind him continued to lumber forward, unable to slow his momentum as nimbly as his buddy. As the ogre charged into his companion, I stepped forward like a baseball hitter and smoothly slammed my hammer into the chest of the human-sized punk. With the ogre acting as a brick wall, the hammer completely crushed the chest cavity with a glorious crunch that sounded more like a car crash than the shattering of bones.

The ogre barely felt the impact and took advantage of my precarious position before I could reset. Huge, invisible lunch box–sized fists closed over my head and picked me up before beginning to squeeze. After a few moments of preparing to mimic the Play-Doh toy where the dough grows out like hair, I was acutely aware that my head was still intact and that my brain wasn't squeezing through invisible fingers. As a matter of fact, I was closer to being comfortable than in any sort of pain.

I REALLY NEED TO GET ME SOME MORE ANGEL BLOOD, YOU KNOW, FOR emergencies. Or after a really long day. Or just because...

You know what? I can feel your judgment, and I reject it completely. I mean, have you tried blood? Didn't think so. Back to it.

TO AN OUTSIDER, IT WOULD HAVE LOOKED COMICAL TO SEE A NORMAL-SIZED dude lifting another one off the ground with one hand. To those with eyes that could see through glamour, it was probably still funny, especially considering the ogre was straining so hilariously hard to pop my cherry.

His teeth were about to fracture, and veins throughout his entire body threatened to bust like geysers.

Feeling perfectly at ease, I separated my hands and willed my blood-hammer to reshape into two gladius-style swords made for stabbing. Even though my head was enclosed in his fist, his glamour was still in function, and I was able to see through his hand. Damn, this really was a top-notch spell. I was almost flattered. Almost.

Using the position of his head as a center, I thrust one blade upward and the other down and to the left, aiming for his throat and liver. The ogre saw the attack coming at the last moment and tried to move. Instead, he screamed loud enough to make the ground rumble as one sword hit close to home. Still grasping my skull, he threw me away and I flipped through the air and landed on my feet just in time to see a chunk of pavement being hurled toward my face. I ducked out of the way with ease and immediately saw why it had been surprisingly no trouble to dodge. One of my blades had found an eyeball, and the ogre was now a cyclops.

I let my swords melt into whips as I strode over to where the beast was spinning in circles, throwing his fists out in a tantrum. Ogres were pretty stupid and weren't adequate at articulating their frustrations—but what they lacked in intelligence they made up for in raw power. The ogre grabbed another handful of the foundation-impaired concrete and prepared to hurl it my way, using his remaining eye and new lack of depth perception.

Flinging my wrist, I wrapped a whip around the thug's throat, his real one. I let my other hand fly forward, entangling his legs, and pulled back with that arm. He fell to the ground with an earth-shattering, "Oomph," the chunk of rock that had been intended for yours truly landing on his forehead. I barked out a laugh as if I were watching a cartoon.

I willed the whips to shorten as I approached, like reeling in a fish, while keeping the pressure tight. The fun was over, and it was time for answers. I brought my hands together and let the whip from my right hand merge with the one on the left so only one hand held both manifestations. With my free right hand, I extended my palm toward the ogre's actual head, fingers outstretched. With a focus of will, I sent my essence into his head. My consciousness flew from behind my eyes and down my arm, using my essence as a train track to my destination between the ogre's eye sockets. I flowed through the barrier of his mind in my incorporeal state and began to search for answers.

There wasn't a lot there. I mean, I knew they were all brawn and no brains, but this was like a warehouse with a single file cabinet in the middle. Not to boast, but I had an entire city, complete with a castle, within my head where I stored pertinent information. One downside about having perfect recall was that I remembered everything I had ever experienced or learned with complete detail that didn't deteriorate over time. This accounted for a lot of useless information that needed to be filed accordingly. Otherwise, I'd simply go insane with all the raw information floating around like a tornado of random thoughts. I still remembered what I had said the day man landed on the moon.

"Neat."

Back to the empty ogre brain. I went to the file cabinet, which was illuminated by a lone spotlight overhead, and opened it in search of who had hired him. Only a crudely drawn image of a man wearing a black cloak was in the particular file I was searching for, aptly named "Kill Fat Vampire." I was pretty sure the picture had been done with crayons as well. I wasn't expecting much, and yet, I was still disappointed.

Hey, wait...fat? I may have a powerlifter's build, but I was far from fat (he tried to convince himself). Besides, dadbods were in.

With an eye roll and accompanying sigh, I pulled out the file and tore it to shreds before dropping it on the warehouse floor. I released my grip, and my essence reversed the roller-coaster ride until I flew back into my own mind. PS waved and gave a thumbs-up in question if I had found anything. I shook my head once, and his shoulders slightly slumped in frustration.

The ogre had stopped struggling at my invasion of his mind. It had never been done to me, but I could surmise that it was like a prostate exam; you didn't want to move for fear of making it worse. I might be off on my comparison, but it was close enough.

Instead of killing my would-be assassin, I retracted my bloodropes while turning to walk to where I had set my bottle of goodness next to the back door. Picking it up, I turned around to see the ogre, still in glamour, sit up and hold his head as if a massive migraine had just invaded his skull. He looked up at me with an expression that seemed to ask, "What just happened?" My own shoulders lifted in answer, suggesting I had no idea, before I set off into the darkness.

Once out of sight, I went into full stalk mode and watched from the shadows. Ogres didn't have super awesome night vision like some of the more predatory supes did—they simply didn't have to stalk their food, whatever they ate. I shuddered as I randomly thought about an ogre eating a unicorn in giant, crunching bites.

After a few more moments of confusion, he stood up on shaky legs and began walking toward the front of the saloon. Fingers slid loosely along the wall, searching for stability, while his other hand cupped the empty eye socket, which oozed blood. It coated his invisible hand, creating a crimson outline that floated above the man-glamour.

Stepping back toward the building, I leaped on top of the roof. My feet landed with barely a sound as pebbles lightly crunched underfoot.

As I approached the edge of the building looking over the parking lot and main road, I heard the purr of an expensive engine approach. My vision crested the roofline, and I could see Mr. Ogre approaching the back window of a stretch limo. The pitch-black tinted window began rolling down, and excitement built in my chest, as I was about to see who wanted me dead, or so I thought. The ogre had other plans, as both his hands grasped the roof above the window for stability. His glamoured body blocked the passenger. It was as if my unlife was a movie.

I spread out my senses and focused on hearing.

"Is he dead?" a hushed voice whispered.

"Huh? Who?" was the ogre's confused response. "Who...who you? Why eye hurt?"

There was a moment of silence and then realization.

"Drive," said the mystery guest, speaking with the same barely audible voice. The window began to roll up as the limo pulled away. The ogre, still confused, kept his hands on the roof for balance and tripped over his own feet as the vehicle moved forward. He hit the ground and sprawled out, giving the rear tire total access to one of his arms. I stifled a laugh as the limo bounced over the mound of muscle.

The window had almost rolled all the way up when two red eyes peered out from beneath a black hood, looking toward the noise I had made. We locked gazes while the window completed its ascension, breaking our brief but intense connection. Then the limo accelerated gracefully down the street while I stood, stunned.

"Who the hell was that?" I asked myself. Probably someone wanting to claim the bounty on my booty.

I took a step off the roof and landed smoothly on the pavement below, my black trench coat billowing like a cape as I did. Ignoring the confused ogre who was struggling to stand up, I strolled down the street toward my lair. It was time to go have a drink and watch *Aliens*.

4

The cemetery was inky black except for a lone light at the old front gate. The crescent moon provided enough illumination for my preter-eyes to see and make my way to my mausoleum. The enchanted bottle of Jack swished audibly in the silence of the graveyard while my footsteps alternated between dirt and grass, crunching with every few steps.

I put my free hand on the cold, white stone of the slab that acted as my door, and pushed to the side. The marble slid easily, as I had installed wheels on the opposite side after Depweg had moved in. Not that he wasn't strong. Oh no, quite the contrary. Depweg was probably just as strong as I was, but with the caveat that it was only while in werewolf form. As a man, he was as strong as several mortals and could leap entire parked cars in a single bound—but a pure slab of marble was still a pure slab of marble.

I entered my gauche mausoleum and slid the door back into place. There used to be a titanium beam that I could lower to further secure my hidey-hole, but after my home had been attacked so easily, paired with Depweg moving in, I thought it unnecessary. Especially now that Locke was gone. To beef up home protection, we had set up security cameras throughout the cemetery that had motion detection, night vision, and even infrared, all in 60 frames per second and 4k quality.

When the door was back in place, LED lights sprang to life along the floor and illuminated the room where I had had a custom marble throne made in the center. There had been a coffin at one point, but it had been knocked over when my home was attacked.

I walked past my marble throne to the back wall, where I pressed a false stone panel that activated the hydraulic system attached to a false door hidden at the back of my huge chair. With a hiss, the door rose from the floor, revealing a stone stairway that I then descended. Once upon a time, torches had been placed along the walls in such a way that I could excite the molecules of the wicks and set them alight, but once again, Depweg. The line of LEDs in the throne room above also graced the sharp edges of the stairs, providing adequate, but not overpowering, illumination.

At the bottom of the stairs, I approached the newly installed iron door with a handle that was wrapped in thick industrial rubber. After our last home invasion, my roommates and I had taken more precautions by adding iron to our defenses to prevent divination or magical attacks.

My Fortress of Solitaire was made from a number of freight containers I had procured on the cheap from Florida. They had even included shipping on the house to sweeten the deal; no mind freaking required. Using my X-Men power of blood manipulation, I had created some hefty, industrial-sized shovels that looked like they belonged on a big yellow machine, and cleared out enough earth to make my home. Now Depweg had his own freight car. I had had to create another massive hole, then set the metal beast into it, and finally redistribute the dug-up soil all over the cemetery to avoid suspicion. Though the place was run down, there was a groundskeeper that kept the grass trimmed and weeds pulled.

Frankly, I was glad the parent company that owned the cemetery did have an employee, because I siphoned utilities such as brand-new, high-speed internet, electricity, and water from the main lines of his modest cabin. Not that I needed to drink water or anything—it was just nice to take a hot shower after a long night. I did suppose that Depweg required water to survive. Probably. I'd never had a dog before. What I could tell you though was that buying doggy food and water bowls hadn't been received quite how I had expected. The early dawn after I had bestowed my caring gift to my best friend, I had opened my coffin to find it filled with hundreds of garlic bulbs. He knew that garlic was a myth perpetuated by mortals to provide them with a false sense of security and control when dealing with vampires—but my coffin still stank to this day.

Grabbing the rubber handle, I pulled the door toward the landing and entered. Once inside, I reached for the opposite handle and secured our home with the heavy clang of some industrial-strength locks.

"'Bout time, man," Depweg said from the couch with a mouth full of popcorn. "We were about to start it without you."

"Yes, John, what did take you?" Da asked. "Didn't get into any more scraps, I would hope."

I didn't answer as I placed my adult beverage on the counter. My silence prompted Da to turn toward me from his favorite recliner and shoot daggers at me with his eyes.

"You didn't..." Da said in disbelief, as if asking a lactose intolerant friend why they kept eating the delicious ice cream.

"It was a hit, orchestrated by a man with glowing red eyes and an affinity for Sith apparel." They both stared at me. I expected my movie references to go over some people's heads, but not these two.

"HE HAD A SITH HOOD ON! Lilith damn it, you guys are dense!" I said in exasperation.

Depweg, being of a military mind, asked that I explain the events of the evening in adequate detail. Da interrupted before I could start and suggested I kept to only the most pertinent of details. A juvenile smile tugged at one corner of my lips.

I explained the entirety of the evening to Depweg, who inched to the edge of the couch, listening intently with a furrowed brow, popcorn temporarily forgotten. I was touched he cared so much about my well-being.

"You're an idiot," Depweg said coldly. Turning his attention to Da, he asked, "Does iron and silver work on angels? Specifically, can they divine John's location right now?"

"Why are you asking him? He doesn't kn—"

"Silver, no. It is a holy metal," Da spoke with authority, believing he was an angel instead of the faerie he clearly was. It drove me mad sometimes. I wasn't the type of person who played along with what people identified themselves as. Live and let unlive, but keep me out of it. Then again, he was a friend, and I had an obligation to put up with some shit, just as, I was positive, he coped with a lot of my own unique mannerisms that some people would find unbearable. Their loss.

Da continued, "Iron, on the other hand, cancels all magic. So, to answer your question directly, no, they should not be able to divine John's location in here."

A thought tickled my mind just behind my forehead. "What about just outside the door?" I asked out loud, both to them and to myself.

We sat in silence for a few moments before the proximity alarms started shrieking in warning. Without a second's hesitation, Depweg set his popcorn on the coffee table and flipped the TV from the paused opening scene of *Aliens* to another source. Several boxes filled the screen, showing every camera broken up across the 80-inch Samsung glory.

"Holy...shit..." I said with eyes trying to bulge out of my skull. There was a squad of armor-clad angels stomping their way through the grounds, their heads scanning left to right.

Depweg chimed in, "Good. They don't know John's exact location."

"You mean *our* location, right? Buddy?" I asked hesitantly. "Pal?"

Depweg's hands went up in a halting gesture, "We didn't kill an angel there, bud."

My mouth hung open in surprise.

"But of course we got your back," he reassured me.

I relaxed visibly.

"As long as you don't do anything else stupid." Depweg's index finger extended my way, accusingly. "Now, they don't know where we are, so let's just lie low."

My life was clearly a made-for-TV movie because, right as Depweg finished his statement, the angels stopped in front of our mausoleum. One of them pointed at the ground, which had footprints in the dirt. In tandem, Da's and Depweg's heads swung slowly my way.

"I've, ah, been meaning to plant more grass there," I said sheepishly. Still synced, both heads shook in amazed disappointment.

Anger rose in my chest, and my hands clenched into fists. "You know what?" I spat. "Fuck this. Let's go have a conversation with them." As I spoke, bloodswords that were infused with rage extended from my fists.

They were horrific, jagged manifestations, as if made from flint, with sweeping sections of serrated teeth.

I turned to face the door and...nothing. I couldn't step forward. I exerted myself like a woman giving birth, or so I assumed from the movies, and only succeeded in making a high-pitched squeal.

"Lily!" I shouted once it hit me.

Depweg and Da shared a chuckle from behind me. This only enraged me further. After a few more non-hilarious attempts to move forward, I sighed and let the bloodswords retract.

"Giving up, are we?" Depweg chided.

"Uh-oh...don't..." Da started, but it was too late. I turned around with a smooth, clear expression; a mischievous smile appeared at the corners of my mouth.

"Oh dear," Da said, placing his face in his hands. "John, please don't. They probably just want to talk." He didn't even bother to look at me, as he knew it would do no good. "If they wanted to kill you, they wouldn't make it so obvious."

I stormed past them both toward the hidden exit in my room. As I did, I said over my shoulder, "Guess I'll go for a walk. But, gotta make sure I use the secret exit so I don't have to fight any punk-ass angels. Hope they don't find me."

"Stop," a silky voice commanded.

"Oh, thank God," Da said. "Please stop him from making things worse."

"Where are you going, lover?" Lily asked.

"Fuck," I whispered to myself.

"Maybe later. But first, you have guests. Play nice and maybe you'll survive the night."

There was a knock on the door. It wasn't overly aggressive, but neither was it meek. "Restrained" came to mind.

Everyone looked at each other curiously. All except Lily, who seemed giddy with excitement.

"Depweg, John, do not mention my presence to your guests. I am only here to observe." As she spoke, her visage disintegrated like she was made out of sand in the wind.

The door sounded again.

"Uh, I'd also appreciate the same courtesy," Da said before winking out of this plane.

"Fairies, man, am I right?" I said over my shoulder to Depweg as I approached the iron door. "Who is it?" I asked in my old lady voice.

"The Archangel Gabriel," a strong, reverberating voice said through the door. "I only wish to converse with the abomination."

Opening the door, I was greeted by a giant, armor-clad angel. Only one though. His helmet was tucked into the crook of one arm, letting long golden locks fall to his shoulders. He looked like a fucking model.

"May I enter?" Gabriel asked with surprising politeness. Caught off guard, I moved to the side, gesturing my permission. He was considerably bigger than the doorframe, and I was humorously curious about how he would squeeze through. Without hesitation, he stepped forward. White smoke, or maybe it was mist, billowed off of him, and his massive frame shrank to normal man size, complete with a charcoal gray suit and black tie.

"Whoa. Neat trick, Gabe," I said.

"Thanks, Jonathan," he remarked with a smirk.

"It's just John," I responded, rolling my eyes in the usual fashion.

"I know." The smirk had grown into a full-blown smile. Damn him and his shiny shoes. "It's Gabriel, and I'm here to deliver a message."

"Last winged dude with a flaming sword wasn't too keen on niceties with his message," I said, crossing my arms. Doubt was written all over my face, like I was waiting for the salesman to tell me the catch.

"A message of peace, of course," Gabriel said with an award-winning smile still on his face. It was surprisingly disarming. I found myself liking him. "I am, of course, the angelic messenger."

As he made his way further into my home, he stopped and closed his eyes. His head tilted upward, and I heard him sniff the air with visible pleasure. He exhaled in a soundless moan as a knowing grin appeared at the corners of his lips and eyes.

Trying to keep his train of thought on track, my arms uncrossed and my tone softened, "Alright. What's the message then?"

"There is concern on our end that you are the catalyst, and that deception which will lead down the path with only one end is at play." His smile had flattened and the corners of his eyes hardened to stone as he turned to face me. There was no joy in his features at that moment.

"Catalyst for what?" I asked, feeling my stomach drop at the implications and expected answer. Angels wouldn't show up at my door to tell me I had just won the Publishers Clearing House giveaway. This was serious if Gabriel was here.

"The Day of Reckoning, of course," Gabriel said. My stomach rushed down to meet my anus, which was clenching upward. I became a little light-headed as his words smashed into my mind like a mallet on a watermelon. Damn it, Gallagher!

"My horoscope said this would happen," I said with a sigh. Gabriel let a quick bark of laughter escape his throat before placing a fist over his mouth.

"Ah! This guy gets it!" I said while pointing at him and looking at Depweg. Damn, he was likable.

Depweg joined the conversation, "In what way is John responsible for the apocalypse?" His arms were crossed over his massive chest, and a dubious yet interested look was on his face. Veins popped out all over his muscles, from the sleeve of his shirt down to his fingers.

"I'm afraid there is only so much I can tell you. Rules, you know?" He looked upward at the last part, referring to the pact God had made with Satan about mortal interference.

"Well, what *can* you share with the rest of the class?" I asked, annoyed that he knew a lot more than he could let on.

"Only this message: You are free to make any decision, in the entire universe, that you wish. It is the consequences that are unavoidable." His emphasis was subtle.

"Sounds like a poster," I said before I could stop myself.

"Exactly," he responded with a wink. "Well, that is all the time for today, abomination." For some reason, when he called me that, it didn't seem to bother me as much. Gabriel turned to nod at Depweg before he started walking toward the door.

"You know, it really throws us off when you say that," I told him while squinting my eyes at him. It's not that I was offended; I was just confused at his demeanor and overall pleasantness mixed with that term.

"What, abomination? My apologies if it offends, of course. It is simply what you are. You'll understand someday," Gabriel said over his shoulder with an award-winning smile. For some reason, the image of him sitting at the head of a corporation formed in my head. "Farewell." The smoky mist rushed to envelop the angel as he walked through the door and up the stairwell.

I didn't respond as I shut the door behind him, my mind swirling with his message and subtle emphasis indicating a deeper meaning to his words.

Lily appeared on the armrest of the couch, her demeanor serious and lost in thought.

Ignoring her, as I knew she wouldn't tell me what was really on her mind, I turned to Depweg. "What did you make of that?"

Placing his hand on his clean-shaven chin in thought, Depweg said, "He added 'in the universe' to that quote, deliberately."

"Was that a hint to seek other planes for help? Or was he suggesting that we do nothing at all?" I asked while starting to pace. "Could it have been a straight-up warning that no matter what we do, we will be punished? That's kind of what the first guy said."

"Hey, hey. There is no 'we,'" Depweg said using air quotes. "He said you."

My jaw dropped open and my hands dropped to my sides, palms facing forward and fingers outstretched in a show of Whiskey Tango Foxtrot.

"Just messing with you, dude. You know I'm in," Depweg said while pointing finger guns at me.

"Damn straight. Who's a good boy?" I teased Depweg.

His smile vanished and was instantly replaced with a scowl.

"Actually," Lily began, "I have a plan."

5

That's a terrible plan," I said with impeccable comedic timing. I had taken an improv class and learned that if you had the right comedic timing, then it was okay to be a complete asshole—just as long as you were funny. That's not what they taught, but that's what I'd learned before I was asked to never return.

"I haven't even said my plan yet. I literally just said 'I have a plan' and you chimed in as if I had laid out said plan."

"Do we plan on not saying plan anymore?" Depweg asked while pinching the bridge of his nose between thumb and index finger.

"Don't plan to," I responded smiling.

"John!" Lily said as much with her hands as with her voice. "You are exhausting," she sighed.

"Plan," I poked.

Lily looked up at me, and I realized I had possibly made an error. "Rip out your tongue," she commanded with amusement. Yeah, I had definitely made a mistake.

Compulsion took over. My smirk evaporated as I struggled against her order. My face scrunched in intense concentration. I could feel my hand attempting to pull an *Evil Dead* and do its own thing. Too bad I didn't have a chain saw lying around.

"Hold up," Depweg said. I could always count on him to have my back. "Want to make sure I get this," he continued while pulling out his cell phone and turning the camera on. My hand was making headway toward my mouth, which was clenched tighter than an anus after eating at a Chinese buffet ten minutes before closing on a Tuesday.

"Wait," Lily said, and I froze in place, relief washing over me. "You're in portrait. Turn it sideways."

"Oh, right," Depweg said while turning his phone horizontally.

Lily looked back at me and cheerfully said, "Continue, John."

"I plan on it," I said through teeth that were refusing to part. "Yup, this is exactly what I wanted to do. Ol' tongue was getting in the way."

Depweg was shaking while trying to control his mirth. Lily just stared at me with a cool smile. I only had one card to play to take control of the situation. Opening my mouth wide, I gave full permission to my rebel hand and reached in, grasping my tongue hard. With a deep breath, I pulled quickly, tearing the tongue in half and sending blood splattering in an arc in front of me. Both Depweg and Lily were now covered in a new polka-dot ensemble. I tossed the tongue onto Lily's lap and made a kissy face at the camera, blood cascading through my lips and down my chin. I walked past the stunned duo and into my room, where I willed the wound closed.

I turned and set my hand on the door and yelled, "PLAN!" before slamming the door shut. Or at least I tried to. Pretty sure it came out as "PAN!" without my tongue.

I physically high-fived myself at having the last words and heard a bemused giggle. Shrieking like a tiny girl, I turned to see Lily sitting on my bed with a devious gleam in her eye. Her clothes and skin were polka dot–free, as if she had just gone through an OxiClean commercial. My hands shot up to my mouth, and I shook my head hard, pleading with my eyes.

"Calm down, John. I truly want to help. Besides, what fun would it be to lose my favorite toy?" she said as her hands found the bottom of her blouse and started lifting it up, revealing toned abs. Wonder if she meant my maw's appendage or me.

There was a knock on my door and I angrily called out with my healing speechmaker, "What?"

Depweg's voice came through the door, muffled but audible enough,

"There's a package for you." There was a hesitance to his words. Probably because he knew he was tongue-blocking me right now.

"There's a package in here too!" I called back. I was met with silence.

Confused, I turned to open the door, my eyes refusing to leave Lily's body as she let her blouse slide back down.

"There's a box for you, man," Depweg said standing in my doorway. Both his voice and facial expression displayed a confounded disbelief interlaced with a growing anger. He was clenching an oil rag in his hand that he had used to wipe off my lightly speckled blood.

"What's in the box?" I asked in my best Brad Pitt voice.

"Funny you should say that," Depweg responded while his gaze dropped to the ground; his face screwed up in dreamlike disbelief. I noticed his mouth twitched in such a way that he unconciously bared his teeth before relaxing again. It was like his mind was battling between confusion and anger.

On the table in front of the couch lay open a plain brown box. I stepped closer to try to gain a better perspective and was rewarded with an impossibility. Locke's burnt, scarred head stared up at me, his face still decimated from our battle. His eyes grew wide when he saw me, matching my own surprised look.

"You!" we said in unison, or would have if Locke had a functioning lower jaw.

IN ALL MY CENTURIES, I HAVE ABSORBED COUNTLESS SCROLLS, TEXTS, BOOKS, and blogs about anything and everything I could get my hands on. I have mastered every language that I've encountered and have read all works of major art in their original tongues. This has afforded me with every conceivable combination of words at my disposal at any time, allowing me what surely must be the vastest vocabulary in the entire world.

"HEA-HEAD...ALIVE!" I STAMMERED ELOQUENTLY WHILE POINTING A SHAKING finger at the box on my coffee table.

Lily came out of my room and strolled over to where I was pointing. Without missing a beat, she almost purred to herself in delight and lifted the destroyed cranium out of its cardboard prison by its greasy black hair.

"Did it...um...come with a receipt? I mean, it *is* burnt," I said dumbly. Both Lily and Depweg looked at me with squinting eyes and mouths in little O shapes, as if I had just asked if the living head that had been delivered in a box had a receipt with it. "Note! I meant note. Oh, and who the hell delivered this?" At this, they let my question slide and pondered the delivery itself. "And perhaps the most important question, how the hell is it still alive?"

Depweg strode to the TV remote and began searching methodically through our security footage. First, he watched the entrance to the Fortress of Solitaire, and when he was satisfied that it showed nothing, he moved on to the others surrounding the perimeter. Not a single one showed a delivery person.

"How did you know the box was here?" I asked Depweg.

"After you slammed your door, Lily disappeared, leaving me alone. I really wanted to watch *Aliens*, so I turned to walk toward the couch, and that's when I saw the box on the table." Depweg pointed to where the cardboard cube still remained. "After sniffing it and feeling for any traps, I decided to open it myself rather than bother you two love falcons."

"HA!" I barked out. "Love falcons. That's awesome." I could see Locke rolling his eyes at that. I walked up to where Lily was still holding him and asked really slowly, "Can you understand me? Give me a thumbs-up for yes or tap your foot for no." I found it easy, even cathartic, to humiliate the man responsible for so much of my and my were friend's pain.

Locke rolled his eyes again, and I could hear the air escape his mouth hole in a pshaw. Lily started to set the head down on the coffee table when I cried out, "WAIT!" She froze in place as I slid a coaster underneath where the head hovered. "Okay, there." With a roll of her own eyes—boy, there was a lot of that going around—she laid the head down. It just sat there, if a head could sit, looking at us. His eyes shifted from person to person, unsure of what to do.

"Do you know where you are?" Depweg asked calmly but with an edge of irritation while walking into Locke's line of sight. There was a bit of restraint in his tone, as if he were trying to forcibly keep his own head on straight. "Blink once for yes and twice for no." Locke blinked once before his brow furrowed. We could all feel Depweg's anger burning white-hot deep in his core, masked by military discipline.

"Do you know how you got here?" Lily asked. Locke blinked twice.

"Do you know the muffin man?" I asked while walking to the junk drawer in the kitchen. Once I reached it, I retrieved what I was looking for, which was right next to a bottle of clear superglue, and then asked over my shoulder, "Did he blink?" before turning and walking back toward the table.

Ignoring my question, Depweg asked, "Will you tell us what your master's plan was?" Locke hesitated and then blinked twice, but not out of defiance like I was expecting. "Then what use are you to us?" Depweg asked as his voice rumbled in the beginnings of a growl.

"None," I called over my shoulder. "Let's kill him...you know...*again*. But first..."

I returned to the coffee table and got down on one knee while removing the cap of the Sharpie. With a few lines and some circles, Locke was ready for a night on the town.

"Is this necessary, Jonathan?" Lily asked while putting her palm over her eyes and rubbing her forehead.

"I didn't do anything," Depweg responded without looking at her.

"HA!" I cried out to Lily while pointing a victorious finger at her. "Not as much fun to use that now, huh?" Jonathan Depweg and I locked eyes for a moment and nodded our heads in silent victory. I realized I was subconsciously trying to alleviate my friend's anger.

Looking back at Locke, I stood and crossed my arms, admiring my handiwork. "Now he really is a dickhead."

Locke had been trying to look at his own forehead, which was both sad and odd, until he processed what I'd said. His forehead scrunched and his eyes narrowed at me while he tried to use his mouth to form words. As his forehead creased, I pointed while laughing and said, "Look! Now it has foreskin!" I looked around, awaiting a high five to be prompted by someone for that epic joke, but there were none to be given that day.

"Fine," I said. "Let's get Father Thomes here so we can get his opinion." At the mention of the holy father, Locke started blinking in rapid two-blink successions bordering on frantic.

"What? You don't want the father to come and exorcise your ass back to Hell? I bet Lucifer is pissed at you right now, huh?" Locke closed both his eyes really hard, his face starting to shake.

Growing tired of his lack of communication I said, "I have a *plan*." At this, both Lily and Depweg cried out while throwing their hands in the air and letting them drop again in a show of disbelief. "No, I'm serious this time," I finished as I put my palm over Locke's crushed lower jaw and willed my blood out and over his face. I focused on my life force, which still had some angel charge, to heal his broken face. The air echoed with the sounds of popping bones and tendons, all while Locke wailed as his face was reconstructed. When the task was almost complete, Locke let out a long "O" syllable that coalesced into, "Oooooooo, you twit! That freaking hurt!" he exclaimed in his motherland accent of Old English.

The remaining blood retracted into my palm, and I stood up next to Lily and Depweg.

"Cool trick," Depweg said.

"Saved your were-ass," I gloated. At least I pretended to. I had been willing and ready to sacrifice my own existence to ensure Depweg survived our encounter with Locke after he had been impaled through his lower torso with a pillar of hellfire. I had doused the flame with my life essence, using all of my will and energy to fight the very flames from Hell itself. Only real problem was I had also been in the process of being eaten alive by hellfire, and had had nothing left in the tanks to save myself. Then along had come Lily. Just as Jennifer Aniston had convinced Ben Stiller to eat that spicy food, Lily had forced me to imbibe her blood, forever making me her slave. Admittedly, it had its perks, though.

"Thanks, brother," Depweg said with full sincerity. Uh-oh, intimate man moment, got to change things up. I punched him playfully hard in the arm while wearing a shit-eating grin. Depweg stood stoically, comprehending what had just happened. Then he nodded in understanding. I think he was more in touch with his emotions and definitely able to control them better than I was.

Turning my attention to Locke, I said, "Tell us what we want to know or there'll be a little head to pay."

Depweg leaned over to me and whispered in my ear, "That didn't really work, man," then leaned back to a straight stance. I motioned for him to come closer, and when he did, I whispered back, "We need to watch *Aliens* after this." He nodded and then leaned once again to his neutral position.

"I love that movie," Locke said, putting his American accent back on while moving his jaw around, testing my work. "Shall we put it on now?"

"Yes, but first, what was Satan's plan? Why did you want me to stay out of his way?" I demanded as I stood up from where I had been crouched. "And don't lie. We'll know if you are lying."

"Seeing as I am in quite a predicament, I will reluctantly tell you what you wish to know. Samael wants to bring the final battle to fruition. He is tired of ruling Hell and wants to destroy Heaven and Earth or be killed in the process, freeing him from his eternal duties."

I was taken aback by the flood of information and leaned toward Lily and Depweg, where I loudly whispered, "Is he lying?" Depweg shrugged while Lily only stared, methodically processing the information.

"But why John?" Lily asked while nodding toward me. "What does a lone vampire have to do with the apocalypse?"

"You are right," Locke stated.

"About which part?" Lily asked, bemused but frustrated. I secretly enjoyed watching the Fae having to play the information game.

"When the last vampire walks the Earth, the gates of Hell will open. This will allow the apocalypse to begin," Locke said.

At the mention of the apocalypse, Depweg visibly relaxed his demeanor while his glare softened to disdain rather than hate. It's like the impending end of the world distracted him from the canine sanctuary that had been burned to ashes by Locke's men.

"Well, here I am, last of my kind. I'm walking and I'm talking and the Earth is still under my feet, so try again," I said while motioning my hands up and down my body.

"That's all I know. Surely you don't think Samael would divulge all of his knowledge to me and then send me to the front lines to do his bidding," Locke pointed out. "By the by, can you heal my burns?"

"No," I said dismissively without giving it any thought. He could have asked what time it was and I would have just as easily turned down his request. Then again, I was the one who had to look at that well-done mug. It reminded me of this one time when I'd first gotten my cell phone and I'd been chatting with Depweg. I'd said to him "Hey, what's that sound?"

When he had asked, "What sound?" I had farted into the phone and laughed at him. "You do realize that you are the one that has to smell it, right?" I'd realized he was right immediately. He was like the Joker, turning people's plans around on them.

"Then, why help him at all?" Depweg continued asking Locke, but now in a more even-keeled tone. "Don't you have a stake in all of this?"

"Great question!" I said while pointing at Depweg. "That, that thing he said. Yeah," I finished by crossing my arms and putting on a Cool Cop interrogation face.

"I'm dead," Locke reported.

"No shit. Am I right?" I said to Lily and Depweg, who continued to ignore me.

"No, you simpleton. I died long ago and was sent to Hell, where my talents drew the attention of some key characters of the biblical persuasion. It wasn't long until the Lord of Hell himself called upon me and made me an offer that was impossible to refuse. He would give me my body back and let me live again on Earth as his servant, or I could spend an eternity in his personal torture chamber where I would lose my sanity. I made my choice, and I challenge anyone else to make a different decision."

"So, you *did* die and actually went to Hell for your crimes?" I asked sincerely. I was under the impression that he had eluded punishment for his crimes until I'd delicately removed his head. It had been maddening to think he had walked this world for centuries all willy-nilly.

"It would appear so," Locke confirmed.

Lily broke the silence that had begun to fill the air, "I don't think it's a coincidence that the Devil chose your archnemesis as his herald, John."

"I agree with Lily," Depweg said, his eyes flicking to Locke before settling back on me. "Seems terribly convenient."

"Why did he burn your face?" Lily asked.

"Well, at first I thought it was to make a point about his power and influence, but then I saw John. It clicked then. Samael was saving his punch line for the right moment," Locke told us.

I thought about this and then stated, "He's right. Had I known Locke was Commander Godwin," I trailed off for a moment, as even uttering the name made my jaws lock together and my fists squeeze white-knuckle tight, "I would have rushed him, damn any army or rules that might protect him."

"You'd be dead," Depweg said, lifting his head to stare into the distance.

"I *am* dead," I said with a shadow of levity. "Well, undead if you want to be technical about it."

"And if you were dead, there wouldn't be a last vampire to start the apocalypse anymore," Lily said, grasping the situation better than Depweg or myself. "Perhaps..." she started while circling the air with an open palm, suggesting the remainder of her thought.

"Don't even think about it," Depweg said, snapping out of his haze to glare at Lily.

"How cute. My puppy wishes to test me. Sit, puppy," she commanded.

Knowing the game, Depweg strode over to the bar, grabbed a stool, dragged it right in front of Lily, and then sat down. Their eyes were on the same level while Depweg sat on the stool. There was a defiance in his eyes that dared her to test his resolve.

"If I die," I started while staring blankly at the wall, "then the apocalypse will be averted?"

Depweg turned quickly to look at me and interjected at the gravity of my statement, "Perhaps, John. But that is to assume a few key points. One, is Locke telling the truth, or the truth that has been presented to him by the Father of Lies? And two, what happens if you die right now? Satan will get his hands on you for all eternity, along with all the zealots and demons you've sent packing, who I'm willing to bet are waiting. Who's to say that the Devil doesn't want exactly that? Maybe as a trophy. Or, perhaps he needs you in Hell to actually start the end of days. You have proven yourself able to handle even the biggest of bastards he can throw at you, and that could be strategically advantageous on the battlefield. Whatever the answer, I would suggest self-preservation until we have more to go on. No reason to be making decisions without all the answers, dude."

I let my mind wander as new pieces of the same puzzle I had been working on for centuries appeared and fell on the already cluttered board I had once thought was complete.

"For the record," Lily said as she looked at me with wanting eyes, "I don't want you to perish, lover. I was simply speaking out loud."

"Just curious," Depweg started, almost cutting off Lily, "but how do you know you are the last vampire? What if one is asleep in Madagascar right now or something? Or even more plausible, what if there are several more out there who are better than John at concealment?"

I feigned surprise while placing a hand on my chest and mouthing, "Me?" Depweg's mouth closed in frustration, and he tilted his head while exhaling loudly. Locke being here, somewhat alive, was taking its toll on Depweg's humor.

"Okay, okay," I began, growing frustrated at this What If game. "Let's just work with the facts we have in front of us. 'When the last vampire walks the Earth.' It doesn't matter if there are more. We can assume that they are being hunted or will be, right?"

"You are the last," Locke said confidently and coldly, being the bearer of bad news. "Though it wasn't said outright, I am confident that you are the last based on the information I either overheard or was told directly." I opened my mouth to say something when Locke continued, "Yes, I am aware that Lucifer is the Father of Lies, but he worked diligently on you and only you. When I was his servant, it was my job to remove certain pieces from the board while watching over you. He never mentioned other vampires."

I dropped my head and took in a deep breath before saying, "I think he's right. Ulric mentioned being the last one when he made me."

It was then that I noticed Lily being intentionally quiet. "Lily?"

"Ulric was the last before he made you. Then you were the last when you killed him in London," she said without her usual playfulness.

"How did you know about London?" I asked. "I never told anyone about that. To either of you." My eyes shifted from Lily to Depweg, who shrugged.

"I had no idea, dude," Depweg said.

"I am Fae, lover. I know what I must and I *must* know." There was a heaviness to her words, as if she were projecting her usual calm demeanor rather than exuding it.

Silence was my response. She had never mentioned me killing my maker before. But I was only slightly surprised at her knowledge. She was, after all, ancient and cunning. I was sure there were plenty of mouths feeding her information for even just a sniff of her perfume.

Something Locke said bobbed to the surface of my mind, and I asked him, "What other pieces have you removed from the board?"

"Samael had me open a doorway to another plane and allow the supernatural community passage off this world."

I glanced at Lily, who remained fixated on Locke. I returned my attention to the crispy cranium, "Why do that?"

"To weaken Earth's defenses," Depweg stated.

"Though he never stated why, and I wasn't foolish enough to outright question Lucifer, I had a hunch that was the reason why," Locke admitted.

Depweg got up from the stool and began pacing as he pieced the puzzle together; Lily didn't object. "We know it's in every supe's best interest, and even their responsibility, to fight demons. They have no compunction about revealing themselves to humans and risk exposing all of us. There must be, what, hundreds of thousands of supes across the world?"

"Not anymore, I'm afraid," Locke said with a sigh. I wanted to ask him how he was able to talk and exhale without a diaphram, but I was sure the answer would make me feel stupid for even asking.

"Are you certain the doorway was opened to Faerie?" Lily asked, placing a finger on her chin in thought.

"Yes. Why do you ask?" Locke questioned.

"If the supernatural community were in Faerie and sought asylum with the Seelie Court, then I would have seen them."

"What are you saying?" Depweg asked as he ceased his pacing to focus on Lily.

"I'm saying there are no creatures from this plane in the City in the Tree."

"Neat name," I said, "but I'm not following."

"If the refugees are not with the Seelie Court, then they can only be one other place," Lily trailed off.

After a few moments of silence, I threw out in agitation, "Look, I *love* suspense as much as the next dude, but can you spit it out, please?"

"The Unseelie Court must have them. If that's the case, they are all dead. Queen Mab of the Winter Court does not tolerate any trespassing on her lands." Lily's eyes, which had gone unfocused in contemplation, snapped back and locked onto the cause of the concern. "Locke, where in Faerie did you open the door? Tell me now."

Locke, sensing her building aggression, stammered as he answered, "I-I-I don't know! I never really thought about it! Lucifer instructed me on how to *feel* for Faerie parallel to our own plane and had me picture a scene in my head. I had never been there and did as I was told!"

"What did he describe? Explain in as much detail as you can," Lily commanded with a tone that suggested to everyone in the room that she was not to be questioned or disobeyed.

Locke closed his eyes and began. "There are evergreens that are in perfect lines down countless rows, as if they were an army on display. The ground and trees are coated with fresh snow that is constantly falling from an overcast sky a shade of light gray. It is quiet, with only the gentle breeze making a sound along with the trees as they sway slightly. There is a castle etched into the mountains—"

"Enough," Lily interrupted. She turned to face me and said, "Satan tricked Locke into opening the gate right in front of Queen Mab's castle. They are all dead."

"Lilith damn it," I exhaled, letting my head drop as I shook it in disbelief. Lifting it again to set my eyes on Locke, I asked, "And this happened all over the world? With other asshats like you opening the doorway?"

"I can confidently say yes," Locke began to explain, intelligently ignoring my jab. "It never really resonated with me why Lucifer needed a warlock at every leyline in the world, until now. I thought he was simply positioning us over this plane's source of focused power—you know, fortifying them before his enemies got to them."

"That still might be the case," Depweg added. "Stands to reason he would kill as many birds as possible with a single stone."

"I need to talk to Father Philseep," I said absently, my mind strained from everything that was being thrown around.

"NO! No, please. That isn't necessary," Locke pleaded. Three eyebrows arched in unison.

"Why are you so afraid of the father?" I asked, tilting my head and crossing my arms.

"Oh, no reason. So, about that movie, then?" Locke segued.

I pulled out my cell phone and unlocked the screen, letting Locke see me go to my Favorites menu where Depweg, Lily, Valenta, Da, and Papa T were the only names listed. Heck, they were the only names at all, so I didn't even know why I had manually added them to my favorites.

I let my finger hover over Father Thomes' name and glanced over at Locke, daring him to lie or avoid answering further.

"Alright, alright, alright. It's because I'm dead and haunting my own body using Hell magic. I am very confident, given what I know about your holy do-gooder, that he would exorcise me in an instant and send me back to Hell. You can imagine that I don't particularly wish to go back. Speaking of, can I crash here with you guys? The iron upgrades would sure help keep me hidden."

Iron upgrades? He had just shown me that he still had some power left in him, at least his senses. I mean, he was also haunting his own decapitated head. I'd have to file that away for later in my information city. Then the gravity of his question hit home.

"DUDE! You fucking killed my parents, you little shit!" I cried out as I pointed to Depweg. "And you burned his house down and all his dogs. Now it's your turn to burn. Depweg, turn the oven on. We're going to have ourselves a Locke-e-que."

"Sounds awesome," Depweg said coldly as he turned and made his way to the kitchen.

"Right, um, sorry about all of that," Locke said quickly. "I did spend a number of earthly years down below, which equate to a fucking long time in Hell years. I paid for my sins and had a lot of time to think about them. The truth is, your father was right."

"Gerald. His name was Gerald," I barked out while fighting the urge to clench my jaw until my teeth shattered. I squeezed my fists until they started to make popping sounds, drawing Locke's attention to the severity of his situation.

I heard beeps from the oven as Depweg turned it to broil while I shot laser beams at Locke with my eyes.

"Gerald was right," Locke said slowly and calmly, like talking down a feral animal. He was drenched in fear, and rightfully so. "We were there only for the land and property that was rightfully your family's. BUT! If it hadn't been me, it would have been someone else! I just did as I was told."

"Another reason Satan chose you, then," Depweg said, returning to the living room. "Doing whatever you're told despite the consequences. You seem to excel at that."

"Forgive me, but were you not a soldier who killed more than his fair share of enemy combatants?" Locke pointed out.

"That's different and you know it," Depweg growled in warning.

"What about the Jewish boy being held prisoner by Nazis the night you raided their camp. In your rage..." Locke began, but Depweg kicked the coffee table in the purest rage I had ever witnessed from him, startling both Lily and me, and sent Locke flying behind the couch with a nose-crunching thud. A throaty growl left his chest, making everything that wasn't nailed down in the living room reverberate. I could see Depweg preparing to change—starting with his eyes, which had turned yellow with black slits for pupils.

"Hey!" I called out, putting myself between the two before Depweg decided to stomp on Locke's defenseless head, or eat him. "Just go to your room for a minute and calm down, brother. No judgment here." Depweg's chest rose and fell with each heavy breath as tears started pouring down his cheeks. I leaned close to him and whispered, "He's giving us some good intel, man...against Satan of all people." Without looking at me, he turned and strode off to his room, slamming the door.

Lily had gone behind the couch to pick up Locke while this was going on. I righted the coffee table, which now had a crack down the center like a fork of lightning. I would have to ask Valenta to either fix it or craft a new one.

Lily sat Locke back down, sans the coaster, and his words started to sink in. This left me conflicted. Yes, he had killed my family, but he had spent what must have felt like a millennium in Hell being punished for it and many other crimes. His excuse of just following orders was not sufficient, and I still wanted to make an enchi-head-a in the oven.

What would the father say to me right now? Probably tell me to continue down the path of righteousness and forgive those who have trespassed against me while also focusing on the big picture—the apocalypse was coming and I was the key. There had to be some truth to this due to the number of supes leaving this plane and hiding—or being murdered by a Faerie Queen. This, coupled with the fact that Satan was clearly trying to piss in my Cheerios, provided all the proof I needed.

"Why does the Devil think I am the catalyst for the end?" I asked somberly while grabbing Locke's nose and twisting it back into place.

"Ow! I don't know, Jonath—" he started before I glared at him with eyes that glowed red, "John. Just John. But I would like to help stop it. Being a bodiless freak on Earth is infinitely better than even dipping my toe back into Hell. It's not all physical torture, you know. Samael is entirely too clever, and personally comes up with the most devious of mental punishments." Locke paused, as if deciding whether or not to continue. "He...he even made me endure the deaths I caused a thousand times over. Including what I did to your parents." Locke's eyes closed in remembrance, and he attempted to gulp. "I feel my mind is barely hanging on by a frayed thread, but the hope of never going back is keeping me sane. Before now, I did whatever it took to stay alive, in a manner of speaking; including trying to keep you subdued, which now I clearly see was an attempt to earn your attention. I was a pawn in his chess game; his sacrifice to lure you out. Now I am free from his influence, and I am just as determined to never go back as before. So please, let me help."

"You were tortured in the bull?" I asked weakly, my voice losing the fight against the lump in my throat.

"Yes," Locke said without breaking eye contact with me; his bottom lip quivered as he remembered each agonizing death.

"You had your intestines pulled out?" I batted my eyelids, trying to free my vision from the blurring scene.

"Yes. Each a thousand times at least. I lost count when weeks felt like days and years passed like months." His eyes brimmed with tears. "I am truly sorry for what I did. Not just to your parents, but also to all those I hurt. I felt each of their pain over and over and over again, and I am sorry!" At that, his tears freed themselves and ran down his face, where they pooled on the table.

"What do you think, Lily? Do we trust this dickhead?" I asked while clearing my voice and wiping my face with the sleeve of my trench coat.

"I think that if the end is on its way, we need all the help we can get," Lily stated honestly and with a slight touch of worry. Her eyes remained fixed on Locke, displeasure marking her features.

It was at this time that Da decided to join us by blinking into existance while holding a comically too big pizza box and saying, "I've brought pizzaaaaaaaaaahhhh! What is that thing doing on my coffee table? And without a coaster, no less?" he exclaimed while dropping the box on the ground and pointing at Locke's head.

"Is that cheese?" Locke asked with genuine interest while sniffling back his tears and ignoring Da's remarks.

Da's gaze quickly shifted between Lily and me, awaiting an answer.

"It's a long story. Well, it actually isn't, but it sounded cool," I said.

A minute and a half later, Da was caught up and picking the pizza box off the ground.

"Can you get him a flowerpot or something? I don't want his neck cooties on my custom furniture," Da said as his eyes stopped on the new crack. "My table!"

"I'll get it fixed," I said before doing a double take and throwing out, "The fuck you mean, 'my table'? Val made that shit for me, bro. That there's *my* table. But yes, I'll get Val to work his magic."

"See that you do," Da said as he bit into a slice that was bigger than him while simultaneously ignoring my correction about the ownership of said table.

"How did you even buy this, Da? Did you float in, pay, and grab the box from the mortals before leaving?" I smiled warmly, thinking about what a sight that would have been.

With that, Da was a normal-sized man. There was no mist or ectoplasm growth, which looked like clay being added to a statue. He was simply a man.

"Nice glamour," I said as I grabbed a paper napkin and set a piece of gooey hot goodness in front of Locke, who glanced up at me with a look that said, "Really, dude?" I patted him on his crispy head and sat on the couch, turning the TV source back to the Xbox where *Aliens* finally awaited. Locke stuck his tongue out and tried to use it for leverage on the slice in front of him. I chuckled—the Devil wasn't the only one good at coming up with punishments.

"And who left the oven on? I leave for a few minutes and come home to pure chaos," Da bitched dramatically as he floated to the kitchen. A few beeps later and the oven was off—which to me felt symbolic of a path that had been chosen on a forked road. It made my skin crawl to allow Locke even another second of existence, especially in my home; but I felt it pertinent to see where this might go.

As I pushed play, I glanced at Depweg's room and thought about what Locke had said about the Jewish boy. Depweg had killed an innocent, and it still weighed heavily on his soul. At that moment, I felt even closer to my brother from another supernatural mother.

6

I lay in my newly repaired iron coffin hidden underneath my fake bed in my room. The LED lights were off. My rotation of books closed. This week's consisted of a series that centered around a shiny, asshole beer can helping out a group of humans in a stolen spaceship. I wasn't sure who I most identified with: the gullible human protagonist or his sarcastic, ancient, and powerful AI sidekick.

I could feel dawn approaching and I fought the urge to surrender to its will. My head was swimming. My emotions were conflicted. The decisions I would make could forever alter this plane of existence, and with it, all mortal life.

I knew I was a key piece on the eternal chessboard, but I didn't know what moves I should, or even what moves I *could,* make. Did I trudge forward and call Mephistopheles' bluff? Did I retreat to my front lines and lie low? What about the other planes in a lateral move? That seemed to be the answer for most supes. Then again, I probably didn't want to show my face to them right now. I was still fair game for accidentally showing my powers to the mortals. Moreover, word was bound to get out about me being the suspected cause of the apocalypse. Any rational being would be in the right if they were to take me out. Like a controlled flame before the big fire.

My foggy mind drifted to recent events and to the hooded figure in the limo with glowing eyes who had hired the trio of comedic relief. I felt there was something there. I knew it like a child knew there was a monster in the closet without any accompanying facts and in spite of his parents reassuring words. Without further thought, the answer clicked into place like a key sliding into a lock; I would find Mr. Limo and have a chat. I hadn't put much thought into him at the time. I hadn't even bothered to chase him down as he drove off. But right now, something was telling me that he was an important piece to this apocalyptic puzzle.

My eyelids won their battle and embraced as I yawned, letting my will relax and accept sleep. Father Thomes' face was the last thing I saw before being pulled under the waves of consciousness, the light fading as I descended deeper into the ocean of dreams.

7

I dreamed, and what I dreamed terrified me. My feet crunched on blackened earth. Smoke blotted out the stars above. Fires of varying colors danced in the distance, some from the hellfires below and others from the heavenflames above. The air was acrid with the smell of sulfur and charred flesh. All around, bones littered the ground as far as the eye could see. Though they had no faces or flesh, their postures made it clear they had died in agony and terror. A skeleton huddled in the corner of a crumbling building, its arms wrapped around a smaller skeleton which returned the embrace.

The wind gusted and pulled at my beard and the hair that spilled out from beneath my gray beanie. It felt uncomfortably warm against my exposed skin, like opening the door to an oven that had been preheated to over four hundred degrees. I walked aimlessly, letting my dream be the guide. It was going to show what it wanted to show, and I had no say about it. I was but a lone passenger on the roller coaster of fate. Sometimes you had to learn to put your hands in the air and enjoy the ride.

At that moment of self-surrender was when I saw them; a gaggle of demons huddled around a fire, cooking what I hoped was a human-shaped deer. I walked right toward them, ground crunching underfoot.

One of them must have heard this over the crackle of the fire, since he looked around, seeking the source. I blurred forward and stood in their circle, looking at the charring man-flesh with feigned interest.

"Hello there," I said to the group, cheerfully.

"It's him!" said a wiry-looking mofo.

"You were supposed to say 'General Kenobi,'" I sighed as I let blood-swords coalesce. "You ruined my dream meme."

"Wait! Don't hurt us!" another one cried out as his hands went up defensively. They all cowered away from the blades.

"What kind of big bad demons are you?" I asked, annoyed and disappointed. This was a dream, so I had no plausible reason to fear a pack of Hell's minions.

"We are what's left," said a large, oily-skinned humanoid.

"What's left of what?" I asked, letting my blades drop to my sides while still leaving them out.

They all looked up at me as if I had asked what year it was and if Elvis was still alive.

"Of anything," said the wiry demon. He gestured around. "This is what's left of the War of Eternity."

"Who won?" I asked.

"No one," he said. "No one won. We all lost. God and Samael were so intent on proving they were right that they didn't consider the possibility that they were both wrong."

I chuckled at this as I sighed and said, "Pride."

"Used to be one of my favorites," said the little one who I was beginning to associate as the leader of this ragtag group of leftover demons.

"So," I began, not knowing what question to ask. "Is Heaven...?"

"Heaven, Earth, and Hell are indistinguishable from one another right now," he informed me while tearing a strip of meat from the body over the fire. It smelled surprisingly pleasant.

"Those are some big words for a demon," I stated.

"What, you think all demons are big and dumb? That's a hurtful stereotype. Not all of us gave into our rage when we had the long fall from grace. There are those of us who kept our minds intact at the sacrifice of brawn."

Even for a dream, this was helpful information. Whether or not it was true was a completely different matter. But for now, I went with it.

"I guess it's true, then, what they say about being big and dumb. At least in regard to demons."

"Mostly," he said around a mouthful of charred flesh. After swallowing, he continued, "There are the rare occasions where you can find those who gave in to their rage while fighting to maintain their minds. They," he shuddered, "are truly terrifying, even for us."

"Why's that? Isn't there honor among thieves or something?" I asked.

"Why? Because we are all demons? That's racist, you blood-sucking abomination," he said with a wry smile.

"The irony of that statement is palpable. But seriously…" I motioned for him to continue while letting my bloodswords retract into my palms.

"The hierarchy in Hell is no different to that on Earth. At least on paper. Those who can, do. Would you agree that there are those who aren't —well…weren't—afraid to slit the throat of their fellow man to climb to the top?"

"Point taken," I accepted while gesturing for one of the demons to move over, allowing me to sit and listen.

"I know this is a dream and all, but I'm confused as to why I don't feel the need to kill you all anymore. Except him," I said while pointing to a particularly nasty-looking beast with tusks, a huge brow, and red eyes. He pointed at himself in surprise, fear somehow evident in his eyes.

"Just kidding, dude," I said. "But for real. Why haven't I ever heard of demons like you?"

"Garlic," the leader said.

"Come again?" I asked.

"All the books and stories say vampires are deathly allergic to garlic, correct?"

"Ah," I acknowledged. "Got ya." I pondered for a moment and asked, "So you are just, I guess, the equivalent of normal dudes? I suppose that it makes sense that most books on demons only mention the super-duper scary ones." I put on a British TV host's accent and added, "Coming up next; we'll follow the demon, Kevin, as he lies about his tax deductions."

"Every plane has their mix of denizens. Keeps things interesting," the smart demon said.

"Well, how do I know you aren't trying to trick me right now?" I asked, only half sincere.

There was a thundering sound in the distance that filled the night.

"Couple things. First, the apocalypse has already happened and the war is over. What good would it be to try to kill you at this point? Second, it's your dream, dude."

The night reverberated again, louder in a staccato BANG BANG BANG.

"Goodbye, John," the leader said.

8

Huh?" was all I could manage before my eyes blinked open. I was in my coffin. Someone was knocking on my bedroom door. BANG! BANG!! BANG!!! Lifting the hydraulically powered iron lid, I sleepily called out, "What?" before yawning and rubbing my eyes.

Da entered the room and said, "It's been sundown for quite some time now, John. It's not like you to sleep in except—"

"Except on Sundays," we said in unison. "That's my day," I finished.

"Yes, we all know that. However, it is not Sunday, now is it?" he said as he crossed his little arms.

"What time is it?" I asked through another yawn, still waking up.

"Half past nine," Da answered while squinting his eyes at me. "Are you feeling well, John? You seem...tired."

"I am tired."

"Right, and doesn't that strike you as a tad bit odd?"

He was right. Something was off. I dove into my information city and couldn't locate a single time when I hadn't been able to awaken within moments after the sun had retreated and let night take control. Except Sundays, when I willed myself to stay asleep as a treat to myself.

"Do..." Da started, "do I make you some coffee?"

"I appreciate it, dude, but no. I can't synthesize the caffeine, which means I'd only be drinking bean-flavored water. Unless we have some enchanted coffee lying around? I mean, we do own our very own warlock now," I said with a smile. "I am hungry though. Maybe I'll go hunting."

"Don't wander too far. We all know how awful you are at managing your time, now don't we?" Da chided.

Yawning yet again, I said, "Yeah, yeah. Got it." I got up, stretched, and went into the bathroom. After brushing my teeth to prevent bacterial growth in the warm cavern that was my mouth, I splashed cold water on my face. Looking up into the mirror, I was greeted by someone I didn't recognize. Water streamed down his face and pooled in his beard, but that wasn't the odd part. Dark bags were prevalent under the eyes of the person staring back at me. Eyes that were questionably purple instead of unmistakably so, as if they were reverting back to brown. With the cold water still running, I leaned back over the faucet and splashed my face again with vigor. I did it again and again, soaking my shirt and the white granite vanity. Water pooled on the floor. I could feel it kissing my toes as I forcefully splashed my face, trying to erase the person that had stared back at me.

With eyes still shut tight, I lifted my head to the mirror, willing my vision to see my normal, beautiful yet still rugged and manly face. My gaze set upon my old self, albeit covered in water. Droplets were falling from my reddish beard and onto my hands, which held the countertop. I looked down and saw a small crack had formed from the pressure.

"Shit!" I said as I pulled my hands away. I stepped back and looked at all the water I had thrown around in my barely controlled frenzy. Surprise and concern tiptoed through my mind, and I looked up to see myself staring back with piercing purple eyes. My hands explored my face, tugging my cheeks down to look at the whites of my eyes. The bags had smoothed to young skin again. Nothing seemed out of place. I flexed my canines and let them elongate easily into my preternatural fangs.

"All the better to drink you with, my dear," I said to the mirror as I let my teeth return to normal. I grabbed a white cotton towel that hung on a rack and dabbed my face and beard dry. Then I soaked up the water on the vanity, cabinets, and floor. I removed my shirt and let it drop to the ground along with the towel. Let Future John deal with that.

I grabbed a fresh shirt and stepped into the living room where Da sat on the couch reading an article on his iPad.

"Where's—" I started before Da answered my upcoming questions.

"Depweg is getting supplies. He waited for you, but he decided to leave before the stores closed. Locke is...*elsewhere*," he let the last word hover with a hint of ruefulness.

"Da," I said like a father sternly talking to his child, "where is he?"

"He had a dirty mouth," Da said without looking up from the screen.

As if on cue, I heard the dishwasher switch from full rinse to super-heated drying. There was a muffled cry that emanated from the stainless steel box. I rarely used the thing as I had no use for dining utensils with my preferred sustenance. I quickly made my way into the kitchen where my hand gripped the handle and pulled on the door. Nothing happened. I jiggled the handle again with some extra gusto.

"You have to hit pause, John," Da sighed from the couch.

I squatted down and looked at the buttons, searching for the correct one to press. I spotted the one that looked like any pause symbol for music or movies, and pressed it. There was a click, and the door opened freely as I pulled it again. Steam billowed out as it opened. I could feel it caress my face as it ran to the ceiling and dissipated.

Peering inside, I saw Locke's soaked head. His eyes were ablaze with fury. He tried to speak, but all that came out were unintelligible vowels around the ball gag in his mouth. My eyebrows went up in surprise.

"When did you get a ball gag?" I asked over my shoulder to Da as I slid the top rack that contained Locke out.

"If you couldn't tell by the size, it's not mine," Da called back from the living room.

I unfastened the sex toy and held it up for closer inspection. I saw two marks made by fangs and said, "Oh, right. Lily went through this Fifty Shades phase and bought all kinds of stuff." One particular memory made my butt clench reflexively.

With his mouth freed, Locke unleashed a torrent of insults directed toward Da. Something about a pretend angel and blah blah.

"Shh," I said as I pressed my finger to Locke's flapping lips. "Don't think you want to go back in there, am I right?"

"Your powers of deduction rival your stupidity," Locke said.

"Not sure how to take that."

"Further proving my point. Now, can you kindly ask your sidekick to treat me with a modicum of respect?"

"Who are you calling a sidekick, you low-level villain. You're one of the minibosses the game throws at you to make sure you understand the simple mechanics of the game," Da chided while floating into the kitchen and pointing an aggressive finger at him.

"We are all pawns, tiny angel. Some of us just have bigger parts to play," Locke said while his gaze shifted toward me. Or I assumed it did. His face was plastered with his usually greasy hair, as if he had just discovered the emo lifestyle. Annoyed, I ran my palm over his face and pushed the hair back over his head, clearing his burnt face.

"Da, please be nice to our guests who are planning to betray Satan and help us stop the apocalypse? Hmm?" I condescended to Da, annoyed that I even had to explain the situation.

"Well, look who has turned the other cheek," Da said approvingly while giving my shoulder a little punch. Though he was only five inches tall, I now knew that the faerie, Da, hid immense power in his little frame. My thoughts drifted momentarily to the boy in the graveyard. In my injured blood rage, I had drained his mother of every ounce of her life force before trying to add him to the dinner menu. Da had miraculously stopped me by throwing me several yards with incredible ease. The icing on the cake was that the boy and his mother had been at the grave of his father. I had made the boy into an orphan and surely scarred him for life. I took pity in knowing no one would ever believe him that a monster had killed his mother. Da had assured me in private that he had taken care of the mother's body by putting a glamour on her that made it look like she had simply died of a heart attack or something else mundane.

"Da," I started slowly, hiding the emotion that was building, "how's the boy?"

"He is taken care of, never you mind," he assured me aggressively. "If you ask again, the answer will remain the same." It was clear that he had forgiven but not forgotten about what I had done. Maybe he thought I would try and intervene in the boy's life out of shame and regret, only to surely make things worse.

Da interrupted my self-loathing. "Now, are we going to play nice, Mr. Potato Head?"

Locke frowned in displeasure but remained silent out of self-preservation.

"Good," I said. "All settled."

A shrill whine shot through the air and invaded my ears.

"The hell?" I asked out loud.

"Motion detectors that Depweg had installed earlier tonight," Da answered. "He was still concerned about how easily our new, um, *friend* arrived," he put emphasis on friend, as if trying it on for size.

"Damn, I love that doggo," I said in reference to my furry companion. "Hey!" I cried out, startling both Da and Locke. "He really *is* my best friend."

Da and Locke sighed in unison.

"I'm telling him you made a dog joke," Da said.

"Please don't," I pleaded sheepishly.

As if on cue, Depweg unlocked the front door and entered, holding several reusable bags of various supplies.

"Did it work?" Depweg asked.

"What?" I responded.

"The motion detection system."

"Look, we both know it works. You're just trying to get praise for a job well done."

"You want me to change the alert sound, don't you?" Depweg said.

"Yes, I do. How about the main theme to *Batman*?"

Depweg looked at me in silence, gauging what I had just said. After a moment, he concluded, rightfully so, that I was undead serious. "Alright, done." Depweg's eyes dropped to Locke's head, who had been nestled in the crook of my arms as we spoke. His hair was still dripping as the drying cycle had only just started when I'd freed him from his clean prison.

"Um, did I miss something?"

"Nope!" Da quickly evaded. "Someone just needed a bath."

"Okay then. Here, try this out," Depweg said, handing me a neck pillow.

"Thanks, I guess?"

"Not for you, dummy. For him. It'll help keep him upright until I can fasten something more permanent," Depweg said until he realized it sounded like he was doing something nice for Locke. He leaned close to his face and whispered with teeth bared in a creepy smile, "This will also hide the gore hanging out of the bottom of your head and making me hungry."

"I'm touched," Locke said to Depweg in a show of defiant submission.

I moved the head to eye level and asked, "Where did he touch you? Show me on the doll."

"On second thought," Locke began, "send me back to Hell, please. I don't know how long I can take these awful jokes."

"You get used to them," both Da and Depweg spoke in unison.

Taken aback, I said, "Well, I don't know what to say to that."

"That's a first," Da responded. "Shouldn't you be out, feeding?" Then he looked at me intensely. "On those who would do evil, correct, John?"

"That's the plan," I said as I turned to Depweg. "Up for some hunting? There's been a lot of armed robberies downtown."

"I don't know..." Depweg trailed off as he laid down the grocery bags, unconvinced.

"An old lady and her husband were both hospitalized this week, and they never found their attackers..." I prodded, letting the last syllable hang in the air temptingly.

"Oh, alright."

Slapping my hands together, I dropped Locke on the ground. "Oops, shit! Sorry 'bout that," I said as I picked up the now angry head and wiped the dirt that clung to his wet hair.

"Da, why don't you make yourself useful and vacuum while we are gone?" I spoke while securing Locke's head on the travel pillow.

"Why? I already did the dishes," he said with a smile.

9

Depweg and I walked the few blocks to the storage park where I kept my white Kia Optima. I glanced up at the bank of clouds that blotted out the stars and sniffed the air, smelling the sweet scent of coming rain.

"Hello, Mortis," I said as the storage door rolled up. The air had a chill to it that cooled my skin, reminding me how hungry I was. My Predatory Self was also beginning to whine inside my mind. *I know, I know. We're going*, I said inwardly, feeling his frustration.

Depweg went to his side and reached for the door handle that still rested in the cup holder.

"Oh, right," I said as I got in and opened his door for him. Depweg got in and we headed off toward downtown Houston.

"I've been meaning to ask," Depweg spoke, breaking the silence. "Why do you call him Da?"

I chuckled before I said, "It's short for Devil's Advocate because the little dude won't shut up about every decision I make. I don't actually know his real name. The only one he ever gave me was of angelic origin, so I refused to call him that. I'm not supporting his delusions."

"What delusion is that, exactly?" Depweg asked.

"That he's a five-inch angel and clearly not a faerie. Have you ever met an angel that can shift planes?"

"I'd never met an angel until yesterday," Depweg said.

"Fair enough. But trust me on this; I've met plenty of demons, and none of them could shift. Safe to say that angels follow the same rules."

Depweg pondered this by stroking his square chin, then made a pointing gesture. "But faeries can't lie, right?"

"There are all kinds of faeries, my friend. From what I have gathered, the Fae of the courts cannot lie. I personally think it was so they could conduct business with each other and know the truths. Otherwise, they might still be at a useless war with one another."

"Peace for the sake of progress," Depweg mused.

"What is that, a quote?" I asked.

"You can quote me if you like," Depweg responded. "But just so I understand, you are saying there are faeries that can lie? That doesn't make sense."

"Can you shift during the day? Can I walk into a church full of crucifixes while chewing garlic-flavored gum?"

"They make those?" Depweg asked jokingly.

"I don't know, probably. I'm sure hipsters would be all over them. But back to the point—don't believe the lies we convinced the humans to believe."

"I was human, once. Stands to reason I would be susceptible," Depweg said with placation evident in his voice.

"Right, which is why you believed these falsehoods, just as you once believed in a fat man in a red suit shimmying down your chimney to give you presents if you didn't drive your parents crazy all year."

"Krampus is what kept kids in line. I used to lie awake at night reliving the events of the day to make damn sure I hadn't done anything wrong."

With a terrible German accent, I said, "You Germans are weird, man."

"Wasn't just us, you damn Scot."

"I'm Irish and you know it!" I barked out. Depweg chuckled as the bait was taken.

As we drove, the streetlights were hypnotic as they raced toward the car and then away from us. The city had just switched to LEDs, which really illuminated the road. I turned on the radio and set the volume low, just to fill the background with rhythmic ambiance.

"So, what did he say his real name is?" Depweg asked.

"Raziel. Can you believe that? I mean, it *is* a cool name, but still." I had my own quirks and internal demons I battled, but at least I was honest with myself about them.

"Raziel, huh?" Depweg said, letting the word linger on his tongue as if it were a fine wine he was savoring.

"Sounds fancy, doesn't it?" I added before pulling down a not-so-well-lit road. Used-tires stores and body shops littered the surroundings.

A question that I had to ask was coming up my throat and heading for my mouth, and like a wave of vomit, it was not to be denied.

"Hey," I began, my voice sounding unsure and meek, "Can...can I ask about what Locke said?"

"Which part?" Depweg asked, cocking an eyebrow at me.

"About...you know...the kid." As soon as the last word left my mouth, Depweg's expression turned sour, and he quickly turned to look out his window. His knee started bouncing up and down in agitation as he thought. I kept my mouth shut, terrified I would make things worse. I was about to take back the question when Depweg's knee stopped moving and he spoke.

"It was just before we met. The Nazi werwolf hunter set a trap for me, and I fell for it in my hubris. I used to think I was the top of the food chain and indestructible. How wrong I was." Depweg shook his head, ashamed of his past self.

"What happened?" I prodded carefully. I knew how hard it was for me to talk about what I had done in the graveyard when I'd been in a blood rage.

"I was hunting Nazis and not being careful about it. I left behind shredded bodies in my path as a calling card. So stupid!" he cried out as he clenched his fists and shook them in the air.

"Hindsight is twenty-twenty, my friend."

Depweg relaxed slightly before continuing. "It wasn't hard to plot where I was heading. By then, they had figured out—or at least correctly guessed—what I was, and set a trap for me.

"I approached the town where the Nazis had set up camp and began stalking my prey. I should have noticed how empty the place was compared to the ones before. I came upon a lone soldier leaning against a flagpole that flew the Third Reich's flag. In front of him were burning mounds of dead bodies of what had to be the entire town's population. The smell of all that decaying, blazing flesh was dizzying. The deafening sound created by the hungry flames was that of a train barreling down the tracks. The soldier seemed to just be standing there, admiring his handiwork, and it enraged me. No. It fucking pissed me off, and I reacted off my emotions. I howled into the night and began sprinting toward the soldier, who just stood there with his back to me.

"I slammed into his back, feeling and hearing a tearing sound, and latched onto the back of his neck with my jaws. I crushed his vertebrae before I heard him crying. It wasn't the type of crying I had expected from a soldier. It was...higher, like a child's. I opened my jaws and looked down at the crippled soldier. His arms were out to his sides, and I could see where his hands had been ripped off at the wrists. Confused, I turned to regard the flagpole and saw child-sized hands hanging from shackles, dripping blood. There was dirt under the nails like you would expect from a young boy. Stacked at the base of the pole were schoolbooks that the soldier had been standing on.

"I began whining as I looked back down at the body that was clearly wearing a uniform that was too big for him. As carefully as I could, I used my snout and nudged the body below me onto his back. He screamed like a teapot as his neck was turned, and all doubt of whom I had just attacked was erased.

"My heart sank as I stared down at a child no older than five years old. Safety pins kept the adult-sized uniform fastened to the boy. He was screaming. His face was cut and bleeding from where he'd struck the ground, and I began licking his face to try and clean him. All I did was make him scream more, but this time in fear rather than pain and surprise.

"I could feel the fur under my eyes soaking with my tears," Depweg said just above a whisper, as if his mind were detached and miles away. "I could taste his blood, and it filled me with despair. I-I couldn't believe what I had done in my rage," Depweg told me with a cracking voice full of emotion. Tears had begun streaming down his face.

"Wha-what did you do?" I asked with a gulp, knowing it wasn't my place, but unable to stop myself. I had stopped the car, and just stared at my friend as he exposed his soul.

Depweg shut his eyes tight while his head moved from side to side as if trying to erase the memory from his mind. "I heard laughing from in front of me, and the bastard who had set the trap walked out from the shadows. The smell of the bodies and the sound of the flames had concealed his presence from me."

"'He was just a poor little boy, monster,' the werwolf hunter said to me. 'Look at how he suffers still. What will you do?'

"I looked down at the whimpering child whose warm tears had melted the snow around his eyes. Drool spilled from his mouth as he sobbed with complete abandon. I knew what I had to do."

My chest grew tighter and I adjusted in my seat, all of a sudden uncomfortable. My mouth hung open as wide eyes watched Depweg prepare himself to tell me his darkest secret.

"I opened my jaws, took the boy's entire neck into my mouth as carefully as I could—he was just so small—and then...I-I..."

My heart sank into my stomach and my eyes began to flutter as I looked around, searching for a way out of this nightmare.

"I released his lifeless, limp body and licked from his forehead to his cheek on both eyes, closing them forever. I whined in regret before the Nazi began tittering again. My eyes shot up to latch onto him, and I charged. That's when he pulled out the silver kukri and slashed at me as he dodged out of the way of my attack. I had never been cut by silver, and I was surprised at how much it hurt. I stumbled and collapsed to the ground as several Nazi soldiers emerged from doorways while others held out long muzzles through open windows. I chuffed as I got back on my feet, not fearing the bullets from those weapons. Then one of them shot me in the chest, aiming for my heart." Depweg lifted his shirt and ran his fingers over a long scar that ran across his massive right pec. I recognized it as one of the wounds I had had to burn closed the night we met.

"My instincts told me to save the knife-wielding man for last, so I exploded into one of the open doorways and tore a Nazi's throat clean out. I made my way upstairs and ripped out the spine of a man standing by an open window.

"The werwolf hunter chased after me, cursing in German. I think he was expecting me to try and stand toe to toe with him as the riflemen picked me off, foolish man.

"I was always one step ahead of him as I made him watch as his soldiers fell by my hand. I burst through walls, leaped into second- and third-story windows, and killed every last one of his men. All that was left was him.

"I leaped from the open window I was at and stood by the flagpole. One of the boy's hands had fallen from the fierce wind that had begun to blow. I howled in both anger and challenge at the werwolf hunter, who returned the call with his own, twisted cry. It was clear to me that he had fought several of my kind, and won.

"Snow had begun to fall, using the wind as a battering ram to beat down the small town. The piles of burning bodies started to extinguish as the wind and snow began their onslaught.

"The hunter stepped out of the doorway that was attached to the building I had jumped from. His chest was heaving from effort. Part of me respected his dedication while the other wondered what his heart tasted like.

"We squared off. Me with my claws and teeth, and him with his silver blade. Neither of us would be able to heal from our wounds before the battle was over. The fairness of the battle excited me. Then I saw the boy out of the corner of my eye and excitement turned to blinding rage. I leaped straight at him, but lower than before, aiming for his legs. He had clearly been expecting me to go for his throat like most wolves would out of instinct, so I caught him by surprise and took him to the ground.

"His blade sliced into my flesh, spilling hot blood on top of him while my claws dug into his torso in wide, deep gashes. I cut through his shirt and flesh like running a finger through fresh snow.

"After we had cut each other several times, I began to win the blood loss battle, as I had more of it to give. His flesh became as white as the falling snow as he lifted his blade like it weighed as much as a gravestone. I swiped at his arm and took it off at the elbow. The werwolf hunter didn't even cry out as his arm and weapon tumbled away. I brought my jaws to his face and bit down on his skull, crushing his face in from chin to forehead before tearing the meat free and eating my prize.

"After I defeated the werwolf hunter, the adrenaline began wearing off, and I became light-headed. I fell to my side and began to change back into a man, unable to stop the transformation.

"As I finished, I lay naked in the blood-drenched slush we had created with our battle. I began to shiver from both the cold and blood loss, and began stripping the hunter of his clothes. That's when I heard the cry of men coming from the distance. I couldn't see them in the blizzard, but I could make out their shouts. I quickly put on the man's shirt and pants before unbuckling his sheath and picking up the arm still attached to the weapon. I ran, then, as the first group of soldiers entered the town behind me.

"I ran for as long as I could before the loss of blood took its toll and sapped me of my strength. While deep in the woods, I collapsed against a tree and tried to catch my breath. I realized I was still holding the arm and decided to try and eat with the hope that I would regain my strength. I pried the kukri from its grasp and sheathed it before looping the blade to my belt on my lower back."

"I think I know the rest of the story," I said, remembering our first meeting. "You sure as shit didn't seem weak to me then, brother. You gave me a run for my money!"

"When I smelled you downwind, my adrenaline shot back up. That and the meat I had eaten helped. But if I recall correctly, you had to help me walk afterward because I used the rest of my tanks on your bitch ass," Depweg said with a dry smile. I took that as a sign that he was coming back from the dark pit his story had thrown him in.

"Thank you for sharing, brother. I'm sorry you were tricked; however, that wasn't your fault. That hunter knew *exactly* how to get you. But you didn't let him, Jonathan. You took out an entire squad of Nazis who had just murdered an entire town even after they had set up the perfect trap! You avenged those people and probably saved countless of your own kind from that, dude. You," I placed a hand on his shoulder to emphasize my point, "are a fucking hero."

"Thank you, John," Depweg said as he looked me in the eyes. There was an immense strength to him, even when he was at his most vulnerable. I smiled, placed my hands back on the steering wheel, let off the brake, and we continued toward our hunting grounds. We sat in silence as the bond between us grew. I knew how it felt to reveal your deepest secrets to those you trusted and who knew you. I could also recall how Depweg had been the only person who had understood what I'd gone through after I killed that woman at the cemetery and almost ate her young son as well. The thought of him holding up his action figure in defense still made me shudder in shame. Thank Lilith for Da.

Another question I had struggled with personally sprang to my mind. "Did you ever find out his name?"

Depweg let his chin drop to his chest in shame as he wiped his eyes and said, "No. It haunts me to this day. Everytime I shut my eyes at night, I see him broken on the ground and *hear* him shrieking...I-I never even found out his name."

I understood all too well what something as simple as knowing a name could mean. Da refused to tell me the boy's name from the cemetery, and it somehow prevented me from having the closure I so desperately wanted —*needed.* At least I had the comfort of knowing Da had taken care of him afterward. Depweg—my brother with the bleeding heart of gold—had no such comfort.

10

Here we are," I segued as we continued down the road where city officials didn't see the need to fix the numerous potholes or lighting.

I parked Mortis in a mom-and-pop chicken shop parking lot (say that five times fast), and we got out. I stretched dramatically, like an Olympic athlete about to break a world record, while saying to myself, "Mom-and-pop chicken shop parking lot. Mom-and-pop chicken shop parking lot." It was my mantra at the moment.

"What?" Depweg asked, clearly confused.

"Hmm? Oh, nothing. You wouldn't understand. Anyway, ready to eat?" I gestured at his clothing.

"Not shifting yet. Don't want to scare them away."

"Oh, right!" I said while palming my forehead. "Forgot these." As I finished my thought, I opened the trunk and handed Depweg a cane.

"What's this for?" he asked, hefting it like a weapon.

"Predators are attracted to weak and dying prey, right?"

"Got ya," Depweg said while letting the cane slip through his grasp from a battering stance to a battered old man stance.

We began walking down the street. I pretended to have a gimp leg while Depweg walked normally with just a cane added to every other step.

"Come on, Mr. Clooney. Put some of those acting chops into it." I motioned at my superb method acting. Rolling his eyes, Depweg leaned into the cane with his alternate steps.

"There we go!" I approved.

We walked for a half mile, which took forever, before Depweg asked, "How long does this normally take?"

"If it's just me, not long at all," I said as I thought. "Maybe I've cleared all the riffraff out of Houston?"

As if I had said, "Can things get any worse?" to which the universe always responded, "Oh yes, they can," before dumping crap on you, that's when two gentlemen wearing pantyhose on their heads leaped out from behind a large bush that overlapped the sidewalk. Each meal wielded comically large knives that rivaled Depweg's epic silver kukri.

Turning to Depweg, I said, "See, this is what happens when we let a law pass letting anyone carry as big a knife, or even a sword, as they want." I turned my gaze to the two men who were twitching slightly. "Great," I told Depweg, "They're druggies. This meal is going to be the equivalent to eating 3:00 a.m. fast food."

"Yeah," Depweg said, "I'm not eating that." At that, he straightened his posture and turned to walk back toward the car.

"Hey! Where the fuck do you think you're going, man? Give us the cash!" one of the tweakers said as his friend lunged at Depweg's back. I shot my hand out, palm open, and a rope snaked out and wrapped around his neck before he got to Depweg. He gurgled and fought as I lifted him off the ground, turning my head back to see his companion's wide-eyed expression, which was hilarious through the pantyhose headwear. As he looked at me in frozen terror, I started to will spikes down the length of the rope. Just as they were about to pierce the neck of the first tweaker, his buddy told me, "Please don't. We weren't going to hurt you. We just need some money for another fix. I-I won't ever touch the stuff again, I swear to God!"

Putting on my best Christian Bale's Batman voice, I yelled, "Swear to me!" as I made my eyes turn from purple to a glowing red. I could audibly hear the man shit his pants over his gasps of terror.

I stopped the spikes and relaxed the rope, letting the first man drop to the ground clutching his throat while coughing up a fit.

"This isn't any fun," I sighed to myself, barely above a whisper.

"We're sorry! Don't hurt us!"

"Pathetic," I said as I let my red eyes fade out. "Get clean, mortal. You only get one life, don't waste it. You never know when you'll take your last breath."

"Than-thank you!" said the man with shit in his pants as he picked up his friend, who I noticed was actually a woman. I was proud of myself for not seeing gender then; equal rights and all. Never mind the fact that the pantyhose skewed their faces and plastered their hair down flat.

"Come on, baby. Let's get out of here," he said as they stumbled down the road and to some assumingly abandoned garage that had a lone dirty mattress as their only furniture. It was only a guess, but one I would bet on.

I turned toward Depweg, who had already made it a few blocks, and bounded after him. After a few leaps, I was standing at his side.

"You did the right thing, John," Depweg declared. "I could smell the fear on them before they even jumped from their bush. They were scared. Their addiction forced them to act with the simplest of goals: get money. I don't think they had it in them to do anything except try and scare us."

"Yeah," I agreed. "Maybe we did a good thing tonight. But I'm still hungry." My metaphorical stomach rumbled in agitation at the tease of a meal.

"I might have an idea," Depweg said as we approached Mortis. He put the cane back in the trunk and climbed into the passenger seat.

"You mean a plan?" I joked as I sat down. Depweg punched my arm, but with a smile on his face. It actually hurt, even though he had pulled the playful punch. I sometimes forgot how strong he was, even in his man-suit. "Head downtown," he said as I pulled out of the mom-and-pop chicken shop parking lot and onto the service road.

As we drove in silence, I had time to reflect on what had just happened.

"I could have drained them and never think twice about it. They matched my criteria. We were walking; they jumped out with weapons. What more could I ask for?"

"You're growing, John," Depweg said, pride evident in his voice. "I believe the more your soul is cleaned, the easier it will be to make the right decisions, and the clearer those decisions will be."

His words sat heavily on my mind, as if a cold piece of ice cream had been plopped on my brain and was slowly melting, filling in the cracks. I wasn't sure if I liked the change. Seemed exhausting to be good all the time.

"Speaking of growing, what are we going to do about our new—*ally*," I asked, spitting out the last word. It was bitter in my mouth, and I wanted it out.

"I'm honestly conflicted. Part of me wants to soak him in lighter fluid and light a match for what he did to the canines. They trusted me to watch over them, and I failed them." Depweg took in a deep breath, held it, and released it while saying, "The other part of me knows we need all the help we can get against the greatest threat to our world. Locke..." He cocked his head to the side while briefly flashing teeth at the mention of his name before returning to normal. "Locke has information and insight that might help us save all of creation." He looked at me then and asked with eyes desperately seeking confirmation, "We have to forgive him...right?"

It was unnerving to see the do-gooder golden boy struggle to take the high road. I felt closer to him as I saw his vulnerability. Ah, damn it—he was asking me for guidance. Where was my map and how the hell did I find the high road?

"I'm with you on both lines of thinking," I admitted. Depweg looked back at the road, but I could see his eyes going unfocused as his brow furrowed. "But what you said is right—about saving the world and stuff. I want to hate him for everything he's done, and I do. I keep thinking about my parents." It was my turn to stare into the void while my mind battled between logic and emotion. "He killed them, brutally murdered them, and I ripped his head off and laughed into his blinking, surprised face as he died. Maybe that's why it's easier for me to say that we should consider forgiving him. I had my revenge." I turned my head to Depweg, hesitant about what I was about to say. I knew my best friend and how he would react, and I was ashamed that I didn't want either of us to forgive the bodyless bastard; but I didn't want the world to end either. "How many innocents, like my parents and even your puppies, will suffer if we don't win against the Devil?"

Depweg nodded slowly and I saw the corners of his eyes and brow soften as my words marinated in his brain. A part of me wanted to yell that

Locke should suffer and pay by our hands for his transgressions. I fought that prideful urge before looking inward into my mind.

What do you think? I asked PS. He crossed his arms and turned away, exposing his back to me.

"So—" I began before being rudely interrupted by a giant blur slamming into Mortis, violently throwing us off the road and over the guardrail. We tumbled down an embankment, rolling toes over teeth repeatedly. I braced my hands against the roof and was vaguely aware of Depweg doing the same. As we came to a rocking stop on all four tires, I let my hands drop as I leaned forward, head resting on the steering wheel. The airbag deployed and punched me squarely in my beautiful face before deflating.

"Are you fucking kidding me?" I asked the universe as I cupped my nose. "Could this possibly get any wor—?"

"Dude, get out. Now!" Depweg commanded as he hastily unfastened his seat belt and pulled on the door handle. Nothing happened. After a few more pulls, Depweg threw his shoulder into the door, forcing it open with a shrill protest of steel on steel. Glass from the sunroof fell from his shoulders and onto the leather seat.

I was still tired from being hungry, but a vampire's energy became permanent after feeding enough times. Much like how protein turned to muscle after being eaten, it took more than one missed meal to lose all the muscle you had gained, but you still needed constant sustenance to maintain and build. Enough missed meals meant your body would break down that muscle for fuel. For blood energy, it was similar. I had energy in reserves, but I hated using those unless it was absolutely necessary.

From the corner of my eye, I saw the rhinoceros charging down the embankment to where we were. Wait, rhino? I shook my head and did a double take. The rhino had black scales on it, like an alligator, and three massive jagged horns that grew in length from back to front. The foremost was nearly half its body length while the middle one was half of that. The one closest to its eyes was half the length of the middle one, reminding me of a bar graph of doubling sales over a three-year period for some reason. Each curved up and back slightly, and had what looked like horrifically sharp tips. Along their lengths, I noticed a haze that sizzled the air around them. I could see flames erupting like tiny geysers. Great, hellfire-infused. Totally awesome! Fuck.

Following the curve of the horns down, I saw two fierce red eyes glowing from their sockets. It was as if someone had thrown a red glow stick into a bucket in a dark room. Along its scaled body, there were three sets of legs propelling the huge monstrosity like a locomotive. As if on cue, pitch-black smoke shot out of its nostrils, billowing outward before its body created a perfect split, leaving behind chemtrails like a 747.

Heh, chemtrails, I thought before Depweg yelled out, "John! Little help!" as he removed his clothing.

My heavy hand reached for the handle and, as before, nothing happened. I threw my side into the door and then grabbed my shoulder whining, "Owwy!"

"JOHN!" Depweg screamed with urgency as he fell on all fours, the change beginning.

"Fuck!" I yelled, willing my energy reserves to flow through me, filling my body with immense preternatural strength. I cut the seat belt with a blade I willed along the edge of my palms and then leaped straight through the already shattered sunroof of the car just as the rhino plowed into the side, ripping Mortis completely in half with a shower of sparks and flames. The two halves flew through the night's air before they hit several yards away and began tumbling violently through the dirt and knee-high grass. My poor Mortis! I wondered if insurance covered demon attacks.

The moon glinted off its scales as the beast made a wide turn back to us.

"Depweg!" I cried out as I let my bloodblade grow into an eight-foot spear, "Turning radius!" I pointed with my free hand and Depweg's freshly formed snout followed. He chuffed in understanding and prepared to pounce.

"Over here, you fat sack of demon shit!" I yelled out, waving my arms as I strode in the opposite direction from Depweg, widening the gap between us. The beast heard me and turned squarely in my direction. I noticed Depweg drop his body low to the ground, blending in with the tall grass.

In my free hand, I willed a meat hook out and bent at my knees, lowering my center of gravity. As the beast charged closer, I ran forward, preparing to use my spear as a pole and vault onto his ample back. He let out a torrent of flame from his gaping mouth that took me completely by surprise. Instinctively, I shoved the pole into the ground and hurled myself up and over. The hellfire caught the pole and incinerated my blood energy, causing an electric sting to shoot up my arm and into my chest, like grabbing an industrial-grade cattle prod.

As I soared through the air, stunned and floppy, the foremost horn lashed up and struck home, carving the Grand Canyon down the left side of my back starting at my hip. Pain erupted and enveloped my every cell as he progressed up my torso and caught my shoulder blade, bone stopping the advancement of the horn. With my momentum no longer pulling me horizontally, gravity took over and I started to slide down the horn. The hellfire-infused obsidian weapon widened in circumference as I slid downward. I screamed in agony as my life force was burned away at the merest touch of the flames. Just when I'd thought I couldn't possibly take anymore, another lightning of searing anguish pierced my back just below the first. As the girth of the horns grew, the two holes through my body widened as I continued to slide downward.

"Heh," I spat through clenched teeth, mouth full of blood, "girth..." My vision blackened at the edges. I didn't even feel the third horn press against my back through my coat. "Oh man, my trench!" I exclaimed weakly, exhaustion seeping into my words.

My head bobbed with each gallop of the hell rhino. I lifted my face to try and focus on a way out of this sticky situation and saw the two horns protruding through my chest, my blood sizzling off like a fajita plate at Chili's. I pulled on my right sleeve with my left hand until my fingers and palm were covered by my leather coat. Reaching up, I grabbed the first horn and squeezed, halting my descent. I let my head drop backward toward the ground, looking for Depweg. He must have seen me searching desperately for him, as he whined just audibly enough for me to hear. The rhino monster heard too and turned his charge toward the sound. I let my left hand, which was still holding the hook, fall over my shoulder and toward the beast's mouth. Like catching and securing a fish, I tried to insert the hook in the ferocious creature's mouth...or nose...or eye. I wasn't very good at fishing and was willing to hook it anywhere I could.

After I felt the tip of the hook hit something, I pulled up, but to no avail. My hand just shot up toward the night sky. I noticed that the wind was becoming cool again even after tapping into my reserves. This bitch was killing me by the second.

I let my hand drop again as we approached Depweg, felt it click against teeth, and then pulled with everything I had. I must have found purchase because the beast's head tilted upward with a roar, raising me like one of those adjustable beds until I was almost vertical with the ground. The beast fought to pull back down, so I let go of the horn with the hand that was preventing me from sliding further down, and grabbed my other hand at the wrist. I pulled with so much force I thought my teeth were going to shatter from being clenched so hard. The third horn pierced my flesh as I pulled, giving it all it needed to violate my insides. The world became a pinprick in my vision as blackness swallowed everything I saw. Sound muffled and then disappeared completely. I couldn't even feel the wind anymore. I just pulled with all my borrowed might, trusting Depweg to do what I could not.

I was aware I was looking at the horizon again as I pulled on my fish, my prize, my trophy. I started to slide off the third horn now that gravity was no longer pulling me down, and allowed myself a brief moment of reprieve before something massive slammed into the rhino, or the rhino into something massive. The smallest horn found renewed vigor as it punched through my lower back and out the side of my stomach. That's when I let my hands relax and drop lifelessly to my sides. The old dirt-covered statue on Father Thomes Philseep's stage came to mind as my arms lay outstretched to either side of me. I was concerned that the horns didn't hurt anymore as I accepted my fate. I was so very tired.

The pressure on my stomach and back started to recede. I had enough energy to barely open my eyes and see the horns turning to ectoplasm and melting away. The searing of blood had stopped, leaving behind the sounds of the night.

After a few seconds, the weight of me broke free from the melting structure that was the rhino monster, and I fell to the ground, face-first. The grass was slightly damp against my face, and the wind made the blades tickle across my cheek. A human foot stepped in front of me and I tried to twist my head to look up. Once I got to Depweg's junk hanging freely in the air, I decided it was better to just let my head relax as the rain began to fall. Unconsciousness took hold of me as dizzying blackness filled my eternity.

11

My eyes refused to open and fought hard to remain closed. They relented after some effort, and my lids pried apart to reveal a blinding light. My hand shot up reflexively to shield my weak eyes.

My nose and ears recognized the atmosphere almost immediately.

"Hey, Doc," I said weakly, letting my hand fall back to my side.

"We need to stop meeting like this," said the veterinarian that had saved my ass twice now. His eyes looked over a pair of glasses at me, the glass—and his balding head—reflecting the light.

I moved my right hand over to my left to find plastic tubes sticking out of it.

"Say, Doc," I started, "How do you manage to pierce my skin?"

"Silver and iron, John," responded Depweg.

I raised my head and squinted in the light to see a cane-wielding Depweg hobbling unsteadily over to me.

"You're getting good at that, Mr. Clooney," I praised with a smile.

"Not acting this time. He got me good," Depweg said, holding his side with his cane-free hand.

"What happened?" I asked as I let my increasingly heavy head fall back to the stainless table I was placed upon.

"When you lifted his head, I charged in and ripped his throat out. Then he fell on me and crushed half my body under its tonnage until it dissolved. Pretty sure he broke something that didn't want to break. But we did it."

"Go team," I said lamely. "When do we get our Cub Scout badge?"

"Cub?" Depweg asked, unsure if to be annoyed or insulted.

"Well, I can't be a Boy Scout because I'm only this many," I said as I flashed ten fingers on both hands and then closed my fists only to flash them again in rapid succession like fifty times.

"I like cubs," the doc said. I couldn't tell if he was joking or not because his face was like stone, but he watched us in silence as if waiting to see if we caught his animal pun. We didn't.

I thought for a moment. "How the hell did it find us?" I asked.

"Don't know, man. But that couldn't have been a coincidence."

"Ah, man," I said, rolling my head from side to side in exhausted frustration. "That fucker burned up a lot of my reserves, brother. It's going to take a long time to get those back."

"Well, since you've been out, I've had time to think about that. The whole reason we were attacked was because we were out hunting."

"Yeah, and?" I motioned for him to continue with my tube-free hand.

"Da let on that you have a great amount of wealth."

"What! And you don't? If you live long enough, it's easy to amass some cash."

"I have always tried to live off the land, John. Material things never interested me. But now I am forced to play the game, as it were."

"Gone are the simple days, huh, buddy?" I asked in remembrance of times long since passed.

"To finish my thought," Depweg continued, snapping back into the now, "why don't you build your own blood bank or something along those lines. Pay people to donate. Heck, if they donate enough times, you can pay for their kids' college or something like that, since you are trying to do good deeds."

"Hmm. You might be onto something here. It would be quite advantageous to have a steady supply of blood from my own personal bank." While looking at Depweg approvingly, I said, "Hey, we might as well build a wing where people can donate their limbs too? Huh? Huh?" We both broke out in laughter as the doc cleared his throat nervously.

"Only kidding, Doc," I said, turning to him. I let my head roll back toward where Depweg stood leaning heavily on his cane. "I will have to get Da to set that up when we get back. For now, though, how am I?"

The doc cleared his throat, catching my attention. "You were gravely wounded by the hellfire tusks."

"Horns," I corrected.

"Excuse me?" the doctor asked.

"They were horns. Trust me. Got to see them up close."

"Right, horns," the doc agreed, not wanting to argue. "They tore through you at three points and cauterized as they did."

"The doc had to cut a lot of you out in order to let you heal. You're going to be weak for a while, bro," Depweg explained impatiently. He was always one to rip the Band-Aid off.

I lifted my head and then rested on my right elbow to get a good look. My shirt had been cleanly cut down the middle, exposing three purple holes that puckered around the edges like little volcano mouths. I explored them with my fingers and was half relieved when I felt pain, and that they were solid.

"When you open your blood bank, be sure to send me some to keep on hand," said Doc.

"If we are going to be seeing a lot of each other, I assume introductions are in order. John Cook," I said as I extended my tube-free hand.

"Doctor James Hunt. You can call me Jim," he introduced himself as he grasped my hand firmly and shook.

"I want to make fun of you for calling yourself a doctor, since you work on animals, but it would appear," I said, lifting my tubed hand, "that you have an advanced knowledge in preternatural physiology. So, no jokes this day, Doc."

A smirk started at the corners of his mouth in response to the acknowledgment of his private prowess. There couldn't be that many people with whom he shared this information with. To regular mortals, he was just a vet. To supes, he was just a mortal.

"But not supernatural," Doc Jim clarified.

"What's the difference between super- and preternatural?" Depweg asked.

"Easy," I started. "They are basically interchangeable, but there are some distinct differences if you want to get technical. Preternatural means beyond natural, but still explainable. I need blood and you need flesh to survive. We are mostly alive, for all intents and purposes. Supernatural means not natural at all. Think of ghosts, poltergeists, banshees, etc. They don't need to eat, drink, sleep, or fuck. They just exist. Most mortals, preters, and supes call anything not human or above human supernatural. Easier that way, I suppose."

"I do believe that is the best explanation I have heard on the subject yet," Doc Jim said.

"What about angels and demons?" Depweg asked.

"Though they can *technically* fall under the supernatural category, they are specifically celestial in nature. Slightly different."

"You impress me still, John the Vampire," Doctor James Hunt said.

"Deppyweg," I spoke, turning to Depweg, "we need to invite Doc Jim here to Risk night. I like him."

"I'm good with that," Depweg said.

"It is settled!" I proclaimed in an obnoxiously loud British voice. "We have just gotten the Rick and Morty version delivered! Doc, what is your cellular telephone number? I shall add it forthwith!"

"Here," Depweg said as he leaned on his cane while pulling out his phone. After a few punches and some swipes, both Doc's phone and mine vibrated. "I just shared your contacts with each other."

"Neat!" I said. "Ain't technology grand?"

"Time to go, John. We've taken enough of Doctor Jim's time. Plus, I haven't eaten yet, and I need to heal."

With an awkward handshake, fist bump, palm-slidey motion in which Doc did his best to entertain, I removed the tubes and began walking to the front.

Doc Jim cleared his throat, loudly. I turned to him and looked at his hand, which was extended, palm up.

"Oh, right. Money," I said as I reached for my wallet.

Depweg leaned in to whisper in my ear, "He doesn't have a set price, but keep in mind he is the only one in the region who can do this type of work."

"The tools aren't cheap," Doc said. "Plus, it is past my bedtime," he finished with a playful smile, pleased with his own joke.

I managed to pull out a small handful of bills, which felt completely inadequate. Doc could see this on my face and said, "I accept Bitcoin."

"Thank Lilith!" I exclaimed as I pulled out my phone. "I had Da invest in this a long time ago. I honestly believe the supernatural community is single-handedly keeping cryptocurrency alive. Text me your code." With a few moves of his nimble thumbs, a text popped up on my screen containing a 64-digit address that I copied and pasted into my trading platform. I decided to reward my new friend by sending him over $50,000. "Use this to expand your facility and make room for supplies just for me, like a freezer for the blood I'm going to have sent to you."

"Very good. Thank you for your patronage," Doc Jim said with a smile as I walked outside.

As we got to the parking lot, I pulled out my keys and looked around confused. I clicked the lock button several times while my head pivoted as if on a swivel.

"Oh! Right. Rhino monster," I remembered as I dropped my keys on a sewer grate in the parking lot. "Won't be needing those again."

"Weren't your storage keys on that ring?" Depweg asked.

My head shot downward to the blackness that was the sewer as an aggressively annoyed and elongated sigh left my mouth.

"Lilith damn it," I said slowly while running the palm of my hand down my face. "Screw it. I'll get another set made."

When I pulled my hand away, I could see the tendrils of sun starting to crest on the horizon.

"Ah, shit. Time to go, man," I said while pointing at the horizon. "I'll take the scenic route. You good?" I asked as I oriented in the direction of home.

"Yeah, man. I'll snag an Uber," he answered as he pulled his phone out.

"Sweet. Catch ya later!" I said as I began bounding away. The wind ripped at my face, so I manifested a snug-fitting bloodhelmet with little slits to keep the bugs from smashing into my face at ludicrous speed. I was sure that if a mortal's eyes could see me, I would be quite the sight. Single ab sticking out from my trench coat since my shirt had been cut off, and with a helmet befitting something from a video game, soaring over houses.

In a few minutes, I arrived to the cemetery that was my home. I sent out my senses to feel for anything out of the ordinary before making my way to my mausoleum. After moving stones and pushing buttons, I made my way downstairs and inside my Fortress of Solitaire.

"Honey, I'm hooooo—" I started but was interrupted by Locke, who all but screamed, "About time! Look what he's done to me!"

I scanned the living room, where I saw Da sitting on the couch watching a how-to video on his iPad. In his little hand was a makeup brush. Next to him was a sexy mannequin body with Locke's head fastened at the top. His face was covered in makeup that had been applied by the equivalent of a five-year-old.

Stifling a laugh, I asked Da, "What are you doing?"

"He spoke to me like a bitch, now he looks like a bitch," Da said with complete seriousness.

"You wouldn't dare touch me if I had my body," Locke said angrily.

"You have a body," Da responded. He stopped applying the stuff that made cheeks look rosy (I'm a dude; I don't know what it's called), and looked Locke in his now pretty face. "Let's pretend that you did have your body, warlock. You would be in the precise same predicament as you find yourself now." As he said this, Da's eyes began to glow white.

"Don't mess with the Fae, dude," I told Locke as I plopped into the recliner closer to the couch. I set my feet on the coffee table and picked up the controller to the Xbox.

"Could you at *least* make it look even?" Locke said placatingly. I was pretty impressed with his ability to read the situation and control his pride. Not sure I would have been able to do the same.

"Where did you get the mannequin?" I asked Da as I thumbed over to the Netflix icon. Titus from *Unbreakable* was my avatar, and it made me giggle each time I saw it.

"Amazon. Same-day shipping," Da said as he turned to me, seeing my clothes for the first time. "What did you do now?" His eyes narrowed at the puckering purple protrusions on my torso.

"Big rhino motherfucker killed Mortis and almost got yours truly," I said as I selected *Stranger Things*. "Depweg saved the day."

"A...rhino...?" Da asked. "Demons are getting creative."

"Oh, I need you to fix the ol' duster again."

"There's only so much more I can do to that— that *thing*. I can't even claim it has any of its original material left."

"Yeah, but I likes it. So, you know, do your Fae thing." I removed and threw the coat on the coffee table and started watching my stories on the television. "When did Samwise get on the show?"

Da set his tools down and grabbed his iPad, closing YouTube. Then he opened the camera app and took a picture of Locke's face before turning and grabbing the coat that I extended out to him. He floated off to his room and let the door shut behind him, muttering something under his breath.

"So, how do I look?" Locke asked.

"Like a burnt turd covered in shitty makeup," I said without ever turning my gaze away from the TV.

"Wait, is this season two? I never finished one!"

"Then look away." In my peripheral vision, I could see Locke's red mouth drop open in shock and disbelief.

The proximity alarms chided a brief alert. I hit pause and then changed the source over to the cameras. Depweg was approaching with two large reusable bags. I could see the sheen of the plastic wrap around the meat.

A second proximity alarm sounded, and I could see Depweg stop dead in his tracks. His head was on a swivel as he searched around. I could see his head tilting up and down slightly as he used his preternatural sense of smell. He dropped the bags, and I could see him talking aggressively, though I couldn't hear anything. I leaned forward in my chair, looking for any movement from the multiple angles.

A man walked into view, wearing a modern black suit. His blood-red tie reflected in the light. A leaf from the tree the camera was hidden in kept the man's face from view, only offering brief glimpses of features as the wind made the leaves dance. He stood with confidence several steps away from Depweg, who was shifting nervously now. He took a step backward with his hands up in surrender, almost pleading, which was uncharacteristic for the militaristic Depweg. I couldn't remember him ever running from a fight.

Another step back and the man blurred forward, subduing Depweg with frightening ease. That's when I saw him. The glowing red eyes that matched his tie. The short-cropped hair with a slight widow's peak evident without the hood on.

"Who the hell is that?" Locke asked as he squinted at the screen.

"Ulric..." I breathed out in disbelief with eyes wide and mouth agape. "DA! EMERGENCY!" I cried out as I ran to the door, throwing it open to slam against the wall. The metal on metal sent a piercing clang throughout the hideout. I raced up the stairs and out the mausoleum, fully aware that I had only been given enough blood to start the healing process. There was no way in hell I could possibly overpower the ancient Ulric. But I had to try, for my brother.

I made it to where the bags spilled their contents over the grass. My eyes shifted, and I sent my senses out, searching for Ulric and Depweg. I couldn't feel anything. My eyes shot to the ground, where there was just as much dirt as grass. I saw footprints and started to follow them, quickly. Panic set in. The footsteps vanished after a few yards. I frantically searched all around, trying desperately to find where they had gone, but their tracks had been eaten by the grass. Depweg had been my best friend for decades, and I was not about to let him die because of me.

Da floated toward me, worry evident on his face.

"Locke told me. Ulric has Depweg?" Da asked, dismayed. "If he didn't kill him here, it means he took him for a purpose."

"Me," I told him sullenly, frustration causing tears to threaten to leave my face. "The sun isn't up yet! We still have time!"

"John. There's nothing more you can do now. The sun will crest in a few moments. Come inside before you burn," Da said as he turned to make his way back to our lair, stopping to pick up the bags in his little hands. He did so with relative ease.

Trailing behind him, I asked, "So, what? We do nothing?" Anger seeped into my words.

"Ulric has the upper hand now, John. He will contact you when he is ready to do so," Da said with apprehension.

"What is it?"

Da sighed as we made our way down the steps. "Let me think a moment longer."

We entered the lair and Da turned to the kitchen, dropping the bags of meat and vegetables on the counter. He began putting away the food into the large commercial-sized fridge.

I shut the door hard and crossed my arms, waiting for Da.

"Two things, John," Da started. "One, he is going to want you in exchange for Depweg. That much I am confident of. Two, there are two vampires."

"And?" I asked, stepping forward with building curiosity.

"Armageddon will begin when the last vampire walks the Earth, remember? If Ulric kills you, or you kill Ulric, the catalyst will be set for the end of the world."

"Technically, it states that the gates of Hell will open, which will allow the apocalypse to commence," Locke said from the living room. After a moment of silence, he added, "You cannot give yourself up to save the wolf. I'm sorry. That's how it has to be."

"He's my best friend. My brother. I'd willingly die for him," I said through clenched teeth.

"And cause the fucking apocalypse while you're at it?" Locke argued with a voice that was growing louder in frustration and worry. "Pretty damn sure that Depweg would not want that."

"He's right, John," Da agreed. "The best course of action is no action at all."

My fists tightened in helpless rage.

"No!" I barked out while beginning to hyperventilate. "I *will* save him or die trying!"

"Let Locke and I come up with an outline of a plan while you slumber. First thing tomorrow night, you must feed. You're going to need all the strength you can muster if you are to face Ulric."

At that moment, I was too bewildered to even point out he had said the P word. Instead, I just went into my room and closed the door, my body doing the motions on autopilot as my mind reeled. Ulric was back and he had my best friend. He was going to kill me or force me to kill him and end Heaven, Hell, and Earth in between. I was dizzy with how momentous the situation was.

I slowly pivoted and sat on the bed, my eyes staring at nothing at all as my mind worked out my predicament. If I killed Ulric, end of the world. If Ulric killed me, end of the world. If I did nothing, my brother died and

Ulric would still come after me. If I brought allies, they would surely die or accidentally kill Ulric. It was as if I were being drawn and quartered—each decision was a rope tied around one of my limbs and attached to a horse facing a different direction. Each horse was pulling at the same time, and it didn't matter which one pulled the hardest, I still lost in every single scenario.

Feeling helpless was more intense for a super- or preternatural creature than it was for mortals. Humans were always a baby hair's breadth away from being completely powerless. A car wreck while coming home from church. A robbery in the parking lot after work. Any of a number of illnesses that doctors couldn't cure. Natural disasters that left them without food, water, or power. Rush-hour traffic. You get the idea.

For supes, it was an almost alien idea. We spent most of our existence being the apex predator, in control of our surroundings and with means of escape or manipulation in most situations. When we were finally rendered helpless, it was truly a long way to fall.

As I sat motionless on my bed, I became dizzy as the reality and weight of the circumstances solidified. This wasn't a bad dream that I could wake up from. I would have to make a decision and hope that I didn't end all of existence in the process.

In my depressed and shocked state, the briefest thought of suicide came into my mind. This woke me up from my pity party, and I laughed at the irony. Sure, I could kill myself. I definitely knew of a cornucopia of ways to do it after narrowly surviving all these years; but then I would just go to Hell, and all this would be redundant. Well, maybe it wouldn't if Hell was also destroyed after my death sparked the apocalypse. Either way, I was not going to let my weak impulses even begin to entertain giving up. Too much was riding on me. At this moment I was Atlas, and the world needed my shoulders to bear its weight.

As my resolve strengthened, the sun rose, coaxing me to rest in preparation for the night of prophecy to potentially unfold.

12

The next night, I awoke and immediately headed downtown without saying a word to Da or Locke, who were still hard at work on their plan. Locke had begun to say something before Da had raised his hand to halt him, knowing how single-minded I was at that moment. I was hangry.

Depweg had suggested a morally approved method of hunting that I was going to partake in.

I took striding leaps in a straight path in search of food. It was of utmost importance that I replenished the reserves that the rhino had burned away.

I leaped over houses, through industrial parks, and over creeks until I got to the edge of downtown. As I entered the city, I shot a bloodrope high up into a concrete building and used my momentum to carry myself upward. This was similar to, but legally different from, that superhero that was bit by the spider.

I landed on a roof while retracting my bloodslinger. Just your friendly neighborhood vampire out for some dinner. I walked to the edge, closed my eyes, and opened my senses. I could feel the wind caress my face and tug at my hair and freshly repaired trench coat Da had left out for me. Footsteps sounded clearly from the few passersby that walked the streets of this early evening. Work was over, and the restaurants and bars were starting to fill up. I could perceive the smell of different types of food wafting from below, but they held no interest for me anymore. Not for centuries now. Though they smelled pleasant enough, the scents were more akin to smelling a cologne or perfume; sure, they were nice and all, but you wouldn't go about consuming them.

My mind kept slipping back to Depweg in my search. Still images of Ulric easily overtaking him. Had Ulric stopped for a fraction of a second and looked at the camera? I couldn't be sure. What I was sure of was that he had my best friend. The yin to my yang. I wanted to find him now and face Ulric, but even PS knew that would be the same as suicide. Ulric was much older than I was, which equated to a multiplicative strength difference, possibly even exponential. Either way, I knew that I had gotten lucky in the alley so many, many years ago. A one-in-a-million shot brought to fruition by Ulric's own hubris, which I was confident he would not repeat. He sought revenge and would not care about the consequences. To him, it would be entertaining to watch the end unfold.

After waiting for several minutes, possibly hours (because I was terrible at time), I heard what I was waiting for. A scream slipped through the night and into my ears, freeing me from my troubling self-doubt. Orienting on the sound, I ran across the roof and leaped to the next one, drawing closer to my breakfast and source of replenishment.

In short order, I parkoured a quarter of the way through downtown Houston then leaped into one of the topmost levels of a parking garage. There, a wild-eyed man was overpowering a woman in a business suit. Saliva bubbled between his lips as her blouse was ripped off like it was made of tissue. He moaned in anticipation as the woman whimpered, red lumps evident on her brow and cheek where she had been struck repeatedly into submission.

"You're in Los Diablos Locos territory now, bitch. You shouldn't be here. Now, you'll have to pay the toll," he said while sucking his saliva back between his lips and then wiping the remainder away with his shoulder. The leather biker jacket only succeeded in smearing the spit.

The rapist gang member had the woman on her back now and was moving a hand up her thighs while I walked right up to him. I didn't even have to attempt to be silent as the foolish mortal was so intent on his prey; so was I.

My hand wrapped around the back of the man's neck and I lifted him. He was as helpless in my grip as a puppy being carried by its mother. I looked down at the woman, who was attempting to pull her blouse back together, and told her in a stern voice, "Go. He will not bother you any longer." I turned my gaze back to the man and waited. She didn't move, unsure which man in front of her was the real danger. I shot my head back at her and willed my eyes to glow red as I shouted, "GO!"

That did the trick. With wide-eyed panic, the woman scrambled on the ground, breaking a heel of her shoe in the process. She hobbled to a nearby car, clicking with every other step, got in, and sped off. Tires squealed and billowed white smoke as a terrified foot pressed the pedal to its limits.

I turned my attention back to the man, placing my other palm on his forehead. It was his turn to whimper as he tried to push me away from him; but to this mere mortal I might as well have been a stone statue, unyielding to his pathetic attempts at freedom.

"Where is your gang's hideout?" I asked coldly while willing my essence into his mind. He stiffened as he sucked in a gasp of breath before relaxing completely after a few moments of pointless resistance.

"A warehouse off Fuqua Street, close to 45," the man said as if floating through a dream.

"What warehouse?" I demanded.

"Los Diablos Car Care Center."

"You...you can't be serious," I asked in disbelief. "Who is your marketing guy, because that title strikes two different emotions."

"We have a Facebook page," he replied.

"I didn't ask, but alright," I said, annoyed. "How many are there right now?"

"At least fifteen locos and maybe some bitches."

"First of all, you're white. I don't know if I should be incredulous or proud of your vernacular. It's nice to see a gang be so inclusive. Second, are all of you crime-laden filth?"

"Yes...why am I saying these things?" he asked in his haze.

"Because I am making you. Doesn't feel so fun being on this end of things, does it, you white cholo."

"That's racist."

"YOU'RE WHITE! I'M WHITE. Fuck, I'm *more* than white. I'm feck'n Irish. That's like the epitome of white," I said, pointing to my reddish beard.

"Are you going to hurt me?"

"I'm not gonna hurt ya. Wendy, darling, light of my life. I'm not going to hurt ya," I told him in my best Jack Nicholson voice.

"Wha...what?" the rapist asked while I let my essence slip back into my being.

"You didn't let me finish my sentence. I said, I'm not going to hurt ya. I'm just going to bash your brains in. I'm going to bash them right the fuck in." As I finished my monologue, I manifested a hammer in my free hand, keeping my other on his neck. With one quick motion, I brought the hammer down with the force of Valhalla and sent the blunt instrument deep into the vein-filled fat sack that once might have been called a brain. White gore sloshed over the broken skull and onto the pavement as I drew his erupting blood into my body. His eyes rolled up and his mouth gaped open wordlessly while his body twitched and shook.

Oh, the power. The ecstasy. Energy filled my every molecule and sent tingles of pleasure shooting down my spine and over my limbs. It wasn't sexual. Rather, it was a whole-body euphoria, like stepping out onto a cool spring night and feeling the evening air enveloping you in a welcoming embrace down to your bones—and then multiplying that a hundred times over.

Once drained, I retracted my hammer-straw. PS rejoiced in my mind as I turned in the direction of this blood bag's hideout. While still holding the sack of flesh in my hand, I leaped through the levels of the parking garage with renewed vigor, and all but flew through the streets at preternatural speeds.

By the time I made it to a warehouse across from the chop shop—I mean, Car Care Center—my leftovers had been torn to shreds by the velocity at which I traveled. My powerful body kept whole while his mortal remains all but disintegrated piece by piece over the journey, leaving nothing behind except the skull, which I still held. I brought it up to eye level, whispered "Thank you," to it before squeezing my fingers into a fist and turning the skull to dust. What fell to the ground I stepped on with my boots and ground with my heel. Perfect way to dispose of a fully drained body. If any large pieces remained intact, animals would surely devour them.

My senses shot out with predatory intensity, and I was easily able to make out every warm body in and out of the warehouse. Big Gulp was right. There were exactly fifteen meals to be eaten.

Don't eat the innocents, got it? I told PS. He nodded in eager anticipation of the Vegas-style buffet that lay ahead of us. *I'm serious. Do not take the wheel from me. Partners?* PS looked at me soberly and nodded once. *Then let's go make the world a better place.*

I shot out from my spot and crossed the street in a single bound. PS oriented on our prey while I sent out my essence to the handful of women whose only crime was being into bad boys. I coaxed some of their synapses to stop firing for a few minutes while I ate, rendering them living statues that wouldn't remember anything.

PS shot a hand out while forming a crude manifestation of what reminded me of a stalactite you could see in caves. It wasn't neat, pretty, or even fully symmetrical, but it pierced through two TV dinners like a chopstick through rice. PS fiercely sucked their life force from their body before their hearts even knew to stop beating. I almost lost control of the wheel as my nerves were kissed with indescribable decadence. I struggled to maintain my grip lest PS lose control and go apeshit on every living thing in a five-block radius. We had lost a lot of energy with the rhino, and we were both desperate to refill our tanks, and then some. Being in a blood rage was nothing new to me, but I was learning to control it the best I could.

I retracted the primitive manifestation while we tackled three men who were standing in complete surprise and horror at what was happening.

"It's all a bad movie, boys," I said with eyes glowing a red so bright that it was like a Mack truck driver had his foot on the brakes. Gang members around us were squinting and trying to shield their eyes as three bloodtentacles slithered out from my palms and into the pulsating necks of the three men I had pinned. They fought and screamed a high-pitched call of unbridled terror before succumbing to their fate.

My hand very nearly came off the wheel that time as the three bodies' adrenaline-filled blood coursed through my veins, absorbing the energy and making me stronger.

Shots rang out, interrupting my reverie, as the remaining wholesome taxpayers broke out fully automatic weapons. One had a Glock with an extended mag that he sprayed wildly in my direction, unable to control the kick in his panic. A few others had AKs and were squeezing the triggers in a death grip that emptied their magazines in a matter of seconds. From a back room, a big motherfucker carried a semiauto shotgun complete with a huge drum for the shells. He unloaded, and those slugs fucking hurt as they found their target. They didn't contain silver or iron, but packed a punch befitting an elephant. It was like being slugged in the arm by your girlfriend, who thought you could take it. You pretended like it didn't hurt, but it did. You knew it, she knew it, your eyes watered a little. Kinda like that.

One slug slammed directly into my head, ripping my gray beanie off and knocking my brain around in my skull. I'd have to remember that shotguns with slugs hurt. Either that or I was weaker from my battle with the stupid horned beast than I'd thought. That bastard had burned off all my reserves, including what little delicious angel blood I had left. These McBadGuys weren't even a fraction as amazing as the angel blood had been. Then again, even a dehydrated man baking in the sun of a desert thought that puddle water came straight from God himself.

I flipped through the air, letting my body go horizontal as I willed a bloodchain with a spiked ball at the end of its length. As I twisted, I used the momentum to launch the ball at the huge bastard with the auto shotty, and shattered the weapon. As the ball found its home in the abdominal cavity of the surprised Goliath of a man, I expanded the spikes in a burst that pierced the entire length of the man's torso in all directions. I inhaled his blood before he died, and oh, he had so much to give. Sending out my essence again, I asked all the entranced innocents to lie on the ground. They did so methodically and uniformly—first dropping to one knee and then the other before placing their hands on the ground and lowering themselves until they lay flat.

While still drinking from my bro-tein shake, I willed a large curving blade to extend from my hand to my shoulder several feet. I positioned my hand across my body, as if trying to touch my opposite shoulder, and then swung my hand out in a blur while extending the blade. It caught the machine gun–wielding men at the waist, and they were bisected cleanly as the blade lodged into the sheet metal wall. Their top halves rested on my blade, while their legs collapsed to the ground, no longer receiving signals from their brains. Crimson life flowed from their organs and severed arteries and into my blade. I focused and willed the surplus of crimson life from their legs to flow into me as well. The motion reminded me of lying on a bed with my head hanging off the side and watching through a window as the raindrops seemed to flow upward.

As I finished the Hungry Man-sized meal, I manifested a javelin and threw it into the bar. It pierced both the bar and the man cowering behind. I finished draining the machine gun goons and the bartender at the same time, letting my bloodweapons retreat into me.

See, bud? That's how it's done. It's called finesse and showmanship. PS rolled his eyes and proceeded to clap slowly.

Should be a handful left. Let's get them before they...

Tires squealed outside. It sounded like two large SUVs had taken off in a hurry for some reason. Maybe they were late for church.

After retrieving and stuffing my tattered gray beanie in my pocket, I willed all the women left to exit out the back hastily, but not before setting the alcohol-covered bar on fire. I should probably still return after I finished, though, and dispose of the mangled bodies at the very least.

PS nudged me and pointed. *Right!* I burst through the sheet metal wall like it was aluminum foil and landed on the parking lot, crouching. After a quick glance around to orientate myself, I exploded off the ground, shattering concrete, and soared into the air in the direction of the SUVs. As I hovered into position several yards up, I shot two bloodspears into the ground on either side of the frontmost vehicle and pulled myself down. I rocketed toward the black, meal-filled SUV like a rocket about to hit a tank. I slammed through the roof and the car flipped end over end from the impact. Their buddies driving behind couldn't stop in time and crashed into the tumbling metal coffin. The impact was deafening, at least to mortal ears.

It was all in slow motion to me. My teeth found the neck of the driver while an ice pick went through the neck of the passenger, siphoning their blood with gusto. It was like when the waiter brought your salad out *with* the meal and you were forced to down it while barely chewing so you could get to your main course before it cooled.

I drained them both in record time and turned in midair while the SUV did a barrel roll around me. The last remaining man, who was in the process of urinating himself, was lucky enough to receive a more personal dining experience. I slammed my fist into his stomach and blood erupted out of his nose and mouth. I got hold of the blood in midair and forced it all into my mouth, a horrific stream of crimson connecting us like a morbid *Lady and the Tramp*. Once his blood started flowing, the rest followed suit like a good little lemming, and I drained him before the vehicle had completed another roll and came to a stop on its roof.

I burst out the back and saw where the other SUV had already stopped and had begun smoking under the hood. The two remaining men were out and fleeing on foot, stumbling as they ran due to their brains getting rattled in the Michael Bay–style crash. They didn't have the luxury of healing as quickly as I did, so I took my sweet time following them while their brains rebooted.

I skipped dramatically with my hands flailing at my sides and my head rocking back and forth as I creepily sang, "La la la. La la la," like a haunting Victorian schoolgirl.

These tough guys, who had committed countless crimes against their fellow men, screamed at the top of their lungs like stuck pigs. As I skipped, I let my tried-and-true bloodropes slither out of my palms, making cracking noises like whips as my hands moved front to back in rhythm with my eerie lullaby.

I lashed out with both ropes and caught the men's ankles. They tumbled to the ground, crying in hopeless dismay. As I stood in place with a serious expression on my face, I let the ropes begin to slowly retreat toward me. The big, tough men's nails broke on the asphalt as they tried to prevent their fate while they screamed "No, No, NO!" Rivulets of blood trailed behind, marking where their breaking fingers had failed to find enough purchase to stop their demise.

"Oh yes," I said slowly and without an ounce of humor, letting my voice grow deep. "We reap what we sow." I let the ropes begin to crawl up their bodies like hungry tentacles until they had enveloped them like spaghetti on a fork, then I let the razors form. Little ones this time. I wanted to savor my delicious meal.

I let the ropes slowly uncoil while still pressing against their bodies, the razors providing a sweet death by a thousand cuts. I sipped their essence like a fine wine as I let my eyes close. I moaned as the energy coursed through my body.

Sirens rang out, breaking me from fully enjoying the rest of my meal. I squeezed the ropes as hard as I could, like draining every last drop from an orange. Only a single exhaling cry escaped the whimpering men before jagged bones pierced organs and the remainder of their life's blood became mine. Finishing my food, I threw the men back into the car that had started to blaze furiously. The night air blew the smell of burning rubber and gas into my nose, making my face screw up. I'd always hated that smell.

I was about to turn and make my way from the crime scene when I noticed the first vehicle hadn't caught on fire. I could see the gas tank as the car was upside down, so I focused my will, asking the molecules to excite. A small section the size of a lemon began to glow a faint red and then a bright orange as I worked. Within a few moments, the tank exploded in a torrent of angry flames ready to consume everything they could get their hands on.

Red and blue lights illuminated the building next to me, chasing each other in a fast-paced dance and drawing my attention. I hurled myself down the street, away from the approaching mortals. The wind tugging at my hair made me acutely aware that I hadn't been without my trusty beanie in several years. At least since the '90s, I was sure. Thank Lilith for Da and his seamstress abilities.

I felt alive and beyond strong, like when a mortal woke up after being debilitatingly sick and realizing how great it was to *not* be ill. Food tasted better, work wasn't so drab, and even traffic was bearable for a day or two until you got used to being well again. Then it was all taken for granted again.

Heading in the direction of my home, I manifested my bloodhelmet and sprinted at impressive speeds, even for a creature of the night. I ran through open fields underneath the main roads and through residential neighborhoods until I made my way to the cemetery. I briefly considered stopping at Valenta's to catch him up on...Depweg. Ulric had Depweg, and here I was, gallivanting around like a drug addict on a huge high. That sobered me up as I made my way downstairs and into my lair.

"Feeling better, I see," Da said to me as I closed the door and strode into the living room with my chest puffed out. I was impervious at that moment, ready to take on anything. Even Ulric, who was several centuries older than I was. Hell, I'd take on Satan himself right now.

"Yes. Tanks are topped off, and I'm ready to fight," I said. "So, what's the plan?"

"I think you need to go have a drink at Valenta's," Da said.

"But...Depweg," I stammered.

"I think..." Da paused and looked at me for emphasis, "you need to go have a drink at Valenta's, John."

"I agree," Locke said. "Bring me back something tasty, would ya?"

Brow scrunched up, I took the crystal clear message to go to Valenta's.

13

After donning a hoodie instead of my trademarked WWII-era, Nazi-stolen trench coat, I was off. I scouted around Valenta's to ensure the coast was clear, as supes were still after me for breaking the accords.

What really pissed me off was that mortals had made up their collective minds since and decided that the footage was fake. In addition, those humans who had actually witnessed what I had done now experienced what was known as didn't-fucking-happen-to-us. I was sure there was a legit terminology for it, but I liked my name better. Basically, when a human saw something they couldn't believe, their brain skipped a beat and didn't let its owner completely recall everything in clear detail. This had happened to me once when I was mortal and I'd watched my mother trip and fall down a flight of stone steps. One second she was walking while carrying a bucket of fresh milk or something, and the next she was writhing on the ground, stunned and disoriented. I'd just stood there, disbelieving what had just happened, and had had to convince myself that she must have fallen right before my very own eyes! Once I'd snapped out of it, I'd rushed to her aid, but it had felt like minutes of just staring as my brain restarted.

I walked up the back steps to Val's, noticing the missing chunks that the ogre had taken out, and rang the doorbell. I waited a full minute, or maybe it was three seconds, before pressing the button again, and again...and again. The door buzzed open angrily, or so I assumed.

Valenta met me in the kitchen, where he nodded once. "Some boys out here I think'll wanna help ya," Valenta drawled while motioning to the main floor.

I went through the swinging kitchen door and followed Valenta to the farthest corner from the front door. At a table were two identical twins who couldn't even be old enough to drink, at least by their outward appearance. Well, I said identical, but there were slight differences between them. Judging by the height of the table, I could safely assume they were about 5'4". One had a buzz cut while the other had a mop of brown hair. The twins were muscular and had black eyes that reminded me of staring into the orbs of a hungry shark. The buzz-cut twin had tight clothing and a tank top that revealed lots of skin, while the longer-haired brother preferred a baggier attire that covered all but his hands and head.

"Boys," Valenta started, "this here's John. John, this's Dawson an' Joey."

"Hi," said Joey while producing a slight smile. His loose clothing felt out of place with how much muscle he was hiding.

"Sup bruh," said Dawson with a huge grin. I could see over the table that he had on a fanny pack with pineapples on it.

"Um, hi?" I greeted, confused.

"John, these boys wanna help ya with yer current predicament," Valenta said.

"And that is?" I had no idea what these twins wanted.

"Dude, we're werwolves," Dawson informed me while pointing back and forth between his brother and himself. I was slightly annoyed that he'd used the German pronunciation like Depweg...who *was* German.

"Yeah. We heard that Depweg was taken, and we don't like that, do we, Dawson?" Joey asked.

"Hell nah, bruh," his brother responded. Dawson was clearly the more animated twin while Joey liked to remain calm. It didn't take long to deduce they were identical but with completely different personalities.

"Plus, Depweg is kind of a legend among the weres," Joey said admiringly. "He hasn't had a pack in decades and is one of the oldest of us."

"He's a fucking celebrity," Dawson informed me, his grin never leaving his face. "We wanna be in his pack."

"We heard about you too, John," Joey added. "Is it true you killed Locke and saved Depweg?"

"Kinda a long story, but let's go with yes," I responded, leaving out the fact that Locke was in my lair playing dress-up with Da, or something along those lines.

"Cool," they said in unison while glancing at each other and then back to me. I didn't speak twin, but I did speak dude, and a single glance could convey entire paragraphs in an instant.

"So, you two are going to help me capture Ulric and rescue Depweg?" I asked.

"Heck yes," Joey answered.

"Ya, man. We are gonna rip that Ulric fucker a new sphincter," Dawson said. I chuckled and immediately knew we were going to get along just fine.

"Can't kill Ulric," I informed them. A look of confusion crossed their faces while Valenta's gaze shifted to the ground. He nodded, understanding the immense difficulty of the situation.

"Um, why the fuck not?" Dawson asked.

"Because when there is only one of us left, the apocalypse will start."

Valenta chimed in, his gaze never leaving the ground, "When the last vampire walks the Earth, the gates of Hell will open."

"Exactly. So, we will have to subdue and imprison him for, oh, I don't know," I looked down at my bare wrist, "hmm, forever."

"Well, this shit just got heavy, didn't it, Joey?" Dawson asked, his huge grin fading to a close-lipped smile.

Joey considered it for all of three seconds before shrugging and saying, "Yeah, but I'm still in. It's Depweg, man."

"Bet!" Dawson responded with enthusiasm.

"Bet what?" I asked. The twins looked at each other for a moment and then back at me before they both burst out laughing.

"It means 'yes,' dude," Joey explained.

"Ah. That word is light alright," I said. Dawson and Joey barked out laughing while slamming their hands on the table in pure hilarity.

"Lit! The word is lit, bro!" Joey informed.

"Damn kids and your 8-tracks," I muttered. Even Valenta cracked a rare smile at that one. "Well, come along then, puppies." As if I had hit pause, their laughter and table-banging stopped. Their eyes focused on me, calculating. "Just fucking with you, kids. Now, shall we, then?"

"Sure thing, mosquito," Dawson said as they both got up from their seats to stand in front of me. They were a full eight inches shorter than me, but they were just as wide as they were tall. Joey and Dawson stood with their massive chests puffed out, stern faces daring me to push more. Words didn't bother me. I actually laughed when demons and their ilk tried to offend me with their name-calling—but these two had intentionally disrespected me. Maybe it was youthful rebellion or an attempt to establish dominance; either way, a lesson must be taught. Since they were wolves, I assumed a show of hierarchy was due. Better sooner than later.

With a blur of motion that was too fast for their human eyes, I appeared behind the mouthy twins. I moved my palms to their necks and willed out my ropes, which curled around their necks like a noose. I could feel them about to turn, which prompted me to lift them off their feet and say, quite authoritatively, "I am more than half a millennium old, children. I have seen civilizations rise and fall. I was on one of the first rickety ships to the Americas. I have walked this earth longer than either of you can even fathom." I willed tiny spikes to push against their skin but not break through. "Might I humbly suggest a quantum amount of respect? Hmm?" Neither twin responded. They simply let their hands fall from my ropes in a simultaneous show of submission and defiance. It impressed me because I knew they had to be extremely uncomfortable being held up by just their throats.

After a few moments of silence, Valenta interjected, "Boy, think they understand. Now yer lil' show's over. Don't skirt 'round the rules an'more."

I willed the ropes to dissolve into a singular mass and retract back into me rather than letting the ropes slither over their necks in the opposite direction. Then I blurred back in front of them, a smile plastered on my face that stopped just under my eyes.

"Dick," Dawson said.

"Seriously, dude. Can't you just use your words?" Joey added as they both rubbed their necks.

"Apparently not," I said. "Now then, I invite you both back to my super-secret lair. You must swear to the utmost secrecy before I let you see where it is."

"You mean the train cars buried in the graveyard? Pretty sure everyone knows about that," Joey said.

My mouth dropped to the floor.

"Ev...everyone?" I asked, deflated.

"Pretty much, dude. I can basically smell the iron from here," Dawson said, pointing to his nose.

"Great. That's great. Just, super," I said, annoyed. I nodded to Valenta and turned to walk out the back door, the twins in tow.

"Shipping containers," I said.

"Huh?" Dawson asked. Joey let the questioning look speak for him.

"Not train cars. Shipping containers," I corrected.

"What's the difference?" Joey asked.

"I don't know. It's just what the ad said."

The night was humid and had the distinct smell of salt from the nearby gulf. Dark clouds rolled overhead, unsure whether to drop their payload over the city or not.

After a few blocks of silence and the were-twins walking just behind me, I broke the tension and asked, "You boys hungry? Got some fresh meat back at the crib," I said the last word with an emphasis of coolness. Or was it lit? To my surprise, the boys didn't snicker this time. Instead, they perked up at the mention of meat.

"Oh man, I'm so hungry I could eat another horse," Joey said.

"Yeah, that first one didn't fill us up," Dawson agreed. The twins were walking on either side of me now.

"I had a pretty big meal tonight and I'm stuffed to the rafters," I said, adding nothing to the weird conversation. A thought hit me as if I were a drunk standing in front of a dartboard. "Hey, what happens if you bite a dog?"

"No idea," Joey replied.

"Yeah, we like dogs," Dawson added.

"But not horses, got it," I said. "What if you bit me?"

"Probably nothing," Joey responded.

"Maybe some *Underworld* shit? Remember that old movie?" Dawson asked.

A puff of air shot out of my mouth in reflex, "Pfft, old? Old movie! How old are you two?"

"Twenty," they said in unison. "What about you, old man?" Joey asked.

"I don't really know. I'm bad at time. But let's see, Ulric turned me in 1480 when I was already a man."

"An old man," Dawson said.

"Dude, I was like in my early twenties."

"Must have been a tough twenty years," Joey added, burning me further.

"Times *were* tough back then, kids," I said, and then added, "How old do I look?"

"Early to late midthirties, at least," Dawson said, cracking a smile.

"Well, gee, guys. Just five minutes ago I was thinking to myself, 'Self, we just aren't self-conscious enough.' Thanks for fixing that for me."

"Maybe if you shaved the beard and got a haircut? You look kinda like a metalhead."

"Good!" I said. "I love metal. Plus, I can't shave. It'll grow right back. I'm just super glad beards are in right now. The fifties were especially hard."

"So you can never change how you look?" Joey asked.

"If I really needed to, I could will mortals' minds to see something else."

"You mean like a glamour?" Dawson asked.

"No. Ugh, I hate that word. Sounds all...Twilighty. I prefer, mindfuck."

"So you don't sparkle in the sunlight?" Joey asked.

"I basically melt in the sunlight. Or maybe it just burns the preternatural essence that is entwined with my human DNA—and if that burns, the rest of me burns too. I'm mostly just spit-balling ideas right now 'cause I have no idea what the fuck actually happens." My mind flashed with the memory of being consumed by sunlight after I had first been made. I had buried my head in the dirt, but the rest of me had burned and smoldered—quite painfully, I might add. Ulric was always one to teach the hard lessons.

"Um, you alright?" Joey asked, worry in his voice.

Returning to reality, I responded with, "Huh? What do you mean?"

"You, uh, zoned out pretty hardcore for a moment," Joey told me.

"Yeah, dude. You were making weird faces and shit. The hell, dude?" Dawson added tactfully.

"Oh, I was thinking about the ending to *Dexter*. Yeah, I'm still pretty pissed that the writers turned him into a fucking lumberjack," I made up—but not really. That was a bullshit ending.

"Ah. Cool. As long as you're alright, bro," Joey said.

We arrived at the Fortress of Solitaire and I led the twins downstairs. As I was about to open the door, something struck me.

"Wait here a sec," I said as I motioned for them to stop just before I opened the door and went inside. "Gotta make sure the place is, you know, um...clean! Yes, clean." A look of annoyance crossed Joey's face while Dawson's forehead wrinkled in confusion. I made my way inside and shut the door.

Locke sat on the couch, still fastened to his mannequin body, and was watching something on Netflix about serial killers. I ran over to him and grabbed his head while putting one hand over his mouth. He tried mumbling, but I motioned for him to be quiet with my index finger over my mouth. Then I used my thumb and pointed at the door, signaling our guests who might not understand why the *head* (see what I did there?) of the regional supernatural gang affiliated with Satan was sitting on my couch. Oh yeah, and he was my archnemesis.

I strode over to my door, opening it to reveal my bedroom. With a few swift movements, the hydraulic bed was descending once again over my iron coffin, with Locke resting comfortably on my pillow...that I was going to burn after this.

"Yyyyyuck," I said with a shiver before turning and making my way back to the front door, opening it for the twins.

In a dramatic MC voice I said, "Welcome to the Fortress of Solitaire, apparently the hottest place around. Don't forget to tip your waitress and leave a review on Yelp."

Joey and Dawson smiled at this, Dawson exposing full teeth while Joey's lips remained closed.

"Yeah, we have a reservation for two. Heard you had some delicious meat," Dawson said.

"That we do. Only the best for Depweg." The last word stung as I said it, reminding me that no matter how hard I tried to be normal, he was still

Ulric's prisoner. And that was only the best-case scenario. I shuttered as I thought about Ulric draining my best friend and gaining his immense energy. I only prayed Ulric didn't know about that little party trick. He had never mentioned it, at least.

"Please, help yourselves," I said as I motioned to the kitchen.

The twins walked past me and I shut the door behind them. Dawson stopped at my locked *Battlefield Earth* cabinet and asked, "What's in here? Vampire stuff?"

"Um, yes. Yes, that is exactly what's in there. Nothing of interest or use to you badass werewolves."

"Werwolves," Joey corrected, using the German term complete with pronouncing the first "W" as a "V."

"You two *really* like Depweg, don't you?" I asked with a touch of jealousy. He was *my* bestest good friend and I didn't like sharing.

"Yeah. Jealous?" Dawson asked as he opened the freezer and rummaged around, inspecting the contents.

"No." Yes.

"It's okay, man. I bet you have a fan club too. I mean, you're old as shit. There has to be a Facebook page or something about you," Joey said.

"Pfft. There's, like, entire Comic-Cons dedicated to me. JohniCons, they call them. I just didn't want to embarrass you guys by bringing them up."

A smile touched Joey's eyes as he looked through my facade, but he was a good sport about it and let it go.

"Liar, liar, coffin on fire," Dawson said.

"Oh ya, coffins!" Joey exclaimed. "Can we see yours? I bet it's badass."

My mind shot to Locke's burnt face drooling on my pillow and I immediately said, "No!" Dawson stopped searching in the freezer and looked at me suspiciously. "I try to not let anyone know where my coffin is," I said, trying to come up with a half truth to keep them off the scent. "You don't live as long as I do without keeping secrets." Score! That was an epic lie.

"Is it in there?" Dawson asked, pointing right at my Lilith-damned room.

"No," I denied, mind panicking. "That's the bathroom."

"Oh, sweet," Joey said as he started walking toward it. His hand was resting on the handle when I yelled out,

"Stop! What are you doing?"

Joey turned to look at me, confusion becoming a permanent fixture on his face. "I gotta pee, bro. That cool with you or should I just go right here on the floor."

"If you do, I'll rub your nose in it."

Joey turned the knob and pushed open my door to reveal my room.

"Is it through here?" Joey asked, pointing to my private bathroom.

I walked to the open door and looked in as if for the first time. It was just a normal room, complete with a normal bed. I never paid attention to the bed and basically forgot it was there, doing its job of hiding my true resting place.

"Yeah. Go ahead, man," I said, relieved.

"What was that all about?" Dawson asked, turning on two of the stove burners and setting pans down. On the counter next to the oven sat a large pile of assorted meats. "You a super private person or something?"

"I suppose that would explain things, wouldn't it?"

"Sure, man, whatever you say. Don't care either way," Dawson said, organizing the meats into two pan-sized portions. "Weirdo," he muttered under his breath.

"Nice bathroom," Joey spoke from behind me, startling me.

"Lilith Christ, you are sneaky!" I pretended to grab my heart.

"All the better to stalk you with, my dear," Joey all but purred as he walked past me and into the kitchen.

"Look, you guys eat your fill. We are all going to need our strength to face Ulric," I said as I sat on the couch and reached into my pocket for my phone. "He is a couple hundred years older than me, which means he is the Thanos to my Hulk."

"Sweet ref, dude. Love that movie," Dawson said as the sound of sizzling meat filled the air.

"Thanks, but it's also apropos," I told him as I texted Da, asking where he was.

"Apro-what now?" Dawson asked.

"It means he's for real about his power level being weaker than this Ulric dude," Joey explained.

"Is your power level at least over 9,000?" Dawson asked.

"Is that a *Dragon Ball Z* reference? Oh yeah, Depweg is going to love you two nerds," I said, rolling my eyes. My phone chimed and Da answered that he was on his way back after picking up some provisions. I responded with a thumbs-up emoji and a skull face. Then, giggling to myself, added an eggplant, water drops, and a dude's face.

I took in a deep breath, allowing the smell of grilling flesh to enter my nostrils. Oddly enough, the blood cooking made me salivate a little. Exhaling, I stood up and said, "You two eat. I'm going to shower and change. I smell like fire and gunpowder."

"Bet," said Dawson. I could hear his stupid smile as he spoke. He'd get old one day. Then we'd see who's laughing.

I went into my bedroom and closed the door behind me. I took off my clothes and separated them into two piles; one for simple cleaning and the other for Da to repair. My poor beanie was split in half, creating a Pacman-shaped disc when I laid it flat on the bed. I frowned as I let my fingers explore the damage. I loved that gray piece of cloth.

I walked to my dresser and pulled out fresh socks, underwear, and some 5.11 Tactical pants. They breathed, stretched, were cut-resistant, and had a shit ton of convenient pockets to keep all kinds of goodies. Plus, they made my butt look good.

I set the clothes on my bed and went to my closet where I grabbed a black cotton shirt and threw it atop the pile on my bed. It was times like this I wished I had a black turtleneck à la *Archer*. As I stepped into the bathroom and turned the shower faucet to hot, I quietly sang to myself, "Danger zone."

The water cascaded down my head and across my body, dragging the dirt and grime of the night away with it as it disappeared down the black hole of the drain. I wasn't ready for this, but I didn't have a choice. Jonathan Depweg would do the same thing for me without a second thought—not even a nanosecond of hesitation—while simultaneously coming up with a military-grade plan of attack worthy of any of the specialized branches.

I stared at the drain as water poured around my face and into my eyes, blurring my vision. Though my gaze was focused on a singular point, my attention was inward.

From within the city of my mind, I made my way to the secured corporate building at the center of town. The automatic doors activated as I walked up, and I was greeted by a long empty desk in the middle of the floor.

"Sup Tom, looking good, man." I gave a quick nod to one of the empty chairs then turned to another. "Juli! Back already? How's the baby doing?" No one gave an answer.

I stepped onto an escalator that carried me up to the second floor while Michael Bolton played on the overhead speakers. On the next level, cushioned bench seats wrapped around garden beds where trees grew, seeming to come out from the silver-flaked white marble of the floor. There were empty businesses scattered along the perimeter of the main walkway. Expensive sugar-laden coffee wafted from the Starbucks, which was right next door to a little one-chair hair and nail salon. Across the path, a Subway tempted nonexistent passersby with a glass case filled with an assortment of fancy breads.

The end of the common area came into view, and I was forced to take a left or a right. I chose the latter and walked right past an empty Chick-fil-A, where I cursed out loud, "Damn it! It's Sunday!"

After a few corridors and some sharp turns, I made my way to a bank of elevators sitting along either side of a hall. I kept walking down the hall to a lone set of doors with a key card–swiper that glowed a faint red next to the Up button. My hand moved over it, and a solid black metal card coalesced into my palm. The scanner turned green, and I pressed the button. After a moment there was a pleasant chime, and the silver doors opened to reveal a tightly spaced elevator. I stepped inside, turned, and pressed Penthouse, which was atop all the other buttons. The doors closed with a sealing hiss, and then I was rocketed upward. The numbers on the display went up ten floors every second. After ten seconds, I stepped out onto the third floor, where I walked past an empty desk and into my office.

"Hold all my calls," I said over my shoulder as my office doors closed behind me.

Walking to a wall of black metal file cabinets, I located and pulled the file that contained the battle between Ulric and myself. After getting what I sought, I turned and made my way back to my office doors, which opened onto the street. I casually walked down the avenue in my mind to my movie theater, trying to procrastinate as much as inhumanly possible. I didn't want to do this. It would be the equivalent of watching your most embarrassing, helpless moment go viral on social media.

Walking by the empty box office, I opened a heavy glass door to reveal a huge concession area, complete with a gelato station. My nose wrinkled at the green pistachio treat and wondered why people ate what looked like Shrek's loogy. Looking forward, I saw the IMAX Theater complete with huge cutouts of Ulric and me in a classic battle stance surrounding the door. Both of us had our fangs and claws out as we seemingly hissed at one another. I glanced at the marquee above the door and chuckled at my own subconscious pun humor: Yesferatu.

As I entered, I sat in the handicap row, which provided the most legroom and was right in the middle of the screen. I had a pang of PC guilt for sitting in a handicapped seat while inside my own mind's city, and willed the stick figures in wheelchairs to vanish. Only the red leather of the luxury recliners remained now, rendering me guilt-free. Lilith, I wish I had never discovered Facebook, as now I was worried about offending people for even thinking about sitting in a seat that was meant for those less fortunate than me (which was everyone, by the way). I could see the headline now on Huffington Post, "Some vampire douche sits in the handicap row inside the metaphorical theater in his own sexist, misogynistic, white, male brain."

PS sat down beside me, which was a surprise, and pointed to the screen.

"Right," I said as much to him as to myself, "no more stalling."

PS nodded his approval and settled back in his seat, eyes on the screen.

"You know in the real world this is all happening in a fraction of a fraction of a second, right?"

PS responded by keeping his eyes on the screen and raising one hand to point forward before letting it fall back to our shared armrest. Damn it, he got there first.

I looked down at the VHS tape in my hands and lifted it up, regarding it at arm's length. It dissolved as the lights of the theater dimmed. The THX intro sounded, really testing the speakers inside my mind. PS hit my shoulder and I got the point. Before he could put his arm back down, I quickly claimed the armrest, smiling to myself in victory. Unperturbed, PS let his arm sink between the armrest and his body.

The screen went blank for a moment and then Ulric was standing in front of us. We were watching from our own point of view as we demanded to know if Ulric knew the date. I could still feel the confused anger as if it were happening in real time. There was no time degradation with vampires as with mortals, so memory was both reliable and unforgiving. Even though I had been mortal when I'd watched as my mother was executed, I'd been immediately turned, and so the memory was painstakingly crystal clear.

PS nudged me, freeing me from my prison of pain, and pointed at the screen. It showed a dark dungeon where I was just waking up to the sound of Ulric's voice.

"Dude! I didn't know I could change the channel just by thinking! I've been getting the videos like a philistine this whole time."

PS stared at me and then pointed, aggressively, to the screen.

"Ah, right." I concentrated and the scene in the alley popped back onto the screen. Since this place wasn't real anyway, I manifested some popcorn and began throwing handfuls back while crunching loudly with an open mouth.

"Oh, I like this part," I said to PS as I prodded his arm with my elbow.

"Ulric," I started calmly but with a flat undertone, "why did not a single camp have a calendar? A dated scroll?" I looked at him after speaking, awaiting his response. My accent had been British at the time, matching my surroundings.

Ulric sighed then did something I wasn't expecting; he looked right at me with cold eyes and said in a tone of finality, "Because I removed them before you could figure out that the mortal commander was long since dead, you petulant child."

That moment still stunned me, my hand freezing in midair with imaginary popcorn falling to my lap. I was vaguely aware of PS growling next to me.

I attacked, forcing all of my rage and fury into a mighty longsword that belonged in an anime. As I soared through the air, Ulric blurred and slammed a fist into my stomach. I was pretty sure he could have grabbed my spine at that moment.

My eye twitched and I willed the scene to replay in slow motion. One moment, Ulric was standing a few yards ahead of me; the next, he was right in front of me.

My eye twitched again and the scene rewound itself. I played it again, even slower this time. Ulric was standing, and then he cut the distance between us in half, culminating with a fist rocketing toward my gut.

Another twitch and I was watching the events play out at a fraction of the first viewing.

Ulric was standing, a frown of concentration appearing on his face, and he began to rush forward, his eyes turning from purple to red like a sunrise over a cloudy morning.

"Okay," I said to PS. "Now we have an idea of speed. Let's watch it again at normal pace."

PS and I leaned forward in our seats, watching the scene. Ulric was standing and began to run toward where we were. It took all our concentration just to keep up with his movements.

"Lilith, he is fast. There's no way we can match that speed. He's hundreds of years older than us!" I said to PS without taking my eyes off the screen.

Predatory Self made a movement in the corner of my eye and I turned to see him pointing at his head and then back at the screen.

Almost defeated, we used our brilliant mind and single-handedly defeated Ulric...by luck. The dude had been caught monologuing and gave us the opportunity to fry him...aaaaaannd most of London, but we didn't talk about that.

"Okay, you're right. We can't match his speed or strength, so we need to set up a trap. The only problem is, we have to go to him, right? Any moment now, we will get a call or a knife on the door pinning a letter about where to meet. Then, he will kill both Depweg *and* us."

PS nodded in agreement while his eyes shifted to the ground, his gaze becoming heavy.

"We'll figure it out, man! Don't worry! I mean, we have Dawson and Joey now, and there's no way he'll see that coming."

PS looked at me, warily. Then he slowly let a bloodrope come out of his palm and slither around his own neck. He pretended to choke and stuck his tongue out.

"Right, we cowed them easily. BUT, they weren't changed! They still had their man-suits on!" I said with hopeful enthusiasm.

PS thought about this as he let his rope slide back into his palm, and then nodded once in acceptance.

There was a sudden Danny Elfman score that burst through the speakers of the theater, and I was snapped out of my city and back behind my eyeballs, where I still stared into the drain. My cell phone was ringing with the *Beetlejuice* theme song. I knew who it was before I even turned the water off, grabbed a towel, and stepped to the sink where my phone lay.

Unknown showed on the screen. I picked it up.

"Hello, Ulric," I said, somberly.

"Please do not hang up. This is not a sales call," a robotic woman's voice proclaimed, "Visa-MasterCard has let us know that..." Click.

Lilith, I HATED those calls. I think I could add the people who programmed these calls to my meal requirements and Heaven wouldn't even bat an eye.

My phone rang again, displaying a local Houston number.

"Remove me from your fucking list before I come down there and fist you like a Muppet!" I yelled into the phone.

"Hello?" a familiar voice asked, unsure about my greeting. "Do I have the right number?"

"Ulric?"

"Yes. Is this John?"

"Yes. I've been expecting you," I said, sighing into the phone as my rage from the spam calls melted into the reality that was despair.

Ulric's voice grew serious, "Good, boy. It has been a long time, and I have been undying to see you."

"That's my joke," I said flatly and annoyed.

"Share and share alike, John, for we are the last two vampires."

"Which, by the way, we should probably keep like that."

"Should we now?" Ulric asked, bemused. "And why is that, child?"

"Long story that you wouldn't believe even if I told you," I sighed again into the phone.

"A penance must be paid for the trespass against me."

"Yeah, yeah. I know. You have my friend and want me in exchange. You don't watch a lot of movies, do you?" I asked, rubbing my forehead with my fingers in agitation.

"I have been asleep for some time, child," Ulric said.

"They are like plays, but better."

"What?"

"Movies."

"I understand the concept. Can we continue?"

"Where are we meeting," I said as much in a statement as in question.

Ulric gave me the exact coordinates.

"That's really annoying," I said. "Can't you give me a cross street or something? And where's Depweg? How do I even know he's alive?" I battled with the anger and the feeling of being helpless in my chest.

"You don't," Ulric responded, coldly. Helplessness blossomed throughout my being. "Be seeing you, John."

Before he hung up, I said, "That's *John Wick*."

There was a pause followed by, "Pardon?"

Being the mature adult that I was, I retorted with, "Last word," before hanging up.

I tossed the phone on the bed—where it bounced and then slid to the floor—when it chimed with a text. I glanced over at it as I put on my Batman boxer briefs and saw an emoji from the same number. It was of a middle finger.

"Figuring things out pretty quickly, I see," I said as I slid into my black tactical pants and normal 100% cotton socks, which were also black. My mind raced with different responses to the postconversation text as I pulled on my steel-toed Doc Martens boots.

As I stood up and grabbed for my shirt, Da knocked on the door. I could tell by the sound of his little fist.

"Intrude," I said.

The door opened and Da came in, his eyes being immediately drawn to the gray beanie still spread out on the bed. He tutted at me with pursed lips before turning back to me.

"Made new friends, I see," Da spoke, referring to the twins who were holding their full stomachs and sitting on the couch. Dawson was eagerly cleaning his teeth with a bone while Joey let out a room-shattering belch.

"Yeah, they were at Val's, imagine that!" I said mockingly.

"Where's Lo—"

"Lo...ki? Loki, right? Thanos killed him, remember? We don't know if he is really dead, though. He's been dead before," I deflected as my eyes shifted to the bed and back to him.

"Dude!" Dawson said. "We know Locke is here. We can freaking smell him, alright?"

"Yeah, cut the crap," Joey confirmed.

From under my false bed, I heard a muffled, "HA!"

14

I carried Locke's, um, body in one hand and my pillow in the other. I set Locke down on the coffee table as I walked to the trash, where I stuffed the pillow into the already overflowing garbage. It stuck out awkwardly as I walked away.

"John," Da said, "what are the rules for the trash?"

"What?" I replied innocently. "There's plenty of room in there!" Everyone's eyes shifted to the can that was leaning precariously. "See?" As if on cue, the trash can toppled over, spilling its contents onto the kitchen floor.

"Right," Dawson said.

"So why is he here?" Joey asked, motioning at Locke.

"Long story short, he wants to stay hidden from Satan, who might not know he's haunting his own head, because he is helping us to stop his former master from starting the apocalypse."

"There's a little more to the story than those brief synopses," Locke said.

"Dude. I said 'long story short.' I said that, didn't I?" I asked as I looked around, waving my hands in frustration.

"Hey," Dawson started with a shit-eating grin, "Simmer down now. Okay? You're coming to a boil. Simmer down."

"Yeah, man. Calm down," Joey continued.

"Calmer than you are," I said under my breath. "Anyway, Locke, this is Joey and Dawson. They are werewolves. I'm sorry, 'werwolves,'" I said with finger quotes using the German pronunciation. "Twins, Locke. Locke, twins," I introduced.

"Sup dude," Dawson said, extending his fist out for a bump.

"Charmed," Locke said curtly with a less than amused look on his face.

"How do you wipe your butt?" Joey asked out of left field.

"Well, it's pretty easy when you lack said butt," Locke chided.

"Then what's with all that shit coming out of your mouth," Dawson said before both twins started laughing while punching each other's shoulders.

I snickered to myself at Locke's torment.

"Miss Hell yet?" I asked Locke.

In all sincerity, Locke said, "No." Not even a smart-ass comment or reply as his eyes went unfocused. Hell must have really messed him up, as one might expect. But you never really understood or even began to fathom the implications until you saw it firsthand. My trust for Locke grew three sizes that day—but so did my weariness. Any man this terrified of something could be a liability if Satan were to get his hands on him again. Maybe he could use him as a spy. Shit, maybe he *was* using him as a spy. That would help explain how the hell he had gotten into my hideout so easily. It would take some major mojo to see past my defenses.

Or maybe Gabriel had snuck him in all hushlike to help counter Satan's machinations. I mean, he *had* just learned exactly where my Batcave was, even the positioning of the coffee table.

FUCK! I yelled inwardly. PS looked over at me in agreement. Three steps forward and three steps back. I didn't know if I could trust him. *Do we kill him? Just to be sure?* PS shrugged with indecision. *Damn, you're right. What if Gabe delivered him to us to help defeat the Devil?* PS looked at me again and then nodded his head in agreement. *You are really of no help, dude.*

"John," Locke said hesitantly. I snapped out of my internal conversation and saw everyone looking at me. I could feel my face scrunched in angry concentration as I looked directly at Locke's head.

"If you betray me," I started suddenly and sternly, staring directly into Locke's worried eyes, "I will submerge what's left of you into an iron box filled with wet cement, close the lid, wrap it in silver and iron chains, and throw you into the Mariana Trench where no one will ever find you. Ever." I leaned forward, inching closer to Locke. "Demons have no patience. You think the physical tortures in Hell are bad? Try being completely alone until the end of the universe at the bottom of the deepest ocean with only blackness and silence as your companions. I wonder how many years you'd last before your mind snapped completely." I placed my palms on either side of his cheeks as his eyes shifted rapidly back and forth between my hands as they lifted him up until we were almost nose to nose. My eyes glowed a fierce red as I willed blood from my palms to slowly start to swallow his entire head. "If you join us completely of your own volition and not because of a lack of options, you will be rewarded. And Locke, to show I mean what I say, in *both* scenarios, mind you," a lump caught in my throat as I continued, the blood now covering his entire face, "I forgive you." A tear slid down my face, disappearing into the mass of my reddish beard.

My blood started to retract, birthing the now unburnt skin of Locke's face. Da put his hand over his mouth in surprise. Then he looked at me with fatherly pride in his eyes and nodded.

"Cool," Dawson said as if watching a CGI-filled movie.

"Can you fix my acne?" Joey asked with half sincerity.

Locke's eyes were screwed shut, and he was holding his breath as if underwater. Letting one eye open, he exhaled and said to the group looking at him in astonishment, "What?"

Joey took out his phone and snapped a picture of Locke, and then he turned the screen around to show him the gift I had given him.

Locke looked at the picture, realization growing in his eyes the longer he looked at his face. His lips quivered, and he attempted to blink away his own tears.

"No one has ever..." Locke started, swallowing the emotions that tried to crawl up his throat, "No one has ever done anything nice for me. I've always had to take what I wanted."

"You were kind of a huge asshole," I said.

"I don't want to be an asshole anymore," Locke said with hope. "Can you help me, John?"

Da interjected at that moment with his infinite wisdom, "Eh, maybe not the best teacher for that particular job."

"Then let's get Depweg back," I said, both ignoring and accepting the accurate assessment.

15

Locke and Da shared their plan with the twins and me. I had questions and concerns that Da and Locke patiently cleared up as if explaining to a child why we had to stop at red lights. The twins, on the other hand, accepted their orders with excitement. Though to be fair, their portion consisted of badass werewolf stuff, while my part was more cloak and daggers. I had never been good at that part. Whenever a game said you could be stealthy or run in with guns blazing, I started screaming at the screen while shooting everything I saw with extreme prejudice.

With the plan set in motion, it was time to face my maker one last time, for the last time—but without killing him or else I would start the apocalypse, and stuff. Jeez, this was not going to be fun or easy, or if I was being frank, possible. Good thing I was not Frank, though. I was John, the last of my kind...except for that other guy. You know what? Let's just get to it.

In the privacy of my room, I held the Home button on my phone until my thumbprint unlocked the screen, where I selected the phone icon. Pressing Favorites, I called Father Thomes and held my breath as I waited for him to answer. When he did, I caught him up on the situation, including the situation with Locke.

"You have allied yourself with a warlock sent by Satan himself?!"

Father Thomes all but yelled into the phone. I had to pull it away from my ear, and even looked at the screen to verify I was, in fact, talking to my friend and not a wrong number. Just as quickly as it had come, his anger receded and he said, "Apologies, my son. I will have to pray on whether or not to inform the Church about this new development; and I fear I can anticipate their answer. The clergy was not pleased when the werewolf came into the picture, but at least he is a good man at heart with only a few blemishes on his soul. Locke's soul, on the other hand, is pitch black and dripping with sin."

"So don't tell them. I seem to recall us having the same predicament when we first met almost thirty years ago." I put on my movie announcer voice and said, "One priest. One vampire. Teaming up to save the world from evil and kick Satan in his dangly bits. Starring Chris Evans as the super buff vampire and Daniel Day-Lewis as Papa T. Coming this summer."

Father Thomes chuckled at that.

"Ah! You laughed! That means it's okay!"

He sighed heavily before saying, "I suppose not wanting to go to Hell or allow Hell to come to Earth are fairly convincing motivators. Very well. But do me one favor, please."

"What's that?"

"Watch him. Question everything he says, even if to yourself. If he committed atrocities in the name of Satan and claimed to not have a choice, then what's to say he isn't being manipulated now?"

"Already thought about that. I'll keep a close eye out," I said somberly.

He prayed for me over the phone and asked the Lord for strength to carry out my mission.

I thanked him for his blessing, pressed the red End button on my phone, and then slid it into my coat pocket.

It was game time.

I slipped into the iron-infused body armor Depweg gave me in that other book, and slapped a magazine into my Glock containing the fresh iron-and-silver rounds. I holstered the Glock before picking up the silver kukri and regarding it at arm's length.

"What's that for? I thought we agreed we absolutely could not kill him," Da said as he floated into my room.

Throwing on my best John Candy impersonation, I said, "Not to kill, no. Just to maim. Take a little off the shoulder. The elbow. Shave a little meat off the ol' kneecap."

Da crossed his tiny arms and glared at me, disbelieving.

"Alright, alright, alright. Look, it's like a condom; it's better to have one and not use it than to not have one and start the apocalypse. Or something like that. You know how the saying goes."

"I don't even know where to begin with that one," Da replied, rubbing his forehead in annoyance.

"Here's the deal, Da. I'll need every advantage against Ulric I can get. And this," I said, turning the glinting blade over in the light, "is a damn fine advantage. If I can take off even one limb that won't be able to heal immediately, we might maybe perhaps be able to take him down without killing him. Possibly."

"I suppose you are right, John," Da admitted with a sigh.

"But know this, my friend; if it appears that Ulric is about to kill me, then I will do everything in my power to strike him down first. At least if the gates of Hell and Heaven spill open while I still walk this flat Frisbee they call Earth, then I'll take as many demons and angels down as I can. Maybe there will be something left of the planet after. Who knows?"

"That's a foolhardy notion."

"I'm just kidding," I said with a wry smile. "The Earth is totally a sphere."

"John!" Da barked, frustration dripping from his words. "This is no time to joke. For once in your unlife, can you please take things seriously?"

Changing my posture and tone, I said, "I am serious, and this isn't a joke to me. But you knew what you were getting into when you said 'I do,' so I don't know why you are so mad at me."

"Follow the plan. Save the world. Don't bring the gun because I know you. You will find an excuse to use it," Da instructed as he floated up to be eye to eye with me. "Think about Father Thomes, about Depweg, about the boy."

Something the size of a baseball got lodged in my throat at the mention of the boy. I tried to swallow but couldn't as I swayed at the impact of his words. He had known just where to hit, and it was a home fucking run.

"Fine," I said through clenched teeth. I was angry, not at the fact that he was right but at the method he had used to make his point. I unstrapped the holster that held the Glock and let it drop down on the bed. "But I'm keeping the knife."

"Agreed," Da said. "Now, they are waiting for you."

I followed Da into the living room, where I saw the twins had changed into...the exact same thing they had been wearing. I pointed at them in confusion and then palmed my head, "Right, man-suits. Okay, we ready?"

"Bet," Dawson said with a mischievous smile and a nod of his head.

"Yup," said the more even-keeled Joey.

"Alright, Da, remember what I always say; if I die, bury me with my things because you know they are mine."

"Go get them, tiger," Locke said, prompting everyone in the room to slowly turn toward him in awkward consternation.

"Dude..." I said, mouth hanging open.

"Sorry, sorry, everyone. I am new to this whole positive reinforcement thing," Locke said, only slightly embarrassed.

"Eh, I'll give it to ya anyway," I said to Locke with a wink. "Okay then. Autobots, Assemble!"

"Those are two completely different franchises," Joey whispered to Dawson.

"Dude, right?" Dawson responded.

"Keep your hands and feet inside the murder train at all times; and please, don't feed the trolls," I said in an amusement park announcer's voice.

As we stepped through the door and into the stairwell, reality snuck in and sat heavily on our minds like a two-ton elephant. This was going to happen, and it was going to happen right now. We all knew the risks and the severe consequences of our likely failure. But what choice did we have?

We stopped at the sliding marble door of the mausoleum, and I turned to the twins and said, "Thank you, guys, for coming. With you, we have a fighting chance to save Depweg and maybe even the whole world."

"Bet," Dawson said while Joey just nodded.

"That word is incredibly versatile, isn't it?"

"Bet," Dawson said again, that stupid smile of his never fading.

"Are you guys ready for this?" I asked them.

"We got your back, bro," Joey said. "Now let's stop holding each other's dicks and go save the world."

The night was humid, and the moon tried to sneak around black clouds only to be overwhelmed after only a moment of success. I closed my eyes, feeling the night, and inhaled deeply. After holding my breath, I let it out in a long stream of air to calm my nerves, and then opened my eyes to see the night again. My eyes had shifted, and the scene was now as clear as day to me.

I extended my arms to either side of me and said to the twins, "Hold on."

Without hesitation, which was kind of touching, they grabbed onto my arms. I squatted down until my knees were at 90 degrees, then leaped into the night. We flew through the air for about thirty feet before landing. Well, I did anyway. The twins had lost their grip and fallen after only a few feet in the air. They hit the ground and tumbled toward me, stopping a few yards away, moaning.

"Hold on tight?" I said with the pitch of the last word going up in question.

"We aren't that strong in our man-suits, dude," Joey groaned as he pushed up to his knees.

"Oh, right. Okay then, let's try this," I said as I walked over to where they were still trying to stand, grabbed them each around the waist, and hooked my fingers into their belts and/or fanny packs. I crouched again and leaped toward the place Ulric had told me. This time, the twins came with. I could feel their bodies tense, but they remained in control enough to not scream as we rocketed through the night at less than blinding speed. I did keep the g-force down to a minimum for the weres. They were stronger than any mortal, but were still susceptible to things like physics.

Several minutes later, we arrived at the location. It was an empty field that had a burned-out home sitting at the edge closest to the street. The house looked like it had been hand built in the early 1900s. The land was mostly knee-high grass, with a clearing in the middle that was about the full length of a football field.

I walked, alone, toward the field, the twins having been dropped off several hundred yards back to flank this position. My hands opened and the grass grazed and tickled my fingers, oblivious to what was about to unfold. Facing death, I thought of Lily. I bet she could have been helpful right about now. Then again, it was characteristic of the Fae to let others do their fighting. Plus, she was more of a lover than a fighter, or so I tried to convince myself. Actually, it was better she wasn't here because that would just be another potential distraction that I couldn't afford.

As I cleared the field and entered the clearing, I called out, "Ulric, come out and face me."

From behind me came my response, "Always so dramatic, John."

I spun in surprise as Ulric open-palm struck me in the forehead, sending me tumbling backward for several yards. Luckily, I was stunned and panicked, because it didn't hurt that much. Either that or it was really bad and my body hadn't been able to tell me the full extent of the pain and damage yet.

With shaking hands, I pushed on the ground and stood to face my maker. My voice trembled as I yelled, "Where is Depweg?"

"Dead," Ulric said coldly. An evil smile graced his face as my pain manifested on its own. The surrounding field and Ulric started to blur as tears welled in my eyes. I went to wipe them and a foot crashed into my face. As I flew back, stunned and dismayed at the loss of my best friend, Ulric grabbed my feet as they became even with the rest of my flying body and then turned me round and round in a circle until the world melted around me like a fresh painting being spun on a finger by a professional plate spinner.

I felt him release my feet as I flew through the night toward the burned-out house, which rushed greedily to meet me. I smashed through the side, blackened wood turning into splinters from the force of impact, and slid on the floor to come to a stop in the living room. I lay on my back in pure agony at the thought of my best friend being killed because of me. I could see the moon piercing the clouds through a hole in the roof. It shone on me, illuminating the home and the man who was walking through the hole I had made.

A giant black wolf with a white patch on his right eye slammed into Ulric. They tumbled into the field, with the were gnawing at Ulric's arm. In pure rage and disgust, Ulric threw the black wolf away with ease just as a white wolf with a black patch on his left eye crashed into him from the opposite side, tearing at his other arm. Ulric cried out in pain as he grabbed the white wolf by the scruff and threw it into the house. It hit and rolled until it landed next to me, whimpering slightly. Then an aggressive growl rumbled in its throat as it got up on all fours and lowered its head closer to the ground, protecting its neck. A piece of lumber flew through the hole at the white wolf, who narrowly dodged out of the way. The lumber struck me right in the forehead as I was trying to get up, knocking me back down. I was numb from what Ulric had done to Depweg. Which was good because that probably hurt like hell. Wait, no—that *did* hurt like hell, damn it.

I raised my head again as I heard a howl from outside. Ulric darted impossibly fast to the side as the black wolf leaped through the hole where Ulric had just been. He skidded on the ground, tearing chunks out of the wood floor. The twins weren't as massive as Depweg, but they were still over three hundred pounds each.

Depweg. Dead. Anger began to smolder in my guts like white-hot coals.

Ulric strode into the building baring his teeth, prompting the twins to attack. The black wolf feigned a leap while the white one went low. Ulric was still too fast for them, and swatted the white wolf away with a heavy thud just as the black wolf made its attack. Ulric slammed his elbow downward, smashing into the black wolf's skull. It landed with a sickening crunch on the ground, where it lay and whined.

The fire in my gut became all-consuming as I let my grip slide from the wheel. Both PS and I were blinded with rage as he took control. One moment we were on the ground, beaten, the next we were upright and screaming incoherently as we lunged forward.

Ulric saw me coming and willed a bloodrapier out of his hand. I didn't care. He had taken too much from me, and I was beyond rational thinking. Either I died right now, or he would. Hell, maybe I would get lucky and we would both die. That would cancel the prophecy, wouldn't it?

As I charged, arms outstretched, he stabbed me right through the heart. Or he would have, had I not been wearing my iron-infused body armor. Ulric cried out in pain and surprise as the blood manifestation's energy was canceled and taken away from him. I finished my charge and took advantage of his stunned state by wrapping my arms around him and tackling him to the ground. While on top of him, I began wildly pounding my fists. Most of my hammer blows missed and shattered holes in the rotted wood floor, but the few that hit home really did damage. Ulric had been starting to recover when the first fist slammed into his forehead.

For an instant, the image of the soldier whose face I'd caved in when my family was taken shot through my mind in rapid flashes.

Each hit stunned him while I continued my onslaught. The white wolf padded up to me and whined loudly. We both knew that if I somehow managed to kill Ulric, the end of times would begin, but I couldn't stop myself.

"He is not dead!" Ulric cried out between fists. I wasn't letting him get full control of his faculties because I knew he would easily overtake me. I had to keep him dazed, or dead.

Then his words sunk in and I slowed. "What did you say?!" I cried out, spittle flying in my rage. I didn't stop the onslaught; I kept smashing his head with blows whenever I felt his body start to regain its composure. With each blow, his chest and arms relaxed under me, unable to receive a strong signal from the brain that was being rattled.

Dawson barked right in my face and then leaned down to grasp one of Ulric's arms as Joey wobbled over to grab the other. They pierced flesh, and blood trickled out of their jaws, staining their fur as they held Ulric in a death grip that even he wouldn't be able to break. A werewolf's jaws were a terrifying weapon to come up against, even for a vampire as old as my maker. The twins pulled the arms out to each side as Ulric grunted in pain and weakly struggled.

"I lied to make you emotional. Just like you were in London," Ulric panted, his eyes rolling in his head. "I still have him as an insurance policy."

I stopped pounding and reached for my kukri. It slid out, hungry for flesh, while humming with raw power. I brought the blade next to his face, pressed it into his flesh so he knew I meant business, and said, "Talk, right now."

"No," Ulric spoke calmly but fully understanding the situation. "If I do, you will kill me."

"I'll fucking kill you if you don't," I said with a tone that frightened even me. I moved the blade down to his ear and slid it under the skin like a white-hot knife through warm butter. It fell to the ground and Ulric screamed through a closed mouth, refusing to give me the full pleasure.

"Where is he?" I asked as I moved to his other ear, slicing it clean off before he could even breathe in for a response. I was going to disassemble him, piece by fucking piece.

The white wolf whined at me, eyes pleading. I knew I should take control back from PS, but I just didn't care what happened to Ulric. He deserved to die.

Joey barked through a full mouth at me and growled. Blood was streaming down his forehead where he had been struck by Ulric. The droplets in his fur glinted like rubies in the moonlight.

"He needs to die," I said with a shaky voice.

Both twins whined at me, their eyes shifting from one another to me.

I knew they were right, but I just couldn't take the control back from PS. It felt too good to punish Ulric, and this was my only chance to hurt the much more powerful vampire.

"No," I said to the pleading twins as I sat upright on Ulric's chest and grabbed the handle of the kukri with both hands, blade pointing downward. "I want his heart." I brought the blade down with all my might.

At least I thought I did. I was frozen in midair, unable to move. Tendons popped and drool shot through my clenched teeth as I fought with all my might to kill this bastard.

I cried out as realization struck. "YOU FUCKING BITCH, LILY!"

Ulric took advantage of the situation and put one foot flat on the ground before he pushed up and over to the side, toppling me to the ground. I was still frozen from Lily's commands. The wolves braced themselves, but with Ulric gaining back full control of his mind, he ripped his arms out of the twin's mouths, bringing most of their teeth with him. They yelped in both pain and surprise as Ulric was up and out of the house in the blink of an eye, leaving only kicked-up dust that slowly settled back to the ground behind.

Once the threat, which had stopped being a threat, was gone, my body relaxed, free from Lily's order. I was so pissed at her, even if I knew she had stopped me from doing something I couldn't take back.

"She fucking knew," I panted as I sat up, bringing my knees to my chest. I went to pull my beanie off, forgetting it wasn't there, and furiously ran my fingers through my hair.

"Knew what?" Joey the Black Wolf asked after he transformed back. His human teeth grew in place of the ripped-out canines. It was a good thing werewolves lost their preternatural teeth when they changed back to human. He sat next to me with blood glistening off his naked body in the moonlight. Head wounds always bled the worst.

"Nothing," I said, embarrassed at being played and because I knew I needed to be played in that situation.

"You had him, man, what happened?" Dawson the White Wolf asked as he finished reverting to his human skin. His face was heavily bruising on one side.

"I froze," I said.

"No shit," Dawson replied as he leaned on a wall. He looked down at the ground in contemplation before saying, "Fuck, he was strong, dude. Like, really, *really* strong."

"Tell me about it," I agreed. "I was so close."

"Okay, let's look at things from a constructive perspective," Joey began. "We know the silver worked against him."

"And the armor," I added, touching the chest plate that had saved my life.

"And the armor," Joey repeated in agreement.

"But he still has Depweg," I said, disappointment and dismay in my words.

"Yeah, but now the dude is bleeding and shit," Dawson remarked. "We can track his bitch ass." He finished his statement by holding up his hands with his thumbs and pinkies outstretched and waggling them back and forth.

Excitement grew in my chest, lined with hope. "You can? Like right now?"

"Yeah, bro. We just need to eat a deer or something along the way," Joey said, leaning forward to get on all fours. Dawson took his cue and dropped to his hands and feet as they both began changing. Hair grew over their entire bodies and then thickened to fur. Their eyes turned yellow as their snouts extended from their face, bones popping like breaking twigs. Wrists extended until they basically became a second elbow as hands became paws. Teeth elongated into razor-sharp daggers while tails sprouted from lower backs. After a few moments the change was over, and both weres shook like wet dogs and chuffed to signal they were ready. I noticed their wolf teeth were back. That's a neat trick to remember, though I knew it was extremely depleting to transform into their wolf skins.

Both Joey the Black Were and Dawson the White Wolf padded outside, sniffing the ground in circles until they honed in on their target's direction. Once locked, both wolves ran full sprint in the direction Ulric had retreated. I followed close behind, letting my senses flow all around us to keep on the lookout for a likely ambush.

We made it almost to the end of an adjoining cornfield before I felt something entering my perimeter senses. Immediately after, Joey's and Dawson's heads shot up as a wave of spiders the size of car tires poured out of the tree line and into the cornfield. Each black mass had eight eyes that glowed red.

"Ooooohhhh mmmmmyyyyy Lilith! That's fucking horrifying! Don't let them bite you!" I cried out to the weres.

Green liquid gleamed and dripped off mandibles the size of steak knives. Lilith, there had to be hundreds.

"Just smash and go. They can't be that strong," I said as I slid to a stop just outside the corn rows, in the space between the field and the trees. I willed two sledgehammers from my palms and into my fists and crouched low. Joey and Dawson lined up next to me in preparation, staying close to prevent flanking.

The spiders started climbing into three piles several yards in front of us, the one in the middle attracting a larger share than the other two. The spiders clutched one another and merged their flesh until two spiders the size of minivans stood in front of us. The third pile was still forming and was already the size of a small RV.

The two minivan spiders charged, front legs outstretched, machete-sized mandibles clicking excitedly. Joey and Dawson darted around either side of me, circling around. The spiders took no notice and beelined directly to me. That was a little unsettling. Maybe if I peed my pants it would help deter them.

I let my sledgehammers grow into broadswords as I brought them up in a defensive stance in front of me. The spiders ran like the creepy bastards from *Starship Troopers*, and thoughts of men being torn to pieces flooded my mind. Damn movies infecting my mind!

The left spider juked to the side, drawing my attention as the right one slowed. I knew this was a trap that would spring as soon as I turned my body toward the left spider. So instead, I turned to the right and jumped forward, sliding on my knees through the earth and grass. As I passed under the spider's body, I let my blades swing out to either side, cutting the demon's legs off at the joint. The spider monster screamed a high-pitched wail that pierced the night. As I cleared its bulk, I pivoted and jumped on the gimp spider's back and drove my blades through its body at a single point. The stump legs shot out in pain as I twisted the blades before pulling them in different directions, splitting the demon in half.

As its body melted into ectoplasm, the other spider pounced on me from the side, knocking me to the ground where it pinned my arms and legs with its massive appendages. I struggled to move as its fangs inched closer to my face. Two wolves slammed into the beast as its mandible caressed my bare throat, throwing the beast to the side. Each wolf grabbed a leg in its massive jaws and shook its head. The legs popped like kindling and broke apart as the wolves did their job before moving to another leg. Dawson got cocky and went for its front legs, putting a front paw in range of the fangs, which pierced his flesh while injecting venom. Dawson howled in pain as he limped away right as I jumped on the spider's abdomen, willing my swords into my oversized Looney Tunes hammer. I brought the weapon down on the spider's red eyes and they exploded in a mass of goo that crunched like a Styrofoam cooler being crushed. I could feel the tremor of impact as my hammer hit the earth. The spider started melting as my attention turned toward the remaining mass that had stopped growing and was now the size of a small house.

"Well, that isn't something you see every day," I said to myself. "Maybe if I shit my pants..."

Joey howled in fury as Dawson collapsed to the ground. He had started breathing hard and rapidly, his tongue hanging out the side of his snout. The house-spider took note of this and began making its way to us. Each leg impacted the ground with enough force to create tremors. Its venom-dripping fangs were the size of Viking broadswords.

"Um, um, um, I don't know what to do with this," I stuttered as I backed away, completely at a loss as to what to do with this monstrosity before me that was barreling down. It reared up as it got closer, and my mind flashed to the terrible movie *Spawn*.

I put my hands together and leaned forward like a diver about to jump into the water. I focused and willed blood to flow out all around me, with half shooting into the ground for support and the other half pointing straight at the beast. The blood sharpened to a point, like a giant spear, and violated the spider's body as it charged. Gore shot out from the impact as the beast screamed with a mixture of agony, rage, and surprise. Its legs pounded on my body-encompassing bloodspear, which had taken a lot of energy to make. I willed the bottom portion of the spear that was in the ground to help provide support before I was beaten to death. I sent more blood into the body of the beast and expanded the tip, creating a wedge to pull the body apart. This only pissed the monster off, and it slammed its many legs with renewed vigor and fury. I could feel the blood protecting my body begin to grow brittle from impact. If it broke, I would lose a lot of energy and would be stunned long enough for the thing to freaking eat me. I focused on the legs and the pattern they used to strike.

Six of the eight legs struck in a succession of front to back, left to right. Between the last legs hitting and the front legs resetting and striking again, there was a brief pause. One, two, three, four, five, six. Pause to reset. One, two, three, four, five, six.

On the third go-around after I noticed the pattern, I sucked in the cover that protected my body and crouched down. As the first leg came down again, I jumped forward with all my might and pierced through the back of the spider's body, splitting it in two. It crumbled to the ground in two pieces and began turning translucent as its driver was sent back to hell, defeated.

As I cleared the spider and flew through the air, the spear I had created arched downward and then stuck into the ground like a lawn dart.

"Looks like he stuck that landing," I said in an announcer's voice as I willed all my blood to return. As I fell to the ground, I took in a deep breath, held it, and let it out in a shudder. "Fuck, that was creepy. Some Stephen King shit. At least it wasn't a clown."

I heard Joey call out in midtransformation, "John! Help!" His voice was deep and strained as his vocal cords reformed.

I rushed to where Dawson lay and gawked for only a moment before a thought hit me. Ulric was going to get away if I didn't stay on his trail. My eyes locked with Joey's, and I could tell he saw were my mind was going.

"Please," Joey begged in a whisper.

Cursing, I pulled out my phone and texted Dr. Jim.

"Emergency. Were poisoned. On our way. Less than 10 min away." I hit send and was almost immediately rewarded with a thumbs-up emoji. I was going to have to learn to use those.

Looking at Joey, I said, "Piggyback. Get on now." I scooped up Dawson's unconscious body as Joey climbed on my back. In his human skin, he was light and only 5'4". As his body pressed against mine, I could feel his junk pressing into my lower back.

"Gross. Impressive but gross," I said as I began bounding to Dr. Jim's.

"Hey, I don't like it any more than you do. And thanks," Joey cried out against the wind.

I knew we didn't have long, so I willed a bloodhelmet to stop those damn June bugs and hauled as much ass as I was comfortable with Joey still in his human skin on my back. My body protected most of his skin from being ripped to tatters by the air.

After a few minutes, we arrived at the vet's—which really seemed appropriate right about now. Joey leaped off as I landed and opened the back door, allowing me to run straight into the back room. I burst through the double metal swinging doors as my helmet absorbed into my body, and marched into the operating room where Doc was prepped and ready. I set Dawson down and Doc used a pair of clippers to shave his arm to find a vein. He inserted a silver-tipped IV and ran a saline line. Next, he grabbed some iodine and cleaned the points of entry, flushing out the remaining venom. After that, he grabbed a big syringe and stuck it in the IV line near the bag where a spot was available for needles to be used to inject solutions.

"What's that?" Joey asked, panic evident in his voice. I noticed his forearms, feet, and shins were bleeding where the air friction had done its job.

"Antivenom, blessed by the Pope," Doc Jim said.

"Holy shit, the Pope helps with this kind of stuff?" I asked, supremely impressed.

"Of course he does. Do you honestly think the most powerful religious figure alive isn't involved in the fight against evil?" Doctor James Hunt said as he moved gracefully from his tools to Dawson. Within a few moments, the wound was stitched and dressed. Dawson's breathing had begun to slow as the holy antivenom coursed through his veins.

"Is he going to make it?" Joey asked, his breathing slowing to match his brother's. I wondered if that was a twin thing.

"I can't make any promises, but I am confident he will be fine, in time."

"How long?" Joey asked aggressively.

"Hey, hey, hey," I tried cooing Joey, "he's going to be fine, man. The doc has saved my life twice now. I trust him."

I saw the corner of Doc Jim's mouth curl up into the slightest smile at the recognition of the work he prided himself in.

"What is his name?" Doc asked.

"Da-Dawson," Joey stammered, eyes still wide in alarm.

"And yours?"

"Joey."

"Well, Joey, there is some meat in the freezer in the other room. Go get some for you and your friend here."

"Brother. He's my brother," Joey said with nerves near fraying.

"You and your brother are going to need to eat, especially him. Also, a room back there has a bathroom, complete with shower, and an assortment of clothing. Wash up and pick your size and then bring the food out here."

Joey went into the other room. I could hear a door shutting and the sound of pipes protesting as hot water started running through them.

"Thank you again, Doc," I said as I transferred several thousand dollars in Bitcoin to him. I could only guess how much holy antivenom cost.

"My pleasure, as always. Your associate has already begun preparations for your blood bank," Doc Jim said casually.

"Da?"

"He used a more…exotic name," Doc Jim said dubiously.

"Yeah, go ahead and forgive him for that. It's easier to just run with it. Unless you are me, of course."

"Noted. You do keep strange company."

A whine escaped from Dawson, which I took for a good sign. It was always bad when you couldn't feel the pain. Ulric had gotten some good licks in that had stunned me, but boy, did I get lucky and get some doozies in on him. Damn, had it felt good to see the surprise and pain in his eyes as

I cut his fucking ears off. Hopefully we would be able to find that spot again and continue on his trail.

After a few minutes, Joey emerged from the back room wearing an ensemble that was too long for his arms and legs. The sweats he wore had to be tucked into his socks, while his sleeves were rolled up a few inches, resting just above his wrist.

"Did I not have your size?" Doc asked, looking Joey up and down.

"I pulled the right ones for Dawson for when he wakes up. This," he said looking down at himself, "will do. Easy to take off when I get my hands on Ulric." He turned his attention to me, gaze fierce as if I had not told the full truth. "How did he summon demons?"

My eyes shot briefly to Dawson, who breathed slowly on the table, before returning to Joey. "I've been thinking about that. I don't think he can. I have been tormented with demons since I first hooked up with the father. He has been pointing me toward the Light and giving me the dirty jobs no one else wants. I had only seen a few demons over the centuries, but now I know where to look thanks to Papa T. Together, we have sent dozens back to Hell with a swift kick in the pants."

"I bet the Devil doesn't like that very much," Doc said while checking Dawson's vitals.

"Tell him what he's won, Johnny!" I said in my prize-winning announcer's voice. "Satan is pretty pissed at us and has recently been sending demons in droves, at least in comparison to the norm. What I don't get," I said while stroking my beard with my hand in contemplation, "is why the demons came out as we had Ulric on the run? Wouldn't Satan want us to kill him and start the apocalypse?"

We all sat deep in thought. The pieces just weren't adding up, at least that I could see, which wasn't saying much. Just keeping it real with myself.

"Perhaps I might be able to offer some insight," said a deep voice with the slightest hint of a lisp. A tall, beautiful man entered gracefully into the room. He had thick blond hair that was made to purposefully look messy, but in a fashionable way. Piercing pale blue eyes looked into mine just over a warm smile. He enunciated each word clearly as he stuck his hand out in introduction. "My name is TalGoid from the Seelie Court, and I am a friend to Midworld." As I stood unsure and quickly looked him over, feeling for trickery, I noticed the points at the tops of his ears that were hidden by his hair.

I stuck my hand out and said, "Cook. John Cook."

"Oh, I am aware of you, good sir, and might I add it is indeed a pleasure," TalGoid said.

"Flattery will get you everywhere, TalGoid," I said with a smile, briefly flashing my fangs in a veiled warning.

"TalGoid," I said again, tasting the words. "That's fun to say."

"Please, call me Taylor. It is my Midworld name," Taylor said, ignoring my subtle warning. He was thin, with arms and legs slightly longer than a mortal's.

"But TalGoid is so much fun," I feigned protest.

"You can call me Susan if you like," Taylor jested.

"You mentioned information," Joey said flatly.

"That I did."

"Stop right there," I said, holding my hands up to both Joey and the elf, Taylor. "Joey, I know you are young, but there are some fundamental rules you gotta follow, man. One of which is to not make deals with the Fae."

"Once again, I reiterate, I am of the Seelie Court." Taylor's intense eyes locked onto mine, hiding ancient wisdom and patience. "Not to be rude, but it would seem we could all learn something from one another."

"Look, I do my best to stay the fuck out of everyone's business," I said. Putting on my best Pee-wee, I said, "I'm a loner, Dottie. A rebel."

"I am well aware," Taylor said, nodding. "But it would appear you are learning to make friends. Which brings me to why I am here."

"Have you tried sending me a friend request on Facebook?" I asked.

"You don't have a Facebook," Taylor answered.

"Exactly."

Unperturbed, Taylor continued, "We have a vested interest in the continued existence of Midworld."

"What! Like a summer home?" I asked in typical John fashion.

"Using your example, I ask; which would be more important to you? A home you own and live in for several months out of the year, pay taxes on, upkeep, and even loan to loved ones—or a random hotel you use for a night or two a couple times a year."

I stood in silence, awaiting his explanation.

"There are those in the courts of Fae that care not for Midworld. To them, this is all a game. The Shadow Court, especially."

"Shadow Court? That sounds foreshadowing as hell," I said while winking at the camera.

"Pardon?" Taylor asked.

"Nothing. Anyway, you were saying?"

Taylor stood in silence for a moment, assessing me. "As I was saying, we of the Seelie Court wish to see Midworld remain as it is. We fancy it."

Frustration began to build as yet another player in this chess game was asking me to trust them based on nothing but their word. Trust was a currency, and once you spread yourself too thin, it didn't take much to break you. There were only a few people I trusted completely; Depweg, Da, and Father Thomes. Next on the list were the twins, and after that at the bottom of the barrel, Locke. But right now, Taylor was asking for more trust than even Locke had. I believed Locke didn't want to go back to Hell. Why should I believe that this elf cared about Midwor...I mean, Earth. Stupid Lord of the Rings jargon. Or was that Odin's religion?

"John," Joey said, walking up to stand next to me. "You've been standing still for like a minute.

"Huh? Oh, right," I said, joining the present again. "Why should I trust you?"

"I would be disappointed if you believed the word of a stranger so easily. So I bring a token of friendship. Might I see your phone?"

"Do what now?" I asked.

"Your phone. I wish to show you something that I am confident you would want to see," Taylor said, extending his hand confidently.

I turned to Joey, who shrugged, before reaching into my pocket and placing my phone in Taylor's hand.

"Could you unlock it first?" Taylor asked, keeping his hand outstretched. I did as was asked but with a scowl.

After pressing my thumb on the button, my phone unlocked with a click. Taylor brought the phone up to his face and gracefully navigated to a built-in app. He opened it and selected one of my contacts on the Find Friends application that most phones came built-in with. I didn't know I had it. Depweg had set everything up for me, like a kid who changed the timer on his parents' VHS player.

Taylor flipped the phone around, wearing a smile, to show a map near Houston with a picture of Depweg as an icon. He was in the middle of the Sam Houston National Park near Lake Conroe.

I stared at the screen, feeling stupid that I hadn't known that I could use the phone like this. It had been with me the whole time, waiting to show me where my best friend was. I could have told Ulric to meet me, then snuck in and stolen Depweg when he was waiting for me several miles away.

Taylor handed the phone back to me, which I clutched in my hands while I stared at Depweg's icon.

"Use this knowledge to save your friend. But please, do not kill Ulric," Taylor said.

"How do you know all this?" I asked barely above a whisper, my eyes never leaving the screen.

"Information is my currency. I know what I must," Taylor said before adding, "With that, I must bid you adieu. Please enjoy a parting gift," he finished with a bow before pivoting and strolling through the front doors. On the table next to Dawson was a clear vial with blue liquid inside.

"What do you make of that?" I asked the room.

Joey responded with, "I don't like his smell."

"Trust until given a reason not to," said Doc Jim, picking up and inspecting the vial.

"I think that was clearly made for Dawson," I said, aiming the statement at Joey. It was his decision.

"I guess it wouldn't make much sense to immediately betray your new friends who are supposed to help stop the end of the world. If he is going to trick us, it won't be until after the real problem is over. Do it," Joey said, nodding at Doc.

Doc nodded and inserted a syringe into the vial, pulling out the 5 cc it held. He inserted the liquid into the IV line and we all waited. I could hear Joey breathing heavily again, as if questioning his own decision; but there was no going back now. His breathing increased until he was near hyperventilating.

"Wait!" Joey cried out, feeling the weight of losing his brother become a real probability. I honestly didn't know what I would have done in his shoes.

Dawson stirred and his eyes fluttered open. He yawned wide and licked his chops. After a moment, he noticed he was in a weird room and began to look around frantically, a growl growing in his chest. Then he saw Joey and he whined in confusion.

"Spider got you, bro," Joey said as he approached the table and stroked the bandaged wound on Dawson's leg.

Dawson sniffed the bandage, chuffed once, and then stood on the table, stretching. Then he began to revert back to man form. His fur fell out along with his oversized, insanely sharp teeth. As his snout receded back to meet his face, pearly white human teeth grew as joints popped and tendons shrunk. Within less time than it took to pee, Dawson was standing on all fours on the table. He offered a perfect view of his hairless ass.

With a gagging sound, I turned my head away and shielded my eyes.

"Don't like it? Then don't look at it, perv," Dawson said, amused.

"There's a nice shower back there, dude," Joey said to Dawson while he removed the IV, which immediately shot blood out like a water gun. Doc raced to him with a bandage and said,

"It doesn't work like that in real life. You can't just remove a needle from your veins and expect nothing to happen."

There wasn't that much blood, but it still caught my attention. I remembered how strong I was after I fed off Depweg, and my mouth salivated.

"Gross, dude," Dawson said as he walked by, noticing me staring at the blood.

"Huh? Oh. Uh..." I was at a loss for words. I had been caught with my hand in the cookie jar, or at least staring at it intently.

"Just fucking with ya, bruh," Dawson said before disappearing into the other room.

"What was in that vial?" Joey asked Doc Jim.

"I can only guess that it was some powerful faerie magic mixed with herbs from the Summer or Spring Court. I will have to try and procure some."

"It's really that good?" I asked.

"The boy was near death," he said as he gave a sidelong glance at Joey, knowing he had not revealed the whole truth of his brother's condition. "Now he is fully up and well, as if nothing had happened."

"Demons are many things," I started, "but they sure know how to kill in the most efficient ways possible." I looked toward the now empty vial. "That stuff is going to come at a cost."

"I will monitor Dawson closely," Doc Jim said.

"For what?" Joey asked, concern in his voice.

"Anything out of the ordinary, such as withdrawal symptoms, changes in personality, or any neurological dissonance, just to name a few."

"Oh," Joey said with a frown as he looked at the floor, his eyes going distant as if he were lost in a churning ocean of thought and doubt.

"Dude," I said as I approached Joey and set my hand on his shoulder, "this is just to be super safe. In most plausible scenarios, it doesn't make sense that Taylor would trick us now, just like you said. If anything, he gave us a taste of something amazing to create repeat customers. There will be a price, of that I am sure, but it won't be today." I finished by patting Joey on the back and smiling as reassuringly as I knew how.

"You're scaring me," Joey said as he slightly recoiled away from me. "It's like in *Terminator 2* when John Connor teaches Arnold to smile at that rest stop in the desert."

"You always know how to make me feel so pretty," I jested to cover my wounded pride. I was pretty, right? Tell me I'm pretty!

The water shut off and Dawson came out of the back room wearing formfitting clothes.

"Are you two ready?" I asked.

"Ready for what? We got our asses kicked," Dawson said, touching his bruised face.

I thought about that for a second. "But he doesn't know we are coming to him," I insisted, eager to save Depweg. "We will have the element of surprise."

"We had that last time too, dude," Joey replied. Dawson nodded quickly in agreement while pointing to his brother to further accentuate his argument.

"Then he won't expect the second surprise!" I said with false enthusiasm.

"But why did you freeze when you had the chance to stop him?" Dawson asked.

"It's a long story. I can't attack him without him first threatening me. He was defeated, by luck, when I tried to, um, grievously wound him."

"Bitch, you tried to *kill* him," Dawson said.

"Yeah, dude. That shit wasn't cool. You gotta, like, get hold of that shit and lock it down," Joey chided.

"Seriously, dude. I kinda like the world the way it is. Know what I mean?" Dawson added.

"I'm...sorry," I apologized, ashamed. I had let my anger almost destroy all the souls in Heaven and on this earth. Sure wish I had a hole just lying around I could crawl into right about now. I could feel the twins' eyes judging me. "But, I'm in control now. Plus, I know that I cannot actually kill him unless I think he is about to kill me. So with that knowledge, I say: let's wound him. Like, a lot," I added as I pulled the kukri from its sheath on my lower back hidden under my coat. Light glinted and reflected from the surgical lamps in sharp patterns across the room. "Once again I ask, are you two ready to go fuck some shit up?"

16

We climbed into the Uber and traveled the several miles to the outskirts of the park near the lake. As we stepped out and shut our doors, I tipped 20% because I was a benevolent preternatural entity—and because Uber drivers rate their passengers. Did you know that? They can see your rating and decide not to pick you up.

"Time," I asked in a statement to Dawson as I pointed at him without even looking in his direction.

"Um, I don't have a watch, dude."

"Where's your cellular telephone?" I asked.

"We don't carry it," Joey said. "You know; the whole naked thing."

"That's why I usually carry a fanny pack," Dawson added.

"I guess that's practical," I said, nodding my new appreciation for the terrible fashion choice that was the fanny pack.

"Practically gay," Joey said with a snicker.

"Whatever, dude. You're just jealous of my sweet pack."

"Does it stay on when you transform?" I asked, intrigued.

"Most of the time. I also fill it with beef jerky, so that makes it easy to find if I do lose it, or if I want a tasty snack."

I pulled out my phone and noted the time before closing it and glancing at the horizon. "Less than an hour to sunup. If I can't stop him, it will be up to you two to save Depweg."

"Question," Joey said with his index finger in the air, "Why don't we just wait until dawn anyway?"

"Because I won't be able to help you, and Depweg is going to be underground or in a fortified structure that will be completely sunproof. A vampire can still be dangerous during the day. Even if Ulric was, for the sake of argument, only a quarter combat effective, at his age, that would still be enough to kill both of you."

"Got it," Joey accepted.

"Plus, that would be a boring story."

"Huh?" they both asked in unison.

"Never mind. Let's move on, shall we?"

We walked to the edge of the water before Joey asked, "What now, Sherlock?"

"Hop on pop," I said. The twins looked at each other, both confused and a bit disgusted. "Look, dipshits, one hook onto my torso and the other onto my back. Trust me."

After a few awkward moments, Dawson called out, "Back!" before jumping on.

"Goddamn it," Joey said, dragging his feet until he was standing in front of me. I extended my arms and made a stupid Jim Carrey type face.

"How about a hug?"

Sighing, he walked into my chest and wrapped his arms around my neck.

"Hold on, you two. This might be really fun." As I spoke, I willed blood to snake out of my hands and down next to me. A little step poked out of both bloodstilts, and I began walking forward. As I met the water, I willed more length to the stilts, and we were raised a few feet above the waterline. We continued forward and more length was created, pressing into the bottom of the lake while keeping us safe and dry above the waterline. I moved forward one step at a time, using my hands to pull the top of the stilts backward and thus forcing the bottom portion to move forward. My feet acted as fulcrums, and within ten minutes of power walking, which did require energy to do, we were almost to the other side of the lake. As the lake's bottom distance decreased, so too did the stilts, keeping us a consistent few feet above the water.

A smell wafted up and pierced my nose. "Oh, dude! Did one of you fart?"

"Sorry," Dawson admitted with an embarrassed laugh.

"Lilith, that's bad!" I said as I tried to blow air from my mouth to force the atomic cloud away.

"Who's Lilith?" Joey asked.

Seeing as how we had nothing but time as we made our way across the lake, I explained, "As legend has it, she was Adam's first wife. She cheated on him with the UPS driver or something, and God kicked Lilith out, which left room for him to create Eve. Lilith walked the barren Earth until Samael was cast from Heaven and fell to Hell. She saw where he'd landed and went to him, and they fell in love. As the ruler of Hell, Samael was bestowed with powers in order to better do his job, which he of course exploited and used as he saw fit. Samael, now Satan (aka Mephistopheles, Baal, Diablo, the Devil, Most Unclean, and a shit ton of other colorful and clever names), wanted Lilith by his side for eternity, but she was now a mortal after being cast out of Eden, and would die someday. Using his new unholy powers, Satan figured out a way to make Lilith live forever by letting her live off the life energy of mortals, which there were now plenty of thanks to her replacement in Eden, Eve. Satan tricked Eve in order to provide an endless supply of energy for his love to live off. It was then that Lilith became the mother of all vampires."

"Sounds like a cool movie," Joey said.

"Or at least a Netflix series," I added while turning to the camera and winking.

"Can I ask a question?" Dawson spoke.

"You just did."

"Can I ask another question?"

"Do I really need to point out the irony here?" I said, rolling my eyes.

"What's with sunlight again?"

"Oh, that's actually a great question, and since it seems we have some time, I'll do my best to explain further. As younglings, you need to learn about this stuff anyway," I said, enjoying the chance to pass knowledge on to the next generation of supes. "Sunlight cleanses all magic. Well, most magic, and vampires are almost entirely made up of energy from the mortals we have fed from, which translates into magic. I prefer to think of it as our preternatural essence being better able to assimilate energy directly from the source, like a fish extracting oxygen from water. Magic is just a way of explaining something in a simple and lazy manner, at least that's my opinion. No one knows for sure, but I fully believe the universe has a checks and balances system that provides counterweights to the super scale. Think about it. Every super- and preternatural being has a glaring weakness, something that prevents their species from overwhelming the population of mortals. Us vampires, we attain sustenance directly by extracting the life energy from the blood that pumps through the mortal's veins. Each cell takes in calories from sources like glucose and glycogen, along with B vitamins, in order to create energy. Every cell in the human body produces energy by utilizing the mitochondria as the powerhouses. I pull energy from the cells in the blood that I drain and store it as my own. The older I become, the more energy I am able to store, therefore the stronger I become.

"You two are in the same process, only the delivery method differs—along with a few minor details. You eat the flesh of living things and gain energy directly from their meat. Depweg has confided that he thinks the were-virus enhances your metabolic rate, allowing you to absorb a substantially greater amount of energy from the same amount of food as when you were simply mortals. I also believe that you are stealing the stored energy in the muscles' cells, and that maybe the glycogen and glucose is being digested and transferred into your own body instead of being shit out. I have seen Depweg eat almost an entire platoon worth of meaty thighs, calves, and biceps before popping a squat and plopping out a normal log. It is like a freaking magic trick to watch him turn what had to be hundreds of pounds of flesh into one little turd. Your virus—and I'm only guessing here—makes your body utilize almost everything you put into it. It would explain your decelerated aging and immense power in were form. Heck, even in your man-suits you are stronger than any mortal alive."

"You just like to hear yourself talk, don't you?" Dawson joked.

"Yes," I said as I stepped off the stilts and onto the beach, letting the blood flow back into my palms. The twins dropped down gracefully and turned to walk with me. I checked my phone again and saw that Depweg had not moved, and that he was due north from our position.

"What did you mean about the checks and balances?" Joey asked, keeping the conversation going. I could tell they both enjoyed learning, but Joey was eating it all up eagerly.

"Well, let's see. How do you make a werewolf?"

"We have to bite someone, and if the virus doesn't kill them due to a mismatch, they become a werewolf," Joey explained.

"Right, but how hard is it for most werewolves to just take a bite of a mortal and not finish the job?"

"Really freaking hard," Dawson said. "It's why we prefer to hunt animals, because we can eat all of them without having to worry about killing someone. Humans aren't keen on other people getting eaten. They start asking questions and doing investigations. I know I can survive getting shot by a gun, depending on the round, but I don't know how many shots it would take to put me down, permanently."

"Exactly my point. As a werewolf, once your...well, I don't know what you call it when you lose control once you are hungry enough...meat rage, I guess? Once you go all meat rage, it's hard to stop, which means any mortal you want to turn into a werewolf must be someone really special to combat that preternatural instinct to feed."

"What about vampires?" Dawson asked.

"Which part are you referring to?" I inquired.

"Why aren't there more of you? How do you turn someone into a bloodsucker?"

"First, you have to drain them to the very brink of death. I can only guess that the soul has to be weak and leaving the body to allow the maker to use their blood to corrupt and change it. It's kind of like upgrading a computer; you have to open the case and remove the old components that you wish to upgrade before putting in the brand-new ones. Once you put the case back on, your computer is still technically *your* computer, but now it's better, faster, and has a tremendous singing voice." I waited for a laugh or even a chuckle at my little joke. Nothing. Moving on, philistines. "Ulric drained me to the point where my soul drifted off toward Heaven. I still remember the change and the pain I felt as my soul was forever altered and corrupted."

"That's pretty deep, bro," Joey said.

I was staring off into the distance as we walked in silence, not focusing on anything as the image of the armor-clad angel filled the theater in my mind. "Heaven is not for you, abomination," he said, his deep voice threatening to burst the speakers and rain sparks onto the seats below.

"So...if you die...?" Dawson asked without tact.

"Right now, I'd surely go to Hell. I have done a lot of bad things in my life that I have no excuse for." The image of the boy and his mother flashed through my mind, leaving behind a wince of pain in their wake.

"But haven't you done, like, some really, really good stuff too?" Joey asked.

"I do whatever Father Thomes Philseep tells me to do. He is helping me use my abilities to keep evil under control. He says God is watching and approves of my actions, but I can't be sure my black soul is being bleached or not. Or at least enough to make a difference in the end." Something struck me with all this heavy talk about souls and whatnot. "Heck, tonight might be my end. At least I'd die knowing I wouldn't have to suffer for long before Hell was destroyed. Along with Heaven and Earth, though."

We stopped at the edge of a tree line. I looked at the twins and nodded once while putting my finger over my lips. They nodded back and began to strip. We were downwind from where the phone said Depweg was, though I couldn't smell anything significant yet. Closing my eyes, I let my Predatory Self grab the wheel as I expanded my senses in all directions. The night transformed like a flat picture turned 3D. Smells became distinct instead of one mixed odor. The cacophony of the woods became separate players in an orchestra, the wind singing through the leaves and grass while insects chirped and the water lightly crashed on the shore. My eyes opened to reveal a forest of singular trees, each with their own markings, growth patterns, and story to tell. I could see the heat signature of birds resting in the trees and small mammals skittering on the forest floor.

There was a chuff next to me as I turned to see a black wolf with a white patch on its right eye looking at me. I pivoted my head to the other side and saw a white wolf with a black patch on its left eye. They were yin and yang; opposites but the same.

We started through the forest, and within a handful of minutes, we arrived at a large and modern house. It didn't belong here at all. Maybe if it had been a log cabin instead of this mansion in the middle of a national park. It was two stories tall and looked modern, with sharp angles and thick glass everywhere, allowing the denizens a view to the outside from all directions. Wait, how the hell did the owner even get clearance to build here?

"Oh, shit," I said out loud. Both wolves looked at me in question. "This is a supernatural safe house. There must be a ward on it or something to prevent mortals from finding it by accident. That means he won't be alone, Lilith damn it!" I cursed in frustration. Then I saw the black limo sticking out from the other side of the house.

"There must be a road on the other side. Stay downwind and stay vigilant. We don't know how many are in there," I warned.

Joey and Dawson split up and walked quietly through the woods, stalking the house. I could see their noses flair, searching for smells they could latch onto.

It's a good thing I practiced super stealth whenever I visited Depweg at his old house—which, by the way, I never lost at.

As if made of shadows, I drifted through the night and to the first-floor window of the out-of-place fortress. Sticking to the darkness, I peered inside only to be blasted with a floodlight from a motion sensor on the underside of the roof. I threw myself to the ground and shuffled out of sight right as a backlit figure went to the window to see what had triggered the light. Panicking, I started chittering like a freaking raccoon while flattening myself against the wall just below the window. I couldn't see the figure, but I was aware of its silhouette. After a few moments of listening to me make an ass of myself, the figure turned and I could see the shadow shrinking.

"Oh, Lilith, that was close," I said as I looked up to see a black wolf lying on the ground while covering its muzzle with its forepaws. "What?" I whispered loudly. "Do you smell something?" Worry grew in my chest.

Then I noticed his body was shaking and little whimpering sounds were escaping through its paws.

"Are...are you fucking laughing at me?" I demanded incredulously while still whispering.

That's when he lost it and rolled over onto his back, kicking his legs into the air with mirth. Tiny howls, barely being restrained, escaped and mixed with the lullaby that the wind was singing.

"Bad! Bad Joey!" I whispered while forcefully wagging my index finger at him. "Focus!"

With that, Joey rolled back over onto all fours and continued to do his job. I mean, what was I even paying him for? I wasn't actually paying him, but you get what I mean.

Looking up at the motion detector, I willed a bloodrope and had it inch its way up the window and onto the underside of the roof like a crimson caterpillar. As it approached the twin bulbs, the rope split into tendrils and latched onto the front of each bulb. I willed each to turn counterclockwise until the lights popped free. I lost my grip on one and it fell to the earth. Without thinking, I shot my other hand out and manifested a catcher's mitt the size of a dog bed. The bulb missed and smashed, loudly, on a decorative rock below. My eyes went wide as I quickly sucked my blood back in, preparing to move. The other bulb hit the same fucking rock and shattered as well. I might as well have been wearing a flashing orange light on my head while singing MMMBop through a megaphone—there was no way in hell those hired guns inside didn't know we were there now.

"Okay, okay, okay, okay," I said calmly. Just kidding. I was shitting my pants. My mind was racing, and then an idea solidified in an instant. A plan, if you will.

Getting up, I scooped up the stupid decorative rock and jogged between the tree line and the house. I turned and howled into the night like a crazed lunatic, aimed at the closest window, and threw the rock with supreme power behind it. It completely missed the window and instead went through the roof and into the attic.

"Hope no one saw that," I said to myself as I prepared for the onslaught that was sure to come.

Ask and ye shall receive. A small flood of different supes poured out of the hideout. The foremost was a dark-skinned face with a glinting short sword in his hand. It was bejeweled and looked impossibly sharp, which I knew it had to be. We locked eyes and the Fae rushed toward me. His skin was the color of a midnight sky under a pale moon. It was black and blue and seemed to change like a chameleon as he approached. I willed my own sword into my hand and took a defensive stance.

Coming in hot behind the Fae were two trolls without their glamours on. They were long and lanky with tusks that shot out of their bottom jaws. They had a mohawk of orange and red hair, and a piercing through their nose that reminded me of a bull's. Each carried a spear that was ready to be hefted toward me.

Standing several feet taller and wider behind the trolls was an ogre, also without his disguise. For the briefest of moments I regretted not watching him squeeze out of the back door like a Great Dane through a dog door made for a Chihuahua. The ogre had brass knuckles that were more accurately described as iron knuckles. Shit, if he landed even one hit with those, wherever I was hit would probably explode like a water balloon.

But, first things first; I pulled my sword back as I stepped forward with my left leg, leaving my right behind me with my sword ready to go. As the Fae started to lunge, I willed a blooddagger attached to a rope from my left hand and threw it preternaturally fast toward the Fae's face. He dodged at the last moment, being incredibly fast as well, but the dagger found a different home in one of the trolls behind him. It pierced his right pec and lodged deep as I began siphoning blood. Now that I knew I could feed off supernatural beings, I was curious to taste from each one like at a Chinese buffet—hopefully without the accompanying horror show of a bowel movement.

As the Fae entered melee range, I willed jagged fishhooks down the rope and whipped it to the right, catching him in his side and latching on. He inhaled to scream from the pain as the hooks burrowed their way into his chest cavity and began draining his life force. While he froze in both fear and pain, I stepped forward and stabbed the sword into his blood-soaked liver. The troll didn't taste good to me—kind of like rubbing alcohol—but the Fae was like a fine wine that cost as much as a car per bottle. I dropped the troll, both because he was dead now and because he tasted like shit, leaving only the Fae to feed on. Mmmm, it was sooooo good.

Two brown werewolves burst out of the doorway and onto the scene. They were both covered in scars from numerous battles—probably for the amusement of asshole supes. Their scars being evident like that meant one of two things: either they used silver or iron in their battles, which prevented the wounds from healing completely, or they fought often enough to not allow time to fully heal. I felt pity for them for the briefest of moments before I saw them lock onto me and charge.

Out of the night burst Joey and Dawson, slamming into the wolves and starting an epic were battle. Joey bit the gnarled ear off one of the wolves while Dawson slashed his front claws down the ribs of the other. The brown wolves howled in fury and pain as they turned their attention on their attackers. Though the twins had the advantage of surprise, the brown werewolves clearly had more than their fair share of experience when it came to battles to the death.

The wolf with the missing ear leaped up onto his back paws and brought one of his front claws down on Joey's nose. Blood squirted from the torn flesh as Joey yelped in pain.

Dawson heard this in the midst of his own back and forth and looked at his brother for the briefest of moments. This gave his experienced attacker all the time he needed as he lunged forward and snapped his jaws around one of Dawson's front legs, which were extended just a little too far. After locking onto his paw, the wolf jumped up and over the white wolf, pulling his leg with him and twisting his body until his remaining legs were yanked off the ground and pointed into the night sky. They turned in midair and the wolf landed on top of Dawson, immediately beginning to dig into his stomach like he was digging for a long-lost bone buried in the yard. White fur stained red as flesh was rent.

I decided I needed to intervene. A spear whistled through the air and found a new home in my guts just below my chest plate. I grunted with the impact and clenched my jaw, but didn't drop my focus from my meal—I knew I would need every last drop of Fae energy to aid in my fight. I finished draining the Fae, whose eyes had rolled up into his head, and let him drop to the ground. Then I willed my weapons back into me as I grabbed the spear and tugged it out easily. The wound closed immediately as I looked up at the stunned troll who had thrown the weapon and yelled, "OW!" before flipping the spear around in a show of prowess and throwing it right back at its owner, but much faster and harder. It went through his neck and into the sternum of the ogre who was charging behind him. The troll went down, clutching his throat as gross blood gushed out and escaped through skinny fingers. The ogre took no notice of his injury and plowed through the troll, his skull crushing underfoot as he knocked him over in his pursuit of yours truly.

Forcing my eyes to shift off the immediate danger charging right at me, I noticed Joey was on his back now as his one-eared attacker went for the kill.

I took the risk of losing a tad bit of energy and flung out a sheet of blood the size of printer paper at the eyes of the ogre, who stopped his charge as he became blinded. With my foe temporarily distracted, I jumped into the air and over to the wolves who had my friends pinned helplessly to the ground. Two katanas formed in my hands as I was descending and sliced cleanly through the neck of the first wolf right as its jaws began to tighten around Joey's neck. It's one-ear head toppled on top of Joey as blood erupted from both stumps. I wanted to imbibe that blood so badly, but had to focus on saving Dawson, who was seconds away from having his insides be on his outside.

I somersaulted into the air, removing the remaining werewolf's head and effectively stopping the deadly onslaught. The defeated twins rolled their lifeless attackers off them and strained to get up. I could see Dawson's intestines were barely contained by strips of muscle. All his fur and skin had been ripped off, some of which remained under the claws of his skilled opponent.

Both twins whined in defeat as they assessed their grievous wounds. Joey had been struck multiple times in the head, chest, and back—blood shone like rubies under the moonlight in his black fur.

Kneeling down between the twin's wolves, I placed one hand on Joey's face and the other underneath Dawson's stomach. I sent blood out and over their wounds, willing their flesh to heal. I was surprised at how much energy it took to stitch Dawson up.

An earth-rumbling roar almost knocked me on the ground as I turned to see the red-eyed ogre lock eyes with me. He had gotten most of my blood off and had started charging.

I healed the twins as much as I could in the time I had, using more energy than anticipated. Dawson's stomach was closed, but the skin I had managed to grow back looked like a burn ward. Joey's multiple wounds had stopped their steady flow of crimson, but still oozed a little. I stood up and faced my attacker while the wolves slunk off, seeming to avoid an impossible matchup. Probably for the best, as my friends were a liability in their weakened state.

I wasn't frightened of the ogre as much as I was wary of his ability to one-shot anything it punched—especially with those iron knuckles he wielded. He swung wide and I dodged low, slicing open his thigh with a scythe I'd manifested while our dance commenced. He roared in blind rage as he backhanded me and send me to sail several feet into the air. I wasn't sure how far because I was tumbling in the air like a rag doll in a clothes dryer. I landed with a thud and a plume of dirt. I raised my head in time to see a comically sized foot rocket toward my face. Seriously, the appendage reminded me of the new *Godzilla* with his thick thighs, ankles, and hilariously fat feet.

Luckily, I had two weres who flanked him from either side, Dawson going for the hamstring of the leg flying at me while Joey leaped to grab the back of the hulking beast's neck. The ogre paid them no mind, fully intent on his target, until a loud twang shot through the night's air. His attack, though diminished now, made contact, and I was thrown backward while stars swam in my vision. At the height of his attack, the ogre cried out in furious pain as he fell to one knee, unable to bend his leg back anymore. His bellow shook the teeth in my head even from where I landed.

The hired gun turned to swing at Dawson while Joey held on like an impromptu ponytail, swinging with the monster's movement. The ogre had less momentum after having his hamstring completely severed, but could still kill the twins with one hit. Dawson nimbly jumped out of the way and then rushed toward his now exposed target as the ogre swung too hard and couldn't easily stop his own fists.

Dawson slammed into the chest of the Fae muscleman and latched onto his throat. Both Dawson and Joey were growling as they squeezed with all they had. Joey couldn't quite break the vertebrae of the ogre, but Dawson had nothing but soft neck. It still took all his might to crush the larynx of his prey. The ogre bellowed again and was cut off when Dawson made headway and gnawed through its flesh. Blood erupted and coated the white of Dawson's face. Joey dropped what he was doing and went for the face, tearing chunks of flesh and popping eyeballs. The ogre's scream was nothing but a whisper as air was unable to escape the clutches of Dawson's jaws. Then the red-coated wolf shook his head from side to side until the sound of tearing flesh silenced even the insects in the immediate vicinity. There was one last horrifically long and wet ripping sound as Dawson detached all the meat he had clutched in his viselike jaws before swallowing his prize. The ogre's hands and feet went still as they dropped to the ground, the only sound left from the big faerie creature being the blood that gurgled out of what remained of his throat. I took note that I could see the white of his spine before blood dyed it crimson.

The black and now fully red wolves started eating the flesh of the ogre, chomping on their hard-earned kill greedily. They had a long way to go until their wounds were completely healed. Meat from a giant faerie beast would certainly help.

The sound of an engine starting and tires slipping on gravel grabbed my attention as I looked up to see the limo take off from the driveway. I didn't care so much about Ulric escaping if it meant I could save my best friend; but something didn't feel right. I pulled out my phone and noticed Depweg's icon was moving in relation to the car.

"I got this," I cried out to the twins. "You two won't be able to catch it. Clear the house of the remaining bad guys so Ulric won't have anyone to run back too." They nodded their heads and began padding to the house, mouths still chewing fresh ogre flesh.

I turned to face the gravel road, crouched down, and then leaped with all my might. I flew through the air in the direction of the vehicle. It was hard to remain in control in my panic and rage at knowing Ulric was in there with Depweg, and I jumped past the limo and deeper into the forest as it took a sharp turn—tires kicking up dirt and rocks as it fled. I shot my legs out and landed on a tree, squatting to absorb the impact before shooting off again toward my best friend. The tree splintered behind me and fell, crashing through its brothers.

As I got closer to the limo, I shot out a bloodtendril and latched onto the bumper. Once secured, I began to pull myself in until I was on top of the trunk. I was about to slam through the back window when a beautiful Fae woman with the same color scheme as the first Fae male I killed burst through the open sunroof and sprayed me with a water gun. I was stunned when I saw her pull the trigger of the bright yellow gun with an orange tip and green water reservoir; then I was screaming. Holy water ate at my flesh, melting my eyeballs and dissolving my skin. I fell off backward, furiously rubbing at my eyes, when my subconscious pointed out that I was about to lose the car. Without even thinking, I shot another tendril that hit somewhere on the back of the limo, and I willed myself to it, staying low and out of sight as I was dragged over the gravel road. I covered my mouth with my melting free hand to muffle my screams of agony. As my cheeks melted away and my lips curled back, I took off my gray beanie and shoved it into my mouth to keep from being heard. Then it hit me. I used the beanie to soak up as much of the water as I could before shoving it into a free pocket on my trench coat. My poor trench coat that was being dragged to tatters.

With the water soaked up and any remainder being air-dried from the speed of the fleeing limo, I was able to use the Fae blood I had consumed to slowly heal. It took its sweet time as my cheeks filled and lips plumped. My eyes were the last to fill like little balloons. I didn't know how long I had been healing as I was dragged, but I became aware that the road was no longer gravel and had become asphalt. Once I knew I was okay, I became really pissed.

"THAT. IS. IT!" I bellowed from below the limousine as I extended my bloodtendril out, letting it form two anchors that led to both my hands. Once my ropes were securely fastened, I set my feet down until my boots were ground away and my bare flesh dug into the asphalt. I set my footing and pulled the limo with both hands until its weight distribution was moved to its front from the quick deceleration of my braking. Then I raised my hands high and slammed them down, sending a huge ripple down the ropes and flipping the limo ass over nose through the air to land on its roof.

I leaped through the air and landed next to the vehicle before it came to a full stop and ripped the back door open. Using preternatural speed, I looked in and grabbed the first being I saw, which happened to be the holy water bitch who had dropped her weapon and was severely dazed. I ripped her out with enough force to snap her neck as she went flying through the night like a train off its tracks.

Repeating the process, I looked in and saw...nothing. The back portion was empty. I strode to the front and pulled the driver out, who was nothing more than a mortal.

"WHERE ARE THEY?" I screamed into his face with enough force to cause ripples to dance on his skin like a pebble being thrown into a still pond. The man didn't answer, only sobbed in terror. Furious now, I put my palm on his forehead and forced my essence into his body. I broke through walls of sanity and thought, like a bulldozer in a library, until I found what I was looking for. Ulric back at the house, telling the Fae girl something and handing her a water gun, and a fucking cell phone that I instantly recognized.

"HOW DID HE KNOW TO USE THE PHONE?" I screamed through clenched teeth, unable to control my rage but trying not to kill him yet. I poured more of myself in, searching desperately.

I'm standing by the limo having a smoke, wondering why these weird fuckers are paying so much to have their own limo driver on call this late. I look up and see the most beautiful woman I have ever seen. She is talking to Ulric through the glass, and appears to be pleading. Ulric is wearing a black beanie over his head with red streaks down his neck under his ears. That's odd. I take a puff of my cigarette as I watch the blonde wavy-haired woman walk out of view for a moment and then return, holding a cell phone. She puts it in Ulric's hand—what kind of name is Ulric anyway—and points at me through the window. I can see she is desperate to make this guy do what she says. This gorgeous woman takes the phone from his hand and pushes some buttons and then points. Ulric takes note of this and walks out of view. I see one of the motion-activated lights in the yard turn on, and I look in that direction to see a giant black thing disappear into the trees. I gulp and rub my eyes with my free hand, unbelieving. There is a crash as glass is shattered. Then another. After a few moments of silence, I shrug it off and pull my suit jacket a little closer—this place is giving me the creeps. The sound of an impact and shattering wood makes me jump nearly out of my shoes. I have no idea what the fuck is going on, and my cigarette burns my fingers. I yelp and let it drop to the ground. I hear the back door being thrown open as it clatters off the wall, followed by several fast-paced footsteps. I carefully walk toward the back of the house, sucking on my burnt fingers, and nearly shit my pants. There's a scene from a horror movie mixed with creatures from that Lord of the Rings trilogy right in front of me. The biggest, scariest-looking dogs I've ever seen are attacking something the size of a brick wall! That's when the chick wearing the weird black-and-blue makeup bursts through the front door and strides up to me, whispering, "We need to go, now." I agree with the plan to get the hell out of here and climb into the driver's side. She tells me to drive like my life depends on it, and I slam on the gas after starting the ignition.

I pull out of the mortal's mind, sickened.

"Lily," I drawled out in complete disbelief. Lily tipped Ulric off. Lily told Ulric how to trick me into following the limo.

The mortal driver fell to his knees, drool spilling from his parted lips. Woozy, he looked up at me with glassy eyes and moaned incoherently. Blood started to seep from his nose and ears as he began to sob uncontrollably. He attempted to form syllables, but couldn't quite connect the dots. His eyes shifted from focused to unfocused and then back again as he wailed one long note. He grabbed either side of his head and pressed in, hard. I fucked up his mind in my rage. I burst into the china shop that was his brain and broke things you couldn't break. This man was innocent, just a hired driver. My stomach became queasy with the realization that I would probably have to kill him right here and now or leave him to a life of endless suffering. He would never know who he was again. He would never recognize his family. And if I had to guess, would always be in indescribable agony. *His family*. My eyes shot down to the gold band on his left hand. Oh no...what had I done.

I could give him my blood. That would heal him; but this close to death, with his soul barely tethered to his body, he would turn. That meant I would damn his soul for eternity. Plus, there was no way he would be able to maintain a normal life with his family after this. No matter if I turned him or ended his suffering now, I would throw black ink on my soul. The murder of innocents was at the top of the list of things not to do. I was about to negate countless good deeds in one fell swoop.

"I'm...sorry," I whispered as I forced myself to look at what I had done in my rage. I formed an ice pick in my hand while kneeling down next to this innocent man whose only wrongdoing had been trying to provide for his family. I placed the pick behind his ear and said, "Tell God I made it quick, would you?" before jamming it into what was left of his brain, killing him instantly. He stopped moving, stopped crying, and fell like a rag doll to the asphalt as I removed the pick—not daring to drain any of his blood. I stood then, forcing myself to take in every moment of this dead man. I could feel the weight of the pain his wife would endure once she was told he was dead. It was sickening to be the only keeper of this knowledge, knowing that an unstoppable fuse had been lit and a bomb was going to go off once she received the knock on her door. Somber faces of uniformed civil servants would tell her everything without having to utter a word.

I felt sick. Not only because of my rage-filled murder, but because I had been betrayed by Lily. Lily, whom I think I was starting to fall in love with, had warned Ulric and even shown him how to trick me into leaving.

"JOEY! DAWSON!" I cried out in panic as I spun around, trying to figure out where I was. "No, no, no, no, no, no, no, no, no!" I repeated in a terrified mantra.

My phone chimed, and without even having to look, I knew what it was going to say. I pulled it from my pocket and held it up, my eyes staring at a spot in the distance and refusing to look at the screen because it would solidify what I already knew.

Gritting my teeth and pulling my lips back in a snarl, I forced my eyes to look at the screen. What it said made me want to faint as my world began to teeter further.

"I have them," said the text from Ulric whose name was flanked on either side by purple eggplants. It had been funny when I'd put them in. Now I wanted to crush my phone between my fingers.

Looking up from the screen, I could see the dawning sun announcing that it was going to arrive soon.

My fingers flew on the keyboard as I responded, "Dawn soon. Finish this tomorrow night. Them for me."

"That is all I wanted, child. Tomorrow night." To add insult to injury, the son of a bitch added a winky-face emoji. Lilith, I hated emojis and I think he knew that.

Feeling the impending dawn, I checked my Map app to figure out a direct path home. That's when I saw the icon that was Depweg's face staring at me. I glanced up from my screen and noticed the icon was directly where the upside-down limo was. I walked over to it, careful not to step on the corpse of the driver, and crawled into the back of the crushed car. There, on the ceiling of the vehicle, was Depweg's black phone. I grabbed it before shimmying backward onto the asphalt. I turned the phone around in my hands as I stood, admiring the choice of case as the screen wasn't even cracked in the least.

"Neat," I sighed absently as I pocketed Depweg's phone before looking back at my own to orient myself. After spinning in place so the phone registered due north, I set course for home southeast of my current location. I put the phone in the other pocket of my road-trashed trench and leaped into the night with no time to waste. I willed a bloodhelmet as I rocketed through the night at Mach speeds.

As I began to run, sun tendrils crested the horizon and waved a warm hello. I was already running at ludicrous speed and was betting I could make it to my lair in time. About halfway home, the first light exploded over the flat landscape, tickling the bottom of the clouds. It was blinding to my preter–eyes, and I was aware that I had effectively become a battering ram. I was traveling at speeds fast enough to cause some serious damage if I were to strike anything, and now I was having to squint to barely be able to see directly in front of me.

It was time to utilize a risk/reward algorithm by taking the assumed amount of time left and the distance needed to trail. A glass building came out of nowhere, forcing me to crash through its tinted panes on ground level and tumble into a hotel lobby where two employees were checking in what had to be a conference full of guests. Hundreds of eyes shot my way, startled, as I attempted to slow my roll—because I was actually rolling from my abruptly halted momentum. I saw that I was about to crash through the first line of guests, so I cartwheeled between two people that gave me some room as they jumped out of the way. As I passed, I noticed one person I'd wheeled past had a slice of pizza, so I said the only logical thing, "Smells good." Then I was through the first line and was forced to jump over the second one as I called out, "Dinner's ready!"

Even though I knew I had made an epic Ferris Bueller joke, I feared what both lines of people heard as I passed by at only semiludicrous speed was, "aaaaaaaAAAAAAHHHHHhhhhhhh!" Guess we'd never know. Oh, look, a stone wall to cushion my body to a soft halt.

"OOOF!" my body said as air was expelled out of my lungs and a deafening crack shot through my head. As my brain reset, I took note that the ground was rushing up to hug me and tell me everything would be alright.

If I'd had any air left in my lungs, it too would have made an exodus to the outside world. Stars swam in my vision as a pinprick of light formed in the center of my eyes and expanded to build a hotel lobby in an outward, circular motion.

As my brain booted up, I thought about the crunching sound and said in an airless whisper, “Please be the wall.” As I looked up, I noticed the quality stone of the lobby wall had but the slightest crack running down its center. That meant...

My hands slowly moved under my armor and up my chest, which felt as if I were smuggling in a bundle of sticks for the campfire. It was time to leave, so I needed to heal quickly before the mortals had the bright idea to pull out their smartphones and start filming me. Having one camera record a preternatural creature in action was one thing, as it could be easily explained away as having been edited. Get enough cameras from different angles recording the same event, and you got yourself some grade-A problems, Jack!

I painfully pulled what was left of my trench coat over my chest as I began healing, the pops ringing out loudly like a potato chip–eating SOB in the middle of a freaking movie. I mean, what theater exec thought *chips* were a good idea in a movie? Oh, and to you lovely fans across the pond, crisps.

Moaning, I rolled to my side, leaving my bloodhelmet in place, before pushing myself up. I glanced at the audience—who was still standing in line, mind you, unwilling to give up their spot—and saw only a few phones pointed my way. Acting quickly, I stood up, bowed deeply, which didn’t hurt at all while my bones were being set, and then righted myself. I pulled out my beanie from my pocket and walked toward the lines, holding the hat out like a bowl. Once people saw I was asking for tips for my planned stunt, all heads shot forward and cell phones disappeared in the blink of an eye. I was actually offended.

“Are you not entertained?” I called out in my best Russell Crowe as I pocketed my beanie and made my way casually to the broken pane of glass.

“Sir! Sir, stop!” a front desk clerk with a little plastic name tag that probably said “Fun Police” called out.

“¿Qué?” I called back as I crossed the threshold, pretending to not understand. Then I pivoted and started running at believable speeds. I squinted at the sky and noticed the sun was caressing the sides of the building, moving down the small of the back to its intended goal; my sweet ass.

Across the street was a Homewood Suites by Hilton, and seeing as how I was a Diamond member due to my horrible time management, I decided it was best to relax comfortably rather than try and tempt fate and run home. I could see it now; all humans were dead, and the few that were left after the Holy War got up from the lunchroom table when I sat down because I'd let the apocalypse start by whistling Dixie and walking home. No, thank you. I didn't need that kind of social anxiety.

I made my way to the front desk, which was blessedly free of a line, and asked for a room whose window faced north or south. This would limit direct sunlight during the entirety of the day. Little trick I'd learned after my last foray into a hotel at the last minute. After a few clicks, the clerk gave me my plastic card and I retreated to my rent-a-lair.

Out of pure instinct, I raced to the windows and closed the curtains, ensuring no light would shine through. At least not enough to do any damage.

Feeling the effects of dawn starting to take hold, I knew I was only a few minutes away from passing out. I quickly made my way to the bathroom, where I stripped off my clothes and hopped in the shower, washing off all the grime and grit of the night before the water even had a chance to fully turn warm. I used an entire bottle of shampoo and slathered it on my head, beard, and the rest of me because I didn't have time to use soap. Moreover, I'd left the little bastard sitting by the damn sink in its little white box. At least I'd grabbed the shampoo in my rush.

I shut off the water and grabbed a towel, feeling my eyelids fill with lead as I moved. I stepped over my clothes, noticing my poor trench, and crawled into bed wearing only my birthday suit and sense of modesty. As soon as my head hit the pillow, I succumbed to the will of the dawn and drifted off, hoping in the back of my head that I had placed a "Shh, sleeping" sign to signal the housekeepers to leave me alone.

17

Around midday, the answer came in the form of a gasping housekeeper. I barely opened one eye and looked over my shoulder to see a Hispanic woman in her midfifties doing the catholic cross over her chest as she looked at my naked body. I was on my stomach, and my legs were spread eagle, providing a full view of my fruit basket.

Letting my heavy head hit the pillow, I loudly slurred out, "No, thank you." As I heard the door shut in a hurry, I became aware that I must have drooled on my pillow because it was wet and cold now. Sluggishly, I snaked my hand up and turned it over, revealing a fresh canvas to paint with my spittle. Sleep beckoned, and I let it take me.

A handful of hours later, I began to stir as the sun began to lose its daily struggle with the night and retreated.

I lifted my head and was surprised when the pillow cover came with me, only to release its hold on me when the weight of the pillow kept it from fleeing to a new life on my drool-covered face.

"Both sides, huh," I asked myself. "Hope you're proud."

I got up and stretched, not for any physical reason that stretching provides, but as a routine that signifies the beginning of the night. Plus, it was a force of habit I'd picked up as a mortal that I didn't see a particular reason to change. Perhaps it was because I fancied myself with the heart of a human in the body of a romance novel model.

I walked to the bathroom where my clothes still lay covered in filth from the night before. Picking up my boxer briefs first, I gave them a quick smell test and determined they were basically perfect. One of the perks of not being a human was that I didn't sweat—though I could cry, and my eyes were lubricated along with my mouth. One of these days I would have to pontificate on the odd features vampires had.

I stepped into the black pair of Hanes and slid them into place, followed by my dirt-covered jeans and torn shirt. Both my boots and socks had been ground off. Glancing at the floor, I said a silent prayer to myself as I picked up my poor trench coat. It was all but decimated. The entire back portion of leather that sandwiched the internal components had been ripped away, leaving behind only the innermost leather that attached to the lining of the coat. The trench was now several inches shorter and frayed. It reminded me of a flamboyant cowboy's gloves with the little strips of leather that hung from wrist to elbow.

"My poor trench," I said in reverence as I crouched to lovingly pick up my most loyal piece of attire in the history of ever. Not many people walking this planet could say they had any article of clothing that had survived countless battles over the span of seven decades. Especially not one they had taken from a freaking Nazi officer who got what he deserved. I was proud of that coat, damn it. It was a constant reminder that there were bad guys that preyed on the innocent and needed...correcting.

For some reason, my brain turned on itself and I said out loud, "Then it makes perfect sense that you would wear it too; bad guy." Fuck, that hurt. Self-burn.

Instead of putting my trench on, I pulled the beanie out of the pocket and left the room as I placed my headgear where it belonged. I left the amalgamation of different leathers draped over my arm as I made my way out. My feet slapped against the stone floors as I did.

As the sliding doors opened, I was reminded of my task for tonight like a gentle sledgehammer to the nuts. I needed to make my way back to the lair and come up with a plan on the fly. Lilith damn it—why didn't I text Da last night what was going on?

I pulled out my phone and first called Da. After explaining the situation as I ran toward Father Thomes' church, Da said he would work with Locke on something before I got home. We had a few hours before Ulric became suspicious.

I landed in the street in front of the church and made my way to the door. It opened as I arrived, and Father T said with a warm, welcoming smile, "I got worried when you didn't call again. How is Locke? Has he revealed anything pertinent about his master?" I had been keeping the father informed on the situation so he could help me keep a level head. He was the one who suggested I forgive the man who had murdered my family. It hadn't been easy, but I trusted the father completely to guide my soul to redemption.

"Not here for that," I said as I walked past him. "Got bigger fish to fry right now."

I caught him up on the situation, which he pondered intently.

"This is very serious, John. You cannot let him kill you just as you cannot kill him."

"Oh, I'm not too worried about that last part. Lily commanded me not to kill anyone unless I feel like they are about to kill me first. Traitorous bitch." I spit the words out, disgusted with my heart for having developed a strong fondness for her.

"If you don't mind my saying, it sounds like she is trying to save you."

"FROM WHAT?" I bellowed out, losing control of my rage momentarily.

At the complete opposite end of the spectrum, Father Thomes softly and soothingly said, "From yourself."

His words struck me in the forehead, and I rocked back ever so slightly as they bored into my brain.

"Even if you were right," I began after digesting what he had said for a full minute, "there were other ways to stop me." I began stuttering and waving my hands in front of me as if I were grasping for the right words to convey what I felt, "She-she could have, I don't know, freaking *commanded* me to stay away. I would lose my mind if I disobeyed her, and she knows it! Why go through all that bullshit trouble?"

"Well," Father T thought for a moment, lighting a pipe he pulled out from his breast pocket, allowing the action to provide enough time to formulate his thought, "What if she cares as much about you as you care about her?"

"Wha...what? I don't..."

"Lying is a sin, my child. Even to one's own self. It is clear as night on your face that her actions have hurt more than just your pride." I appreciated his vampire metaphor.

I thought about it as my throat got tighter. I was in love with Lily, and she had prevented me from saving my best friend and stopping my maker.

Father Philseep continued, "If she were to directly command you, it would remove your free will and effectively make you her slave. As you have explained it to me, she didn't used her full power against you until recently, when she asked you to not go looking for a fight. She still gave you free will and an intentional loophole about self-preservation. And what did you do, child? You immediately used that loophole she gifted you with to slay an angel."

His eyes glowed orange from the embers as he took a heavy puff of his pipe.

"I cannot say with any certainty that I would have been as, let's say, lenient, as she was. And because of that very act of kindness, you have found a whole new avenue for trouble."

"I don't know what to do," I said as I put my face in my hands. This was all too much for my supermodel brain to handle.

"I am confident that you will find a solution. But know this; if you kill Ulric, you are killing every human being on this planet. You are also damning every soul that has ever existed throughout all of history to potential nonexistence. Control your emotions, John." He looked at me a moment longer, ensuring what he had said sunk in. I raised my face to look at him and he nodded, seemingly satisfied that the impact of his words had found a home in my mind.

Father Thomes slowly stood from the pew and began limping to his chambers. It seemed worse than before.

"Father Thomes," I called out. He stopped and turned his head slightly, looking at me over his shoulder. "Are you okay?" I asked, fearing the answer.

"Don't worry about me, my child. You have enough on your plate as it is. Now, go save your friend." He turned and began limping away again, though this time it seemed he was focusing more on not showing how severe it had become over the years. “Oh, one more thing,” he said as he turned fully to face me. “Bring Ulric here and I will keep him safe.” As he finished, he stood looking at me without having to say another word.

“Hopefully you’ve made some improvements. I was able to get out pretty easily,” I boasted.

“You lost a leg getting out and lost the other against the church’s gargoyles,” he smiled. “But yes, I have made some substantial improvements. I never thought I would need to use the room before. It was built, how do the kids say it, half-assed?”

“So you’ve rebuilt it whole-assed this time?” I said, smiling.

“Oh yes,” he confirmed as he turned and continued his way to his chambers. “I borrowed some from you, as you seem to have plenty to share.” I could hear him stifling a chuckle as he walked. I sat, open-mouthed. That was twice I had been called fat lately!

I used my best go-to weapon for times such as these. “Your mom!” I called back. There was no answer as I stood and made my way outside. The concrete was surprisingly cool under my bare feet. I took in a deep, contemplative breath, and started walking home. My brain raced with the realization and admission of my love for Lily. Lily, who had betrayed me and potentially doomed my were friends. Lily, who had manipulated me from the beginning. Lily. My Lily. A lone tear of frustration escaped my eye and ran down my face. I didn’t bother wiping it away.

18

I made my way home and noticed it was empty. Da's room was closed, and I could see light dancing off the laminate floors under his door. The TV was on in there, and he was watching something, loudly.

Odd, but still in the realm of normal, I suppose. I took a few steps across the living room in the direction of his room, draping my poor coat over a barstool, when I saw something out of the corner of my eye. Willing a sword into my hand, I turned toward the couch in a defensive stance and saw her. Lily was sitting on my couch, waiting for me. She was wearing modest clothing and had her hair and makeup fully done in a businesslike fashion.

"You!" I cried through teeth that threatened to shatter. My jaw flexed and I began breathing heavily out of reflex and rage. "How *dare* you come here?"

"John, I know. Please listen to me," Lily stood, pleading.

"No! I don't have to listen to shit from a traitor. Ulric now has three of my friends because of you."

"I didn't know you had the twins with you!" Lily cried out, frantic tears in her eyes. She was aware that my rage was legendary and how what she had done looked in my eyes. There was no way I was going to listen to what she had to say.

"I should kill you, right here and now. Stab you through your liver and drain you dry for what you did." I began walking forward, not in control of my actions. I realized I had let the wheel go and turned my back as PS took control—hungry for revenge. I was only a spectator in my own body, and I was scared. I loved her, and what the father'd said made sense, but my pride was overwhelming, and I wanted to hurt her for hurting me.

"John, stop right there," Lily commanded, her own anger rising. She thought she had done the right thing and was only trying to explain her situation.

My body stopped...and then a foot stepped out and down. Then the other. I raised my sword arm, straining to fight against her command. Inside my head, I collapsed to the ground, wordlessly crying in immense pain. PS was driving while I was writhing on the ground clutching my skull, which threatened to cave in on itself. I could feel my mind tearing at the seams.

Lily's eyes widened at how easily my body kept moving forward, intent to kill her. PS looked over at me and shook his head, disgusted, before turning back to the windshield that was our eyes. I was screaming in anguish and rolling on the ground. Each step intensified the pain by a multitude that I could never have fathomed before now. My cries became high-pitched and panicked as I felt my mind begin to fray at the edges, unwinding to leave the precious core vulnerable.

STOP! SHE'LL KILL US! I cried out to my Predatory Self, who took no heed. Oh, shit, if I died, would he take full and complete control over my body? He would have no restraints or compunctions about killing who he wanted, when he wanted. He would be a feral beast with a mind that only knew hunting prey in a body filled with aged power.

LILY! I CAN'T STOP HIM! I cried out in my head. Just when I thought my mind was about to snap, PS screeched and grabbed his own head as he tumbled backward to the ground. The pain in my own head subsided as I threw up in my own mind, moaning loudly. The world that was boiling in rage around me began to settle, and I focused on healing my torn mind as I stood up on shaky legs. After I could see straight, I strode over to where PS was writhing and kicked him in the ribs as hard as I could. With a yelp and an audible crack, he sailed through the room of my mind and crashed into the wall, where he collapsed to the ground. Without breaking stride, I stomped over to where he was holding his head with one hand and holding the other out to stop me. I bent, grabbed the extended hand, and then threw him in an arc to the ground just behind me. There were more cracks as metaphorical bones broke. Bones that felt every bit real to PS.

You will do as I say or I will end you. Am I understood? I said as I grabbed him by the neck and threw him against the wall at the other end of the room. Predators only understood stronger predators.

You almost got me killed, you fool. What do you think would have happened if I'd lost my mind and died? You think you'd get control over this body full time? How long do you really think you would last with your blatant lack of self-control, dickhead? Yes, you can fight, but you can't think worth shit. At least I can think more than five minutes in front of me. Now, are we on the same fucking page now or do I need to continue?

PS shook his head desperately in submission. Sometimes I needed a reminder that he was akin to a wild horse that had been tamed; yes, you could trust it, but you still never walked behind it and slapped it on its ass.

I extended my hand and PS looked at it warily, his head no longer splitting in two now that my body, *our* body, had stopped advancing toward Lily. PS had earned the right to co-drive this sexy sack of flesh I called John. He had saved our lives numerous times over the centuries, and I was indebted to him for putting up with my stupid mistakes.

My hand never wavered as I gave my Predatory Self all the time he needed to decide. *Come on, brother. I can't do this without you.* With that said, he nodded once and grasped my hand, allowing me to pull him up. As we stood eye to eye, I kept our grip as I placed my other hand on his shoulder. I turned to face the viewport and put one hand on the wheel. PS mirrored my actions, and I was brought back to Lily.

"John? Is it still you?" Lily asked, taking a step back.

"Who?" I asked in a creepy voice.

"Shit," Lily said as she began moving her hands in a pattern in front of her, trailing a path of sparkling energy.

"Juuuuuust kidding!" I said. "But seriously though, fuck you. I don't care about your reasoning. Next time, trust me."

"Trust you?" she exclaimed as the light faded from her hands. I wondered what she was about to do to me. "You have proven yourself untrustworthy, John," Lily scolded.

"Name ten times," I said. Lily began ticking off her fingers without even a second's pause.

"Okay, okay! I get it! But Joey and Dawson are in trouble now, and I offered Ulric the only thing he wanted to keep them all alive."

"John, you can't," Lily said breathlessly.

"I can and I will if it means saving my friends."

"You're a fool. Can't you see you'd be dooming them to a fate worse than death? Ulric is going to kill you; he told me as much. I couldn't convince him otherwise."

"And why would you even begin to think that he would trust a Fae he'd just met?" I asked sternly.

"Because," Lily started hesitantly, clearly unsure if she should continue her thought, "he hadn't just met me." My world spun as the implications of her words whispered doubt and deception in my mind. I had to grab my recliner to steady myself, but I entrusted too much weight into it, and it unfolded into a full reclining position, allowing me to fall to the ground with grace. As I sat on my ass, I brought my legs up to my chest and wrapped my arms around my knees before compiling my next sentence.

"You knew Ulric?"

"I know Ulric," she corrected.

When she let the silence linger, not revealing more information than she had to, I pressed on, "In what fucking capacity, Lily?"

"I knew him when he was a mortal," she said with an intentional cessation at the end.

"Lily, stop playing with me." My rage was starting to blossom once again in my core like a well-maintained garden of hate. "You need to tell me everything and not hold back. You want me to trust that you have my best interests at heart? Prove it. Right now. Prove to me that I can believe anything you say, ever again."

As her eyes shifted to the ground momentarily, Lily nodded once in acceptance of my request. I could tell she was taking a risk and that this very moment would define our relationship for the foreseeable future—which, for all intents and purposes, could potentially be an eternity.

"As you wish, John. I will tell you the truth and hope that you can see past your own emotional fragility and see things from my perspective," she said before taking in a deep breath and closing her eyes. As she exhaled, opening her eyes, she continued, "I found Ulric as a man in the thirteenth century in Denmark. He was an ally of King Sverker II of Sweden, who was Danish-backed. Ulric, his brothers, and father fought at the Battle of Lena in 1208 and were subsequently crushed by Prince Eric's army. Ulric lost his entire family in that war, having never known his mother, who died giving birth to him." I felt a pang of familiarity and already knew where this story was going. "I found him, broken and desperate to avenge his brothers and father, whom he adored completely. I influenced a vampire who had grown tired of ruling Africa to convert Ulric and make him his companion. I instructed his maker to tell Ulric that, if he were to join him, the war that would follow would be like none he had ever seen."

"What was his name? Ulric's maker, I mean. He never spoke about him."

"Cimeries. I can understand why; he killed him."

After taking all of this in, I said, "I'm beginning to notice a twisted pattern with vampires. Are we like the Sith of the supernatural world?"

"There are those who are much worse, John," Lily the Fae said coldly.

"What happened after Cimeries made Ulric?" I asked, fascinated.

"Cimeries spent the next two years teaching Ulric how to control his abilities and hone his instincts into a weapon of revenge. When he was ready, Ulric convinced King Sverker to arm peasants and farmers and attack again. It did require some special manipulation of the vampiric persuasion, but Sverker agreed. Ulric and Cimeries almost single-handedly wiped out over ten thousand soldiers in the battle that followed. To this day, history books suggest it was a mere five thousand peasants who overthrew a trained army that more than doubled their numbers," she finished with a smile touched with pride.

I let all of this sink in before saying, "So you helped make Ulric."

"I guided Cimeries to him and persuaded the change. It wasn't the first time," she said with eyes that locked onto mine with hesitation, "and it wasn't the last, John."

"Huh?" I said, face scrunching in confusion as my brain struggled to piece together what she was implying. "What are..." It hit me in the chest like jumping into a frozen lake. The theater in my mind showed me the first time Ulric and I had met.

"So you must be John," the calm voice of a cultured British man said with mild entertainment.

But he's British! Didn't Lily say he was from Denmark? I said as I looked at PS, who responded by slowly pointing to me. I was Irish and currently had an average American accent. Over the years, I had adopted the tongue and cadence of whatever area I resided in order to blend in. My preternatural mind made it a seamless transition, just as Ulric's did. Hell, even Locke forged a perfect American accent even though he was the Brit, Godwin.

"You..." I said to Lily, mouth agape and eyes wide in realization. "You led him to me."

"I did," Lily said. "I felt your pain and knew I could help. Ulric was close by, asleep in the dirt, so I awoke him and did for you as I had done for him two hundred years before. He had grown bored of life after getting his revenge and killing his maker, and decided to sleep for a few decades until the world became more interesting to him. You provided the perfect excuse."

Something tickled at the forefront of my mind and I asked, "Do you love him?" My chest tightened at the potential answer.

"I did," Lily said sighing, her eyes going unfocused for a moment as if reliving her past in an instant.

"Do...do you love m—" I was cut off by my phone, which startled both Lily and myself. The *Beetlejuice* theme song rang loud, demanding my attention. Both of us looked at each other, knowing precisely who was calling.

The eggplant-surrounded Ulric popped up on the screen as I slid my finger to accept the call. I pushed the speaker button and held the phone up so Lily could hear.

"Salutations, John," Ulric said in his clipped British accent. Every word was enunciated in his own special diction. He reminded me of John Malkovich mixed with Bill Nighy.

When I didn't respond, Ulric continued, "He was innocent—the driver, I mean—and you killed him. I thought you only killed bad guys, John. He had a baby on the way, which was why he needed the job. His wife will have to raise the child alone now—because of you."

I saw red. Lily stepped forward as I took in a deep breath to scream at Ulric and pressed the mute button.

"Can't you see what he's doing?" she asked frantically. "He's using your emotions against you so you'll make mistakes. Fall for it and he will win."

I looked her in the eyes and said, "It's your fault he's dead just as much as mine. You told Ulric to use Depweg's phone and trick me." I was losing the battle of control. Ulric had stabbed me right in the sweet spot and I was lashing out in pride. What's worse was that even though I could recognize what was happening, I couldn't stop it, which only served to piss me off more. I hated being so fucking weak.

"John, please," Lily pleaded, letting my comment glance off her before pointing back at the phone.

"Hello? Can you hear me?" Ulric asked. His voice grew distant, as if he'd pulled the phone away from his face, "These bars mean he can hear me, right?"

"No. They mean you're a dickhead," I could barely hear Dawson saying.

I unmuted the phone. "I'm here," I said quickly before Ulric punished my new friend. "Where are we meeting?"

"At my house. Just you, not that it matters," Ulric said confidently.

"I'm on my way. Let's finish this," I said as I pressed the red button.

Lily looked at me intently as I slid the phone into my pocket. "Do you want me to prove that I trust you, John?"

"Right now, I'm not sure what I want from you. You've put me on a roller-coaster ride that I can't get off of," I said flatly. "I don't know if there's anything you can do to make me trust you again."

Lily thought about this for a moment before taking in a deep breath and saying, "You are free from my previous commands. When you face Ulric, you are free to do whatever you wish."

"Wow," I said dumbstruck. "I was not expecting that." She was trusting me to not cause the apocalypse by killing Ulric. That is to say, get lucky enough to even be able to kill him, again. Pretty sure I had better odds as a lifeguard in the middle of summer than being able to get impossibly lucky for a third time. Either way, Lily was showing me the ultimate trust in a situation where I didn't even trust myself to do the right thing. Maybe I should see a therapist about my emotions or something.

"Don't make me regret this, John," Lily said. She took a half step forward before returning to her stance, as if she had been going in for an embrace. Though I longed to feel her arms around me, I was not ready to forgive her; but that was my damn pride talking. I gritted my teeth and stepped forward, beating my pride in this tiny battle, and wrapped my arms around Lily, who gave a little gasp before relaxing and throwing herself into my embrace. It felt good. Not only because of my growing affection for her, but because I had taken a step in controlling one of my faults.

I breathed in her hair, which smelled of flowers, before breaking the embrace and walking to the door.

"John," Lily started, unsure of her next words. I turned to look into her beautiful eyes. "Be careful, okay?"

"No promises," I said as I turned back to the door and made my way outside. Then I went back inside and past Lily, who stared at me in confusion. I opened my bedroom door and grabbed my spare pair of boots, putting them on after a fresh pair of socks hugged my feet.

Walking out of my room and to the front door again, I looked at Lily, who was smiling, and I shrugged. I stopped undead in my tracks and palmed my forehead, hard. Turning—again—I went past Lily, who was now shaking her head with a smile, and stepped into my room. Opening my closet door, I selected a super nice and thick hoodie. I had used it a few times in the past when Da had been fixing my trench coat, and its thickness stood up to how hard I was on clothes. Being faster than Superman came at a cost. You really had to spend the pretty penny on high-quality clothes.

Standing outside, my mind raced, digesting and organizing everything Lily had said. She had helped to make Ulric, and me. She loved Ulric, at least once. I had no choice but to trust that she was now on my side and not of the immortal man's she had known for a handful of centuries longer than me. That was a big damn pill to swallow.

As I made my way toward Ulric's place in the national park, I thought about what I could possibly do to stop him without dying or killing him. My only hope was to reason with him, which I knew in my heart would not go over well. Different scenarios played out in my mind, most of which ended in Ulric attacking. Fuck! Da and Locke were supposed to have another plan for me. A plan that probably wasn't going to work, just like the first one.

"Why the fuck am I doing this?" I cried out as I came to stop at the edge of the park.

"Doing what?" a casual voice came from the trees.

"Who's there?" I demanded, willing a sword and stepping into a defensive stance.

"Whoa, whoa, whoa, man. You don't need that." The voice reminded me of Jeff Bridges in *The Big Lebowski*.

"I'm not playing. Don't test me right now!" I called out, searching for the source of the voice.

"Over here, dude," the voice said with complete ease. I saw movement by a large tree and slowly stepped toward it, letting my eyes shift to have a better view.

What I came upon made me stop in disbelief. A tree waved at me as my eyes followed the split trunk up to a face that had moss and herbs growing from it like a long goatee. It looked down at me and smiled warmly.

"What's up, man?" he said.

"Oh, shit. A talking tree," I said, rubbing my eyes as if to clear them of this ridiculous sight. He was easily twenty feet tall.

"Treant, man. I'm a treant. I protect these trees and all the life inside," he said as he pulled some herbs from his face that looked oddly familiar and put them between his wooden thumb and forefinger. He ground the herbs together until they were almost a powder and dropped them into a rolled-up piece of bark he pulled from his forearm.

"Do ya mind?" he said, holding the organic joint out to me.

"Uh...huh?" I asked, confused.

"Lite it, bro."

"Ah." I focused and excited the molecules at the end of the joint and it began glowing orange.

"Thanks, man," the treant said as he brought the weed up to his mouth and took several long drags. He inhaled deeply as he spoke, trying to not let any smoke out just yet, "Vampire, huh? I knew it." He bent and offered the joint to me as he exhaled.

"Um, no, thanks. I try not to take supernatural drugs from strangers."

"Preternatural, man. I am of this plane," he said as he coughed out a laugh, still holding his offering out to me.

"I really can't. I'm about to go fight someone who is older and stronger and I kinda need to be able to focus and shit. Know what I mean?"

"This *will* help you focus, my friend. I sense great fear in you. And as you know, fear leads to anger. Anger leads—"

"Are you quoting *Star Wars* at me right now, tree?" I asked incredulously.

"Does it matter if it is? Shit's still on point. You have a lot of fear in you, and this will help you calm down and clear your mind. Help you see things that you couldn't see before," he said, still holding the joint with the smoldering end pointed toward him. "I may be a creature of Faerie, but I was born on this plane, alright? This shit right here," he said, shaking the joint at me, "is not your mortal weed. It's magic."

"I don't really believe in magic."

"Said the fucking vampire talking to a fucking tree," he said ironically. "Name's Richard, by the way."

"Richard the tree?"

"Treant, man. I'm a fucking treant. And yeah, I like Richard, so that's my name." I looked at him doubtingly before he said, "Look, you can call me Tiffany if you like. What's in a name? When you grow as old as me, you—"

"Break up the monotony of existence," I finished, recalling an earlier conversation with Valenta.

"Yeah, man. You get it. Now, are you going to take a hit off this and calm yourself before you go storming the castle?"

I grabbed the joint—which looked comical in my hand, as if it had been made by a twenty-foot-tall Snoop Dogg. "How did you know what I was here for?"

"I know a lot more than most creatures would give me credit for, man. That is, until they get to know me." There was a gleam in his eye that hinted that he was far wiser than he was letting on.

Shrugging in placation, I took a small hit off the Fae joint, held it in, and then let it out in a long exhale.

"There ya go, man. Soon you'll be feeling right as rain."

"May I partake?" asked a familiar voice. Startled, I turned while coughing up a lung to see Gabriel standing behind me at human height and in his nice charcoal suit.

I held up the joint in question with a raised eyebrow, to which the angel nodded. "You are allowed to do the marijuana?" I asked playfully.

"Who created the plant? Hmm? Oh, right, it was Father." I handed the joint over to him and watched in awe as he took a large hit. As he sucked in and held his breath, he said without letting any smoke out, "Dad created the human body and put intricate receptors that are made specifically to receive this." He exhaled the smoke and held up the Fae weed, appreciatingly. "This was supposed to be a practical cure-all for mortals, and what did they do? They created harmful pharmaceuticals that weren't needed to mask symptoms instead of fixing the problem. On top of that, I know Richard has the best stuff. How are you doing, my old friend?"

"Good, man. Living the life." He turned his attention to me and said, "Just trying to make sure this one doesn't do anything stupid and kill everything in existence."

As he spoke, a calm washed over me, starting at the top of my head. It felt like a blanket enveloping me, stilling my agitated nerves. I felt...peaceful. I didn't feel the giggles come on like TV would have you believe. Instead, I felt...prepared. I knew I had to save my friends while preventing the end of times.

"John," Gabe said, stepping in front of me after passing the faerie joint back to Richard. "You are free to make any decision you want in the universe. It's the consequences you can't avoid. Remember that."

It all came together then. Lily trying to protect me from myself while still providing me with the freedom to choose. Gabriel showing up to warn me of the consequences of my actions. The fate of the world and every soul that had ever existed throughout all of time depended on me. In this moment of clarity, I became aware that I was my own biggest enemy, and not even PS. PS *was* me. My anger had been a constant veil that blurred my path, which only served to infuriate me further. It was a vicious cycle that I knew I could end when I *really* wanted to. The truth was that it felt good to give in to my pride and hurt those who hurt me, to the point where I would cut off my nose to spite my face.

This was bigger than me and my petty problems. Ulric was waiting for me, and I knew I had to face him. Now that my mind was still, something nagged at me—something Lily had said.

"That's it!" I said excitedly as I turned to face the angel, Gabriel. "I know what I have to do."

"Excellent," Gabriel said with a smile as I turned to go face Ulric. "One thing before you go."

"What?" I asked.

"A test, mostly for my own curiosity. I've seen what you can do to angels and creatures from this plane and others," he said as a flaming sword manifested in his hand. The light shone bright, almost blinding, to the point where I shielded my eyes. "Sorry about that," he said as the flames dimmed to a low but constant flicker across the gladius. "Here," he said as he turned the weapon over, holding the hilt out to me. I took note that the heavenfire didn't burn him where it touched his body. I looked at him with a shocked expression, which he found humorous. "It's just a weapon, like many others you have held in your hands. Now, try and take it, for my own intrigue."

I did as instructed and grabbed the hilt of the blade. As soon as I lifted the sword from Gabriel's grasp, the flame went out after contact was broken.

I looked at the blade, confusion evident on my face as Gabriel said, "Oh, well. It was worth a shot. I owe one of my brothers five dollars now." As he finished, he reached out and took the blade back, which immediately vanished.

"What did you think was going to happen?" I asked Gabriel.

"I don't really know. That's why I wanted to see. Besides, it might be the last time we get to try."

"No, it won't," I said as I turned once again to face Ulric. As I leaped through the forest, I called over my shoulder, "Thank you for the enlightenment, Richard. I will come back to see you again!"

"Peace, man!" I heard the treant call back.

"Consequences," was whispered into my ears by the wind, though it sounded suspiciously like this angel I happened to know.

In short order, I arrived at Ulric's lame aboveground fortress. Depweg, Joey, and Dawson were there, standing stark naked on a handmade wooden bench with their hands tied behind their backs. Around their necks were silver cords that formed a noose and rose into the branches of a tree above. I followed the ends to see that they were anchored around the trunk of a tree. I didn't think the silver was being used to actually hang the werewolves, but to prevent them from shifting to their were forms. They would die if hung by the neck in their man-suits.

"Jesus Christ, John. Where have you been? He's had us standing here since dusk," Depweg said.

"Hang in there, guys. I got this." At that, all three let out a moan of annoyed frustration at the joke.

"Welcome to the end, John," Ulric said as he stepped from the shadows and into the light cast down from the spotlights around his stolen home.

"Which end?" I asked, probing how much he knew. Maybe if he knew the true impact of what was to come, he would rethink his actions.

"Yours, child," Ulric said coldly.

"Well, come on then," I said flatly, showing no emotion. My hands were steady as they hung by my sides.

"Gladly," Ulric responded, raising his hands to either side of his body. Nothing happened at first, and then a rumble sounded in the distance. There were thuds of impact that sounded like they should have been in a particular Steven Spielberg franchise.

From the tree line burst a giant demon, clad in obsidian armor, with glowing red eyes that expelled fumes from its sockets and over a horned helmet. Lilith, he was over fifteen feet tall and dragged a sword behind him that was just as long as he was tall. It was jagged, being made from obsidian and forged in the forges of Hell. I was quite confident that it was also infused with hellfire.

My confidence began to wane as two more broke through the tree line on either side of the first. One of his brothers hefted a double-sided ax with blades the size of a car's hood while the other carried an enormous mace with spikes all over it.

Normally I would lose control over my faculties and make a little teetee or even poopoo, but the fate of the world was resting on my shoulders. It was time to man up and face my destiny head-on. In addition, what Richard had given me and Gabriel had convinced me to try had really steadied my nerves and kept my mind focused.

I didn't wait to react like I normally would. I rushed the demons, pulling out a bloodgladius in one hand and a circular shield in the other. For shits and giggles, I put Captain America's emblem in the middle, which surprisingly gave me more confidence. Good thing I looked exactly like Chris Evans, too. Well, truthfully, it was more like Chris Hemsworth in *Avengers: Endgame*.

The demons were surprised at my charge—as was Ulric, who stood, shocked. All three demons quickly regained their composure and charged in a V-pattern for a tactical advantage. The mace-wielding demon lifted his weapon high to attack, and I threw my shield at his throat while keeping a fishing line's width of blood attached. This helped with both retrieval and maintaining the connection. As it smashed home, the demon dropped his hands and clutched at his throat, dropping the mace behind him. I willed my shield back to me by reeling in the line as I thrust my blade at the chest of the surprised beast. My sword bounced off his obsidian armor, throwing me in a spin to my right. I went with the momentum, allowing the blade to be swallowed by my hand as I reached for the mace at the completion of my turn. I hefted it, admiring its weight, as the ax-wielding demon swung down. I risked pouring a lot of energy into the shield and held it up at an angle. I knew that if he made a direct hit with his hellfire-infused weapon I would lose the energy in the shield and my arm, as he would surely slice through, probably even right through me. My plan worked and the blade ricocheted off the shield and embedded itself into the ground with a resounding thud that was felt as much as heard. I used the opportunity to swing the mace down on his helmeted head with the force of Valhalla. As he looked up at me in wide-eyed rage, the mace made contact and took the demon to the ground with ease, obsidian spikes piercing both the helmet and his brain. The giant corpse collapsed to the ground, unmoving.

A sword connected with my mace-wielding wrist, severing my hand. I was astonished at how numbly I reacted to the pain before backhanding the sword beast in the face with my impossibly hard shield. His head whipped back in surprise and pain as hellion blood shot from his broken nose and torn lips. Shattered teeth sprinkled to the ground in a way that reminded me of fish food over a tank for some reason.

A large pair of hands reached around my chest and pulled me in for a bear hug. I dropped the shield and stuck my hand under the arms of the mace demon before he fully took hold. He grabbed each of his forearms across my chest as my back met his armored torso. I took in a huge, deep breath before he began squeezing and did my best to keep my chest expanded; but this son of a bitch was strong, and I could feel my lungs about to burst like balloons under the pressure. The monster grunted with effort as he began to make headway, air escaping through my clenched teeth with each second that passed. This allowed the sword demon with the pretty face time to regain his senses after I'd bashed the front of his skull in. He picked up his blade and positioned himself to ram it into me, smiling—at least I think he was. His grin resembled a dilapidated graveyard with neglected tombstones crumbling to pieces.

An idea struck as I remembered in a flash what Lily had forced me to do in the alley. I focused on my hand sandwiched between his crushing arms and my chest. Concentrating, I began to fill my fingers and palm with blood. I could feel him struggling to hold on as his grip weakened, my hand becoming the size of a softball then a bowling ball. It hurt. Not only because of the expanding hand that felt like it was about to explode and had to keep healing so it wouldn't rupture but also because my ribs were beginning to crack and cave inward.

As the sword demon stepped forward and thrust his blade at my chest, I sucked in all the blood from my hand in a fraction of a second while emptying my lungs in a rush, momentarily creating room between his bear hug and my broken chest. I slipped down toward the ground as the blade stabbed and cut through the top of my shoulder. As intended, the mace demon got the full brunt of the attack. The sword baddy crashed into his brother and they tumbled to the ground, both screaming but for vastly different reasons.

I tried to will my wound closed in the brief reprieve, but the hellfire prevented that for now. I had precious seconds before the battle was to continue, so I focused on growing my other hand back. Only one itsy-bitsy problem: it was also burned by the stupid hellfire. I lifted my stump hand into the air while yanking my shield back into my good hand, willing the edges to become razor sharp. My eyes shot to the stump above my wrist, and I mechanically raised my shield arm at the elbow and brought it down above the hellfire-burned flesh, allowing nontainted flesh to regrow my favorite hand. The remaining demon began picking himself up after he'd overextended his attack and fell on top of his now very dead brother. Extremely dead, even.

Taking advantage of my remaining time, I used my new sandwich holder to form a small hook and bloodthread, and quickly moved to stitch one section of flesh to the other. I cinched the wound closed to prevent further blood loss. A quick rotation showed me I still had control over my chest and arm, but with limited range of motion above my head. My fingers grazed over my skin, then I realized that I was *directly* touching my skin.

"My fucking coat!" I yelled out in anger, only to realize that I hadn't put it on. "Oh, right—my fucking hoodie!"

I turned, willing a bloodwhip out of each of my hands, and threw them around the remaining demon's throat as he fully stood up to face me. I sent razors down their lengths before willing the two ropes to merge into one that connected at my hands, and began sawing his head off. Still holding the shield, I pulled one arm back while the other shifted forward, and then reversed the motion. He bellowed in rage and fear as the razors cut through flesh and veins before inching their way to his vertebrae. His hands were shredded while his base instinct to survive overrode the pain as his fingers were sheared off. His arms dropped to his side as the razors finished sawing through bone and his head toppled to the ground, black blood erupting like a demonic volcano.

I stood, watching the bodies with a sense of pride and satisfaction, and waited for them to melt into ectoplasm. My ribs started popping back into place as my sternum healed itself, filling the cave-in that was my chest. Once completed, my head tilted and an eyebrow went up when the three bodies lying in front of me began shuddering and convulsing.

"Um...what?" I asked out loud as the three demons started rolling and crawling to one another like jerky puppets on invisible strings. As they came together, their armors popped off, allowing for more flesh on flesh contact as their eyes began to blaze to life again. The three melted into one another; the ax demon with the mace still in his head formed the bottom portion, with his arms and legs acting as four feet for the forming monstrosity; the headless demon was in the middle, his arms and legs melting into the back of his brother, while the mace demon climbed onto the highest point, his legs merging into the forming mass just as his brother's had done. The beast before me had four arms and four legs and stood over thirty feet high. It bent over, picking up the decapitated head, and placed it on its shoulders right next to his brother. The heads merged, their touching eyes forming into one larger, glowing orb while the jaws also came together to make one giant, fanged mouth. It smiled at me with its three eyes and enormous maw.

"I don't have time for this," I said as I willed the bloodsaws into one hand, until just enough stayed out to form a spartan spear. I positioned one foot behind me and crouched with my lead leg as I set the weapon on top of my shield and aimed.

The horrifying monster in front of me bellowed a roar that shook the ground beneath my feet and covered me in warm strands of saliva. I screamed back at it as it began to charge.

I created a notch in the shield where the spear touched it, allowing it to sink just enough to act as a guide. Aiming with my shield arm, I let the beast approach before attacking. I didn't thrust the spear like any enemy would. Instead, I willed more of my blood into it and elongated it in the blink of an eye until the beast's middle eye was punctured. This only pissed the monster off as he grabbed me with his four arms and lifted me up, positioning each of its hands to grab a limb. Realizing my predicament while my mind raced to formulate a plan, I pulled my blood back, confident I was going to need every drop.

The deformed hellion began pulling my limbs in different directions as its massive jaws began taking chunks out of my exposed stomach just below my armor. Ribs were crunched like sticks of celery while intestines were slurped like spaghetti. I refused to scream as my mind tried to focus through the pain, desperately trying to figure a way out of this. My friends were counting on me, just as the rest of the world was.

My head cleared at this thought. This wasn't about me but the fate of everyone that had ever lived up to this point.

Blood oozed down my legs, and I focused on the gaping wounds. My limbs began to tear and I quickly forced my blood to flow from them and into my chest. My arm was ripped off along with one of my legs, sending agony through every nerve in my body. I didn't let it stop my unstoppable train of focus. The blood gushing from my stomach began to decrease, and it stopped its descent as a pained smile crested my face.

The demon took notice that something was happening and paused briefly enough for me to say, "Fuck you," before sending greedy tendrils of blood shooting out from my gaping wound. They grabbed the beast's upper and lower jaws like an octopus, prying them open as more blood slithered its way down the fucker's throat and into its center mass. I sent so much that I could feel my face begin to become sunken at the cheeks—it was an odd feeling being aware of each individual tooth touching the inside of my cheek, as if my skin were made of cellophane.

Once enough blood was filling its cavernous stomach, I weakly manifested jagged spikes to form in all directions, piercing every important, blood-soaked organ in the massive body.

I willed the huge monstrosity's blood to flow through my manifestation and into my body, refilling my reserves. The blood felt like sludge in my veins, but I didn't have a choice. I needed to filter the energy and repair the damage that had been done. I kept sucking as the beast's two remaining eyes began to flicker out as its body started to turn translucent and melt into ectoplasm. Once the blood was no longer tangible, I pulled my tentacles back into my chest, willing the gaping wound to close. I fell through the amalgamation's weakening grasp and collapsed on the ground while ribs grew around exposed organs and blackened skin healed. Staring at the stars while on my back, I stuck out my nubs as black sludge grew from my body until it grasped the fallen limbs, pulling them back to me and reconnecting them where they had been torn. Those too turned black where the blood healed my body. I was vaguely aware that my cheeks weren't wrapped around my teeth anymore.

"Gross!" I cried out as I realized the tainted blood had stained my healed skin. Once the limbs were back in place, I bent over and hurled up the filtered demon blood. Black oil exploded from my mouth and out of my nose, coating the grass in front of me in vile that immediately turned the grass brown, decaying it in an instant. It was like a year's worth of dog pee on the grass you spent several thousand dollars on because the salesman said it would survive your puppies peeing in the same damn spot. Liar.

I posted myself up on my arms and legs as I watched the rest of my enemy melt into ectoplasm before it evaporated into nothing. The monster had enough blood energy to get me back to normal, but man, was it disgusting. I was going to have heartburn for sure.

My beard was dyed black where the toxic waste touched, which meant that smell was not going to leave anytime soon. Being right under my nostrils, it reminded me of a mountain of tires that had been coated in cat piss and then set on fire. I was still hunched over, spitting intermittently in a futile attempt to get the last remains of demon blood out of my mouth. I covered one nostril and blew out black chunks of snot and hell-slime before doing the same to the other.

I looked up to see Ulric, who proceeded to golf clap in his arrogant way as he walked to inspect the plank that was holding my friends. His message was clear.

"Give yourself up and I will make your death a swift one, John," Ulric said. Confidence exuded off him. It felt like he'd sprayed an entire can of Axe body spray on him, to the point where even cocky frat boys in salmon-colored shorts and Sperrys would wrinkle their noses in disgust.

"Ulric," I started, taking in a deep breath, knowing what I was about to say would do nothing to change the events that had been set in motion, "you don't have to do this."

"Why do they always say that?" Ulric asked, shaking his head as his mind played the footage of all the people he had murdered over the centuries.

"Bitch, you are *not* about to quote *No Country for Old Men* at me." His face answered for him as confusion crossed his expression. I opened my hand and waved it in a quick circle, signaling that the fine details were irrelevant but that I would explain anyway. "It's a movie where the bad guy asks why people say, 'you don't have to do this,' before he kills them." Frustration set in that I had actually explained the quote to him. "Look, it doesn't matter. What *does* matter is that if one of us dies, then Armageddon will start."

"And why should I believe you, child? You would say anything to stop the inevitable."

"I'm giving you a chance, Ulric," I pleaded.

"Boy, I am two centuries older than you. I will cut you down like any mortal before me."

"Don't say I didn't warn you, dick."

Without further preamble, Ulric charged forward, manifesting a rapier, his weapon of choice. I willed my own personal favorite—a gladius—as I shifted into a fencing position. With my body turned sideways, I snaked a bloodwhip out of my hidden hand and let it curl on the ground at my feet. Ulric didn't notice as his eyes stayed intent on the sword in front of him. He landed in front of me and immediately began his attack, thrusting and parrying with an expertise that was both preternatural and honed from years of practice. I stood my ground, deflecting his attacks while feigning my own. Ulric's face melted from an evil, gleeful smile glowing with confidence to intense concentration as he realized I was just as skilled as he was.

After a three-step barrage of strikes that I easily deflected, he leaped back a few feet before trying on a familiar strategy for him. "How does it feel to know you will never get the revenge you sought on Commander Godwin? Hmm?"

I laughed and his brow furrowed deeply. I stepped forward with my hidden foot at impossible speeds and whipped my bloodrope around Ulric's feet before manifesting long, gruesome hooks. They pierced through his flesh as I pulled, yanking him off his feet. I willed Ulric's blood into my body as he realized what was happening with wide-eyed horror. He grew his rapier into a broadsword and began chopping at my thin rope. My laugh began to rise in pitch and volume until it was a maniacal bellow of hysteria—which prompted my prey to lose his well-maintained control as he threw an insane amount of energy into his bloodbroadsword, intent on freeing himself from the parasite wrapped around his legs. Oh, his blood was delicious and powerful—the perfect palate cleanser after the demon's vile juices.

As he began his downward swing, I pulled on the rope, hard. His swing missed as his body rocketed to where I stood. I let the bloodrope melt around his legs and retreat into my hand as he tumbled toward where I stood. A strong wind tore at my coat and the hair that stuck out from my beanie as my laugh filled the night. Just as he was about to crash into me, he adjusted his sword again and swung at my throat. The blade stopped just at my neck. Ulric's eyes widened in horror as he saw why. I had stopped the blade by grabbing his wrist with one hand. He mouthed the word "No" before I stopped my creepy laughter and my face went stone-cold. Without uttering a word, I ripped his arm off at the elbow, breaking the energy he had poured into the sword. Stunned, Ulric dropped to his knees, grabbing at the gushing nub with his remaining hand. He didn't speak, didn't cry. Ulric only shook in indescribable pain and loss of massive energy as his eyes managed to climb my body to lock gazes with me, struggling to form words.

"How..." was all he could manage.

"How?" I asked with a frigid tone of finality. "What, you think you are stronger because you are two hundred years older than me?"

He looked at me with his mouth agape and his nub still pouring blood, and I said, "You may be older than me, dick, but you slept for over three hundred years, didn't you? Not to mention however long you slept before you and I first met. I remember your clothes and how old they looked. But you know what? I haven't slept, Ulric. I've been awake, feeding and growing stronger with each drop of blood. You may be technically older than me, but I am over one hundred years stronger than you, child." I finalized my point by picking my maker up by the neck, who struggled to get away. His eyes flicked frantically around him, searching for something, *anything*, to help him—but there was no gas lamp here. After a few pathetic moments, he stopped fighting and looked me in the eyes. His face was calm but his gaze was filled with rage, and doubt began to creep into my mind. His hand had crept behind him and pointed at the bench where my friends stood.

"Um, dude?" Joey said while Dawson stood in stunned silence and Depweg set his jaw, preparing himself.

As I realized what was happening, I grabbed Ulric by the collar just as he shot out a bowling ball of blood that solidified and rocketed toward the bench. I saw it fly from his palm in slow motion, unable to stop it. It slammed through the middle of the thin wood, and the remaining sections crumbled, just as they were meant to do. All three dropped down only to hang a few inches off the ground, the nooses around their necks having tightened. Joey and Dawson's eyes bulged from their heads, and their mouths gaped like fish out of water. Depweg's body hung loose, eyes closed tight and face turning bright red. He wasn't going to give Ulric the satisfaction of a dramatic death.

"Now you have a choice; kill me, or save your friends," Ulric managed to get out. The bowling ball took a lot of his remaining energy out of him, and he hung limply from where I grasped him.

"Why not both?" I asked as I pulled the silver kukri from its sheath at the small of my back. The blade hummed with power, and Ulric's eyes widened slightly, even in his exhaustion.

"You would let them die?" he panted. "You are not the man I found in that prison cell."

I leaped to the tree in one bound, bringing Ulric with me, who was rocked by the unexpected momentum. I slammed him into the tree where the silver nooses were tied and dropped him on his ass in front of the trunk. I took the blade, remembering what Gabriel had said about consequences, and stabbed Ulric right through his stomach, severing the ropes tied around the tree. The tight ropes snapped loudly as they were cut and rushed away from the blade.

Depweg, Joey, and Dawson all dropped to the ground, gasping violently. I stood and strode over to each of them, in turn removing their nooses and unbinding their hands with a blooddagger I manifested. They were being held tight by the thick zip ties you saw cops use on TV. I turned to see Ulric sitting at the base of the tree, pawing at the blade with his remaining hand and unable to remove the silver from his body. He had lost too much of his precious energy and was verging on unconsciousness.

After I made sure my friends were alright, I embraced Depweg, who squeezed me back. I tried my best not to cry from relief, but a tear or ten snuck out.

"Dude," Depweg said, nodding his head toward where Ulric lay, bleeding out.

"He'll live," I responded in my Arnold voice. I wiped my face as we broke our embrace and sniffed some fleeing snot back home. Depweg just stood, looking at me. "Alright, go. Save his life like the good guy you are."

Depweg jogged into the house while I crouched next to where the twins were still panting on the ground.

"Thought we were goners, man," Dawson said.

"Yeah, dude. I thought Ulric was like, way stronger than you or something," Joey said.

"Well, my naked friends, he was—at one point. But he slept for a long time. Hell, the second time he slept I thought he was dead. He probably used every bit of energy he had ever stored to keep from fully dying."

"That's a crazy plot twist, bro," Dawson said as he stood up, one hand caressing his throat.

"Think I could sell the story to Netflix yet?"

"I'd watch it," Joey said, rubbing his neck, which I noted had violently bruised in the few moments they'd been hanging.

Joey saw me looking, glanced at his brother's perfectly matched neck bruise, then said, "Don't you dare make a leash joke."

"Damn! Beat me to it."

Depweg came out of the house carrying an armful of supplies that he dropped where Ulric lay unconscious. He wrapped a hand towel around the stump that had slowed its bleeding but still leaked life fluid, securing it in place, ironically, with a zip tie. He reached for the silver blade jutting out of Ulric's stomach, prompting me to call out, "Wait!"

Depweg did as asked, watching me pick up a silver noose off the ground and jog over to the tree, where I placed the rope around Ulric's neck. I tightened it before nodding to Depweg, who pulled the blade out. Ulric didn't move, which was kind of worrisome.

"Lilith damn it," I said as my mind began to race with solutions to the major problem in front of me. An idea struck me that was so poetic that it was delicious. I put my hand over Ulric's slack-jawed mouth and willed blood to flow from my palm and down his throat. I was going to give Ulric a second chance, just as he had done for me all those years ago. Well, this was like his third chance or something—but who's counting? Me.

As I fed Ulric some of my life energy, which I had stolen from him in our fight, Depweg worked to burn the wound on his stomach and back closed by lighting another dish towel, which he held with a pair of tongs. Ulric's face barely contorted in response, signaling that I had provided enough blood to keep him from dying. I willed my palm closed and held the rope close to the knot, just in case. Depweg handed the blade back to me and I cut several feet of the rope off before sliding it in its sheath at the small of my back; but not before first wiping it on Ulric's clothes to clean off the blood.

Ulric's eyes fluttered, and a moan escaped his lips.

"Stand back," I told Depweg. "Take the twins and go see if there's anything of value in the home, like clothes, and then burn it down. I'll deal with him."

"You mean rob him?" Depweg asked, testing my comment to see where I stood on the moral ground.

"See if you can find any pertinent information, like who he was working with. He got this house—which is not supposed to be here, by the way—and had a small task force of hired goons, including fucking demons, man. Look for anything that shows where the money came from to pay for the muscle, and then burn it down."

"What do you mean it isn't supposed to be here?"

"It has a ward on it that prevents mortals from finding or remembering it. Bad guys use it as a hideout," I explained.

"Got ya. Guess I should burn it down, then."

"Say, that's a damn good idea. Do that. I'm going to take this sack of shit to a special place at Papa T's. You guys good here?"

Depweg and I looked over at Joey and Dawson, who were piling electronics, cash, and weapons on the ground just outside the front door.

"If this is a supernatural bad guy hangout, then yeah, we're good," Depweg said.

"Check the garage for a ride before burning the place down," I called as Depweg walked toward the house to find any information he could.

As if on cue, Father Thomes pulled up in his hearse and I walked over to it, dragging Ulric behind me, who clutched at the noose as it tightened. "What's wrong, princess? Don't like that?"

I set Ulric in the passenger's seat and then climbed in behind him, keeping the noose tight around his neck to discourage any violent outbursts. He didn't need to breathe, anyway.

"You did well, John," Father Thomes Philseep said, pride brimming in his voice. "I had prayed you would be strong enough to win the battle."

"Turns out, I'm way fucking stronger than this piece of shit," I said, tugging lightly at the rope, which prompted a moan from Ulric.

"I wasn't referring to him," Father Thomes said as he looked meaningfully at me through the rearview mirror while putting the hearse into drive.

"Oh," I replied, feeling conflicted at everyone's faith in me to control my emotions. I was happy that I had (barely) done the right thing and rewarded the faith my friends had in me; but it was still sobering to know how they really felt about me.

We rode in silence back to the church as my mind replayed all the events and coincidences of the evening. Richard the treant showing up where and when he did, followed by the angel Gabriel, who convinced me to imbibe the faerie-juana. I had been more anxious and fearful than I had thought, probably because my pride blinded me from reality. Richard and Gabe had allowed me to relax, control my emotions, and realize the truth —that I was the stronger person; not only physically but mentally as well.

I'd beaten both my enemies in one fell swoop—Ulric, and my own inner demons. Oh yeah, and stopped the end of the world.

I DRAGGED ULRIC TO HIS NEW HOME IN THE CATACOMB DUNGEON belowground. Father Thomes wasn't kidding; he had made vast improvements after my escape. There was no bed, only a simple down mattress and pillow. The door was no longer hinged. Instead, it was a sliding door similar to that of a jail cell but with a solid iron door. There was a small hole with a sturdy cover where items could be placed inside without having to open the door. There was also a bar that fell into place that braced the edge of the door once it was closed, providing further sturdiness and guaranteeing that no one could possibly get out.

As we placed Ulric on the mattress and removed the noose from around his neck, he opened his eyes and looked around, frantically.

"Where am I?" he cried out weakly as the door started to slide shut. Before it closed, I flipped him off and smiled. His eyes blazed with fury and confusion. The iron shut with a thud that reverberated in the stone, sending dust tumbling down from lamps that littered the catacombs. I noticed there was a red button with a clear plastic cover on it. So, of course, I lifted the plastic and put my finger on the button while asking, "What's this do?"

"Please do not press that button," Father Thomes calmly but sternly said. "It releases enchanted iron dust into the ventilation of the cell. Enough to reduce the supernatural occupant to ashes.

"Neat," I said in awe before realizing that the room had been made for, and then modified, for me. "Oh, shit." I looked at Father Thomes with a mixture of emotions.

"Are you really that surprised, John?"

"I guess not. You gotta do what you gotta do. But damn!"

"Thank you for understanding. Now then, leave Ulric in my care and try not to get yourself killed."

Without thinking, I embraced my friend who was trying his best to save my black, stained soul. He stiffened in surprise, as I had never hugged him before, and then relaxed while putting his arms around me.

"I'm proud of you," Father Thomes told me. It meant so much coming from him.

"You know, I'm kinda proud of me too," I said as we separated.

"Go. Be with your friend you risked everything to save," he said with a smile.

I took his hint and headed home, stopping to have a drink at Valenta's first. I wanted to let him know everything had turned out okie dokie. As I entered through the front, Valenta nodded at me as I made my way to the bar and sat on one of his custom-made stools. His place was empty. I could only assume supes were still hiding.

"Give me the usual, please, sir."

"Glad yer still with us, boy," Valenta said as he poured my special mixture of enchanted Jack and Blood. "Thanks for not doen nothen stupid."

"I hope all of you know how hard it was to not kill him."

"I hope ya'know how grateful we are that ya didn't," he said as he slid a second drink over. It was a subtle show of gratitude that meant mountains coming from Valenta.

Holding up the glass, I said, "Skool," before downing the first and starting on the second after the burn dissipated, sipping it to enjoy the significance of these drinks. The world had not ended, and I was growing, which fucking sucked. It was so much easier to be stubborn, prideful, and full of rage. But damn it, I really enjoyed *Game of Thrones* and all these bitchen superhero movies that would cease to exist if the apocalypse happened.

After a few minutes of blessed silence and self-contemplation, a tall figure entered through the door and came to sit next to me without pausing. I recognized his smell before I saw the pointy ears in my periphery.

"Hey, Taylor."

"Greetings and salutations, hero," Taylor said, placing an admiring hand on my shoulder.

"Hero? I don't know about that," I said, taking a long pull from my drink, finishing it. I held up the empty glass and shook it slightly while scrunching my face with the sweet, sweet burn. Val nodded and began pouring a fresh one.

"Allow me," Taylor said, placing a crisp hundred on the counter and sliding it toward Valenta.

"Don't know if I want any Fae to pay for my drink there, bud," I said, setting down the empty glass and picking up the full one.

"No strings. And once again, I'm a friend of this plane and don't play the Fae games of the other courts."

"Well then, cheers," I said, taking a sip from the glass, letting it slide down my throat. I was beginning to feel the effects. "So the Seelie Court is a friend, huh?"

"Yes. I would very much like to be your friend, which is why I am here."

"Oh, Lilith, here it comes," I said, rolling my eyes.

"The Shadow Court is upset that you didn't kill Ulric, or the other way around. Well, not as much 'upset' as they are 'pissed,'" he said with air quotes. "They don't know where Ulric is, but they know where you are."

"What do you mean?" I asked with words that were beginning to slur, setting my drink down hard, and turning to fully face him.

"They know you are in one of the largest ley lines in the region; Houston. They have countless shadow Fae they can send, and will send, to kill you and erase this plane until only darkness remains."

"Let them come," I said, emphasizing each word, and turned back to my drink.

"They will, but know you have friends with the Seelie. We will be watching," Taylor finished before blinking out of this plane.

"Oh, goodie. The fun never stops for John Cook. Lilith, can't I get five fucking minutes to myself?" I said in cursive, my words slurring together.

"God only gives what we can handle, boy. Some can take more than others."

"Yeah, yeah. Father Thomes and you should write a damn book."

"Don't need ta. One's already been done," Val said, turning to clean the bar behind him, leaving me to my thoughts.

I finished my drink, thanked Val with a nod, and stood on wobbly legs to leave. The air was calm and the stars were out in full force, no longer afraid of the end that almost happened tonight. I took in a deep breath and began casually strolling to my home, enjoying the world around me as if for the first time.

As I walked in a completely straight line to the graveyard's entrance, I immediately noticed an out-of-place, blacked-out Ford Expedition parked out front. The back was open and I saw Joey and Dawson carrying various valuables toward the mausoleum. I could hear them talking with one another, excited at their loot, and to be alive. I wondered if they got any good movies or games out of the deal. OH! Or maybe an incredibly rare relic from some ancient civilization that was haunted or something. Killer book idea, or maybe Hulu.

I drunkenly walked to the entrance of my home and descended the stairs, flattening against the wall as Joey and Dawson made their way back out for another load. Joey high-fived me as I passed, while Dawson moved his hand back and said, "Too slow, old man!"

"Could use some help," Joey said over his shoulder.

"I'm managerial," I said with a slur. "You guys are doing great! Keep it up! We're only as strong as the early bird that gets the moss."

"Dude, I think..." Dawson started.

"Don't engage," Depweg warned from the bottom of the stairs. He sniffed the air as I got close. "How's Valenta? Did he say anything?"

"A lot," I said as Depweg led the way to the kitchen where he turned to face me, waiting for the rest. Da and Locke were in the living room looking at the goodies we'd salvaged. That's the legal term for stealing, right? Salvaged? Anyway.

Rolling my eyes, I took in a deep breath and managed to get out, "Taylor showed up and bought me a drinky-poo. Nice guy, I like him. Mentioned something about the Shadow Court *really* wanting to cast the world into darkness, or something bleak like that."

"The fun never stops for John—" Da started.

"Yeah, already said that," I interrupted while trying to keep the world from spinning. "So everyone take a day or two to rest and get ready for a tidal wave of scary ass Fae monsters coming to kill us."

"Um, can I have a body?" Locke asked. "I can help. I *want* to help."

"Maybe for your birthday," I said dismissively.

"My birthday is actually tomorrow," Locke said. Depweg and I looked at him, assessing his comment. "Seriously!"

"Maybe for Christmas," I amended, ignoring him. I was a little (a lot) drunk and tired. It was exhausting, doing the right thing, and even more tiring that there was a horde of faeries that wanted to kill me. "I need a vacation. Da, how many weeks do I have accrued?"

"Not enough, I'm afraid," Da said.

"Lilith! Why do I even work here? No 401(k), shitty hours, and no vacation."

"Actually, your retirement is substantial. More than most countries, actually. You're lucky to have me, you know. It's dreadfully hard to run all these shell companies and spread the wealth over several companies around the globe."

"That's why I pay you the medium bucks," I said as I moved toward the couch. I turned my back and pretended to have to squeeze between the couch and coffee table, saying, "Excuse me. Oh, excuse me. Sorry about that. 'Cuse me," as I stuck my ass out in Locke's face, who could do nothing but take it on the chin, literally.

"Dear Lord, man," Locke said, scrunching his nose up futilely. "You smell rank. Were you at a Grateful Dead concert or something?"

"Huh?" I asked, sniffing my armpits and taking in a whiff of the organic holy weed Richard had given me. "Oh, right. That smell is what saved the world, my friends."

I picked up the remote and began sorting through shows to continue watching. When I didn't continue the odd statement, Da asked, "Care to elaborate further?"

"Not really," I answered, feeling their judgment wash over me. I didn't have the energy to confess out loud that I hadn't been confident if I could restrain from killing Ulric or not, and that it'd taken a foreign substance of mind-altering origin to mellow me enough to not cause Armageddon.

"Oh, man, what season is *The Walking Dead* on now? I got bored after the Governor," I said, changing the subject.

Knowing there was no winning when I was stubborn and drunk like this, Da and Depweg continued sorting items on the kitchen table.

"I understand," Locke whispered. "I've known you awhile and I get it. No judgment here."

I looked at him then, as if for the first time. Then I picked him up, tearing away the mannequin body, and put my palms around both sides of his head just as I had done before. Blood flowed out and surrounded his neck before moving downward. I focused and sent my energy into expanding his flesh. It took a lot of what I had left in my tanks, but since I was on a roll with self-betterment, I figured why not learn to trust.

After a full minute, the blood retracted back into my being, leaving behind a brand-new body for Locke. Tears began to well in his eyes that he instinctively wiped away with his new hand.

"John, I…" he began, fighting back the oncoming wave of sobs. "What the…" He looked at his baby hand with its cute little chubby folds, then his other. As I sat him on the couch, he looked down at his naked body and gaped incredulously. "My penis! It's the size of a Lil Smokey!"

"Don't give yourself too much credit, kid," I said, stifling a laugh. He looked at me with a pleading look that also had anger mixed in. "Look," I said, "You'll grow into it." With that, the whole room burst into laughter, all except for Locke, whose mouth was permanently affixed open in what I assumed was gratitude.

"Dude! They have a bootleg disk of the new *Avengers* mov— Holy fuck! What is that?" Dawson yelled, dropping his spoils and pointing at Locke. "Why is there a man's head on that baby?"

"Cool," Joey said, shouldering past Dawson to drop his load on the table.

After a few minutes of laughing, I wiped the tears from my eyes, looked at Locke in all seriousness, and said, "Look, two things; I don't know if I can fully trust you yet, and I used all the energy I had left to give you that. Plus I'm fucking drunk," I said, motioning over his body. "Now, how about you cover up your Tic Tac and test the body out."

Locke grabbed a throw pillow and put it over his junk. "Not like that!" I said, noting that particular pillow would soon meet Mr. Fire.

Locke waved a hand in midair and whispered to himself. A ball of fire the size of a marble appeared in his hand, making his eyes go wide with joy. "Thought I'd never get to do that again! OW!" Locke said as the fire began to burn his delicate baby flesh. "Oh, right. I'll have to toughen up again. Damn it, that took years the first time!"

"You have nothing but time," I told Locke. "No Master pulling the strings this time, forcing your every move. Dobby is a free elf."

"Hey! I can feel my heartbeat! I…I'm alive!" Locke exalted.

"Do…do we need to get diapers?" Da asked in all seriousness.

The End

EPILOGUE—PART 1

The new Avengers movie was in the loot pile; but, alas, it was dubbed in Danish. Fine with me, but I didn't think anyone else could speak the language.

"Guess we'll just have to wait for it to come out on iTunes or something," I suggested.

"Oh, John, before I forget," Da started, "the blood bank is awaiting permits from the mortal authorities, and then we can begin construction. It may take some—"

"Bribes," I interrupted.

"—greasing of certain wheels," Da finished politically. "I am confident the project can be completed within the year."

"Make sure you get a steady supply to Doc Jim," I said.

"Of course," Da responded. "Depweg had already shared his information with me. You'll be pleased to know that he has made substantial upgrades to the clinic as well."

"Neat," I said while chuckling at the hilarious translation the Danes had done.

"Why are we watching this?" Locke asked.

"Aw, does someone need a time-out?" I retorted without taking my eyes off the screen.

"That's never going to get old for you, is it?" Locke stated more than asked.

"No," I answered as I rose from the couch and walked the few steps to my room. No one questioned me leaving, though I could hear the movie change to something else that wasn't horribly dubbed. I shut my door and clenched my fists until they shook and tears welled in my eyes. Veins bulged as I tried not to scream at the thought of the man I had killed in my rage. I had done to him what had happened to me so long ago.

"What is it, John?" asked Lily in a soft, concerned voice.

"I don't fully know, Lily. I killed an innocent, and it's weighing heavily on me. I don't...I don't understand."

"You're growing, my dear. Being good isn't about helping old ladies cross the street, you know. Believing you are good and being good are two completely different things, John. Your heart is changing, and with that comes the clarity of what is wrong. Embrace the pain, for you deserve it. I'm not going to sugarcoat it for you. What you did was wrong. But if you truly regret what you did, and you learn from it, then it is a lesson and not simply a mistake."

"A lesson that cost a man his life, and a family their provider," I responded coldly while shutting my eyes to avoid looking at her. I didn't deserve her compassion. I deserved to be slathered in cooking grease and left in the middle of Death Valley at dawn.

"A lesson all the same, John," Lily said a little more harshly. "Now stop being a victim, learn from your mistakes, and grow." Her words were stern, but she was right.

I cried then. Like, ugly cried, with snot oozing out of my nose while drool escaped my mouth and ran into my beard. Lily embraced me as I collapsed to my knees. My head rested on her stomach as she stroked my head.

After a full minute, it was over. I wiped my eyes with my hand, and my nose with my sleeve. "Growing sucks."

"I understand. Feel better?"

Sniffling, I said, "Yeah, actually. Thanks. I needed that."

"Now," Lily began, a wry smile forming, "you were saying something before we were interrupted when we last spoke?"

"Give me time," I answered, staring into gorgeous eyes that made my knees weak.

"I understand. Luckily, we have all the time in the word." She planted a loving, gentle kiss on my lips before shifting planes, leaving me puckering the air.

"Being immortal has it's perks," I said with a warm smile growing on my face.

EPILOGUE—PART 2

From the darkness, perched on top of a building overlooking an alley, sat a featureless black cat. Fierce purple eyes the color of glowing amethysts watched with interest as the fat vampire got lucky and killed an angel before stumbling around like a drunkard. Taking advantage of the vampire's lack of attention, a shadow paw was held up and extended into the alley, stretching like taffy at the fair. While being careful to avoid the light, the paw morphed into a massive clawed hand and grasped the angelic sword by the hilt. With the vampire still distracted by his own actions, the shadow hand smoothly lifted the sword from its concrete sheath before pulling it into the darkness; there, the large hand reverted back to a normal cat's paw.

Scowling at the abomination with an intense hatred, the feline watched as the foolish vampire realized the weapon was missing before starting to panic and stumbling to a white car that had pulled up. The cat made of shadow lifted its front legs into the air and began to grow like Alice after she ate the cake labeled "Eat Me." Unlike Alice, however, the cat began to morph into a hulking mass as tall as a house and the color of midnight. A Cheshire grin with gleaming white teeth as sharp as razors spread on its face. Hands that ended in three thick fingers extended from above the roofline to wrap around the angelic body covered in celestial armor. The shadow monster reeled in its huge prize as easily as a child picking up their favorite stuffed animal.

As the lifeless body and holy sword began to be swallowed by the darkness on the roof, the shadow monster shrunk back down to once again become a featureless black cat. The stupid vampire noticed, then, what had transpired in his distracted state, and almost made the cat cry out in delighted mirth.

With everything in place, the cat began to fade into the darkness, amethyst eyes and gleaming smile winking out.

If you enjoyed John's shenanigans, turn the page for a sample of **SHADOW OF A DOUBT**—*book 3 in the Preternatural Chronicles.*

Or get your ebook copy HERE:

argentopublishing.com/l/1306080

TEASER: SHADOW OF A DOUBT (BOOK 3)

Water dripped incessantly every few seconds in the dark, freezing prison. There were no windows in Queen Mab's dungeon, so Oberon—the once king of all of Faerie—had no idea how much time had passed since his imprisonment. Had it been years? Decades? Only the water kept him company.

Oberon refused to scream or lash out, knowing Mab would relish any show of emotion. Instead, he sat in meditation, dreaming of what he would do once he escaped. As he closed his eyes, his estranged wife flowed to the forefront of his thoughts, and he remembered.

Oberon had danced with the idea of absorbing the Unseelie Court for centuries. Though he had proclaimed himself King of all Faerie, he had known in the back of his mind that it was only in name. Everyone had been aware of Queen Mab and her unquestioned rule over half of Faerie. Therefore, the time had come to stop fantasizing over being the one true king. The time had come to attack and make it a reality. No one would dare question or doubt King Oberon. Not even in private.

Tatiana had argued with her husband over the necessity of the Winter and Autumn Courts.

"We could rule them *better* than that bitch sitting on the throne," Oberon had roared in his blinding anger. Tatiana had simply stood with arms crossed and glaring at her husband. Taking a deep breath, Oberon had softened his tone and pleaded, "Imagine it; Spring and summer in perpetuity! Flowers would always bloom, while full trees would wave in the warm wind! We can make it that way, wife."

"There can be no light without darkness, dear husband. We need the winter and autumn just as they need the summer and spring. It is this perfect dance of balance and equality that gives way to life in Midworld."

"Who cares about Midworld!" Oberon had bellowed, losing what small semblance of control he had had over his emotions. "I *want* that throne, and there's nothing you can do to stop me!" As Oberon had turned to leave and prepare his private army, he had been surprised when his opinionated wife had said nothing. Now he knew why. She had betrayed him by warning Mab about his intentions of overthrowing the Unseelie Court. Mab had been waiting with Tatiana by her side. The loyal army of King Oberon had faltered and kneeled before the combined queens of Faerie, leaving the king alone to face the Unseelie.

Oberon had refused to accept his fate and had battled everything that had been thrown at him. Frost giants wielding ice clubs, elves with blue eyes and skin casting dark magic, shrieking banshees, and even a cyclops had fallen to Oberon's blade and prowess. It wasn't until Tatiana had stood in front of him as he swung his sword that he had hesitated, allowing for Queen Mab herself to cast the powerful spell that had frozen the king in place. All of Faerie had known about his defeat and subsequent imprisonment.

"Bitch," Oberon barked through bared teeth. His face was sore from scowling for so long in the darkness. "You're going to pay for this, dear wife —*both* of you will."

Oberon could feel his fists shaking as wrath built a fire in his core that made his skin crawl.

"Maybe I can be of assistance," purred a smooth, female voice from the darkness.

Startled, Oberon's eyes shot open only to be flooded with absolute blackness. Two amethysts appeared a few feet away from him, followed by a gleaming smile of sharp teeth. Oberon was perplexed at how teeth could shine in the complete absence of light.

"Who might you be, specter?" Oberon asked in the tone of someone who was used to being the authority in the room.

"A humble servant of the one true king of Faerie," cooed the voice as the smile grew to a full Cheshire grin.

MAKE A DIFFERENCE

If you enjoyed this Urban Fantasy eulogy for Sir John Cook[1], would you consider leaving an honest review? Every genuine review means the world to me, and helps new readers find my books.

It only takes five minutes, and it can be as short as you like. Just head on over to my Amazon page.

Thank you in advance for giving John *unlife* after death. The series dedicated to my bromego will be 13 full novels with a handful of novellas and short stories for good measure. So until next time, John On!

---

1. *John is not actually knighted.*

DEDICATIONS

To my loving wife, who has supported and believed in me while I follow my dreams of crafting stories.

To John, for making me promise to write a book about you as a vampire. You didn't have to die for me to hold true to my promise; but then again, you never half assed anything you did. It was whole ass or no ass. Miss ya, bro.

And to you, epic reader, and whatever challenges life has thrown your way. Remember, when life gives you lemons, make orange juice and leave life wondering how the fuck you did it.

ABOUT HUNTER BLAIN

Hunter Blain is an author and entrepreneur who has spent his entire adult life—before writing—in the retail industry. At the age of 24, Hunter became the youngest Regional Sales Director at GNC before joining one of the largest supplement companies in the world. He is swole, ladies and gentlemen. *So. Swole.* After a few years, he had accumulated enough knowledge, beard length, and confidence to open his own brick and mortar store, *Empire Nutrition*. As of 2020, Hunter is in the midst of franchising the business to budding entrepreneurs.

One day, a teenage Hunter went to visit his mother at work (*because he's a good son*), and met a goddess in the flesh who went by the name Amanda. She was one of his mom's coworkers, and Hunter's own age. She also happened to be the most beautiful woman Hunter had ever seen. On an unrelated note, Hunter decided to visit his mom at work a whole lot more after encountering Amanda, and somehow convinced her to marry him after spending nearly a decade together. "Finally!" their family members screamed in exhausted relief at the wedding.

As of this writing, they live with their two adorable puppies, Bella and Shimmy. To shamelessly maximize fan adoration and *awww* factor, Hunter's pit bull terrier, Shimmy, was one day away from being euthanized when Hunter swooped in to rescue her at the very last minute! He reminds Shimmy of this fact almost daily, demanding that she realize how lucky she is and to "get a job!" Shimmy is currently unemployed.

In 2018, Hunter began writing **I'M GLAD YOU'RE DEAD**, which is an Urban Fantasy eulogy for his childhood best friend, John Cook, who was taken from this world in a horrific car accident. Writing the novel was both cathartic and the fulfillment of a promise that Hunter had once made to John before his sudden passing. The *PRETERNATURAL CHRONICLES* is a way for John to live forever in the minds of countless readers across the world.

In June of 2020, Hunter signed on with Argento Publishing—run by the urban fantasy world's greatest supervillain, Shayne Silvers—and the rest, as they say, is history.

Or…the *future*.

Get Down with Hunter Online. T-shirts, signed books, new release updates, and Hunter's blog awaits at:

www.HunterBlain.com
info@hunterblain.com

facebook.com/HunterBlainAuthor
amazon.com/author/hunterblain
bookbub.com/profile/hunter-blain
goodreads.com/hunterblain

BOOKS BY HUNTER BLAIN

PRETERNATURAL CHRONICLES

DELIVERANCE (Prequel novella #0)

I'M GLAD YOU'RE DEAD

DAWN AND QUARTERED

SHADOW OF A DOUBT

MOONLIGHT EQUILIBRIUM (Book 3.5)

MOUTH OF MADNESS

WHAT THE HELL

HOLY SHEOLY (*coming soon in 2020...*)

Audiobooks by Audible Hall of Fame narrator, Luke Daniels:

Listen to free samples HERE.

DELIVERANCE

I'M GLAD YOU'RE DEAD

DAWN AND QUARTERED

SHADOW OF A DOUBT